ECHO
SPECIES INTERVENTION #6609

J.K. ACCINNI

E.K. Publishing

Bradenton, FL

This is a work of fiction. Names, characters, places and incidents either are the product of the author's imagination or are used fictitiously and any resemblance to actual persons, living or dead, business establishments, events, or locales is entirely coincidental.

ECHO
SPECIES INTERVENTION #6609
J.K. Accinni

ISBN: 978-0-9899769-1-6

An E.K. Publishing book published in arrangement with the author, Bradenton, FL.

Copyright © 2012, 2013 J.K. Accinni
This edition published 2013
Editing by LionheART Publishing House

All rights reserved.

Books by J.K. Accinni:

Baby (Species Intervention #6609, Book 1)

Echo (Species Intervention #6609, Book 2)

Armageddon Cometh (Species Intervention #6609, Book 3)

Hive (Species Intervention #6609 Book 4)

Evil Among Us (Species Intervention #6609, Book 5)

The One (Species Intervention #6609, Book 6)

Alien Species Intervention Books 1-3

Dedication

I would like to thank my mom, Jane, for her unflagging support. She never once thought to even question my capabilities. I owe so much to my one true love, Wil, whose honest clear sweetness and support gave me something to live up to.

I would like to thank the phenomenally talented artists who granted me the rights to their work for my covers, Adam Taylor, , United Kingdom—Baby; Larissa Elise Bergsma, Netherlands—Echo; Jonas Jedicke, Berlin, Germany—Armageddon Cometh and The One; Terry Rogers, Gainesville, Florida—Hive.

And lastly, I want to acknowledge my four-legged children, Barney, Toby, Molly, Teddy and Echo, and all of my children that are waiting for me over the Rainbow Bridge. They are what bring all the richness and laughter into my life.

Chapter 1
2044 AD

Scotty slipped out his front door unnoticed, easily overlooked if you failed to notice his ringworm and impetigo scars. Barely three and a half feet tall, even at six years old, it put him in the underdeveloped category, another result of the wicked fall his mother had taken while pregnant with him. The fall had initiated his premature birth, keeping him in a grossly understaffed neonatal hospital unit where his tiny body had contracted a number of skin diseases which had left him scarred and disfigured.

To add to his misery, his left eye muscles had not fully developed, allowing his eye to wander in its socket, giving him headaches, vision problems and disfiguring facial effects. The fact that his father continued to deny responsibility for his mother's fall illustrated the truth of his sister, Abby's, claims. His mother had married a full-blown leachy weasel.

Scotty looked up and down the bleak empty hallway, dirty graffitied walls, a testimony to the futility of the lives packed like termites in the ugly utilitarian monstrosity he called home.

He cautiously peeked in the stairwell. Seeing it empty, he scrambled down the cold metal stairs, his tiny worn sneakers masking his footfalls. Emerging from the gloom of the stairwell, he recoiled from the sudden glare of an unexpectedly sunny afternoon.

Scooting around to the back of his building, he dodged empty beer cans, used condoms, and piles of dog feces to hide in the big cardboard box he currently used as his fort.

Yesterday, Chang Appliance, the largest Chinese appliance chain in the world, had delivered something to an exceedingly lucky tenant in his building. He and his buddy, Germaine, had quickly claimed the treasured empty box, dragging it to the back of their tenement in the giant public housing neighborhood of Short Hills, New Jersey, hoping they could hide it from the big guys—at least long enough to have some fun with it.

Short Hills, formerly a bastion of affluent homes in the early part of the century, no longer boasted anyone who could afford them. As a result, the Socialist New World Party had strengthened the urban renewal and eminent domain laws. When the real estate market for large expensive homes (the most visible trapping of despised capitalist pigs) collapsed due to the exodus of the wealthy to more welcoming countries, the homes were appropriated. After removing the squatters and gangs, the bulldozers made way for what some called inevitable progress. The kind of progress that produced nasty government-subsidized housing projects: pretty ironic for a state once known as The Garden State.

Now New Jersey blossomed with one huge hideous urban ghetto after another. Just like many other states undergoing a similar renaissance. Not everyone agreed to call this progress. Like his mother.

She remembered the stories her grandmother had related to her about growing up on a working family farm with cows and hay barns and wide open meadows, replete with the simple harmonies of sunrise crows, twilight crickets and the exceptional fragrance of newly mown grass and wild wood violets.

His great-grandmother had spent her summers as a child delving into the woods, looking for wild strawberry patches and black caps growing along the side of the road, probing waterholes and brooks for magical polliwogs, turtles, minnows, even snakes, which she invariably dragged back to the farmhouse—a favorite pastime.

Instead, Scotty lived with the perpetual smells of hot air brakes, big rig exhaust and alley-rat infested garbage. He heard the sounds of gunshots and screams as the bullies of the neighborhood beat on their latest victim. His playground consisted of hot smelly asphalt and discarded cardboard boxes as his playthings.

Luckily, his mom knew of a few areas that had missed out on the progress. Like Sussex County. Full of rolling hills, mountains, packed trout streams and bucolic lakes. It even bragged some surviving timid black bears that penis-challenged hunters had failed to eradicate in their perpetual attempts to prove their manhood by putting food out for them in the woods, waiting in trees with their weapons, then shotgunning them down, cubs and all.

Hardly convenient, the wealthy found the remoteness objectionable, leaving no albatrosses for the government to tear down. The lack of access to mass transit, actually the reason the area had stayed rural, undesirable to the masses for the same reason.

An hour before dinner, Scotty's parents started fighting again; the same old thing. His mother, one of the four million polio victims in the United States from the epidemic of 2018, had frequently yet unsuccessfully tried to convince his father to relocate. She dreamed about better healthcare and quality of life in a less populated area. Like Sussex County.

His big sister, Abby, a dialysis patient, needed to get to the hospital three times a week. As a toddler, she had developed chronic kidney disease, acute and undoubtedly fatal, requiring her to be in and out of hospital since a baby. She really needed a kidney transplant, but they didn't have the money to buy one from China or South America as did other patients of loftier financial means.

When the country decided to worship at the altar of socialized medicine, an understandably desperate shortage of doctors ensued. Over-utilized emergency rooms, with a standard back up of thirty six hours on any normal day before the polio epidemic, suddenly morphed into requiring an appointment to get in. Dying before your appointment became common, creating a huge underground market which sold these appointments to the highest bidder. Family allowances limited the amount of doctor visits per year. Inevitably, rationing became as necessary as breathing.

Simple sore throats or innocuous coughs, easily overlooked by busy adults trying to avoid burning a valuable medical visit, still spread germs. Unfortunately, polio was highly contagious. An airline passenger can infect an entire plane with one phlegmy throat. The government burden of bloated bureaucracy put the final nail in that coffin.

The epidemic started because of a Muslim law, passed in 2005, in Northern Nigeria. They issued an Islamic Fatwa, declaring the polio vaccine part of a secret conspiracy by the United States and the United Nations against the Muslim faith. Their claim declared that the vaccine drops, secretly designed to sterilize the Muslim true believers, stimulated the virus. It then reappeared in Nigeria and spread throughout Africa. In this world of high-speed airline transportation it didn't take long to span the globe. Legal immigration figures show the number one source of immigrants in the good ol' U.S.A. to be from Africa. And who could blame them?

The SNW Party now exercised iron control over the government. The exceptionality of the United States had started its decline long ago when the masses realized they could use their vote to elect officials willing to rape the country in their efforts to buy those very votes. So they elected the politician and party that promised them the most swag. They didn't care that someone must inevitably pay for it, so long as it wasn't them.

As a result, availability of capital to grow the private sector diminished. Small businesses suffered and disappeared. Taxes shot through the roof. Large corporations left the country along with the wealthy. The Hollywood elite bailed quickly; France, London and Mexico their preferred destinations. A pound of chopped meat in a grocery store (if you could find it on the shelf) now cost $33.00. And it was mostly pink slime fillers at that. Thank heavens for food stamps.

The country now consisted of a populous that couldn't catch a break as rival political parties outdid themselves robbing from the taxpayers. The country, no longer a melting pot, became a nation of fighting tribal factions and competing ideologies. The SNW Party, the Muslim Brotherhood, the Green and the smaller Republican Party perpetually slandered each other in their quest to control what remained of the country while the people did their best to hold their families together.

There no longer existed a national language. Children attended school for four hours a day, eight months a year; the average work week was a mere twenty five hours. The public insisted that politicians respected their need for rest and recreation. If they didn't, they lost their jobs—voted out. Capitalism reigned no longer.

The outdated pieces of paper called the Constitution lost their relevance and respect. The new law of the land required the courts to consider the beliefs and requirements of all global groups when assessing legal responsibility. Political correctness ran amok. And the deficit—stratospheric. Why do you think China had such a large economic presence? They owned the United States. Yes, what a lovely country the people lived in.

The Chinese depended on that. Money for research and development in the U.S. had vanished. Our scientists had moved to other countries, as had the best doctors, the rich, Wall Street, and the entrepreneurs who had found their spirits crushed by taxes and burdensome regulations. Everyone needed capital to survive. There was no capital in the U.S. The government would spend, spend and spend on entitlements and kickbacks to their donor cronies. It didn't matter who was in power—they *all* did it and there was no way to stop it. A ruling class of vampires that threw a few trinkets to the people to keep them quiet and willing to hold out their arms to have their blood sucked. Surprisingly, the world's superpowers, China, Russia and Iran, still allowed the U.S. to borrow money, even though repayment of the principal appeared unlikely. And the interest sure was a doozey.

And then the polio came; the U.S. the hardest hit. Over ten million children and four million adults died in the U.S. The highest percentage of adults came from minority communities, mostly immigrants from third world countries. Another three million were left maimed and crippled to one degree or another. Urgent medical care meant emergency rooms came under siege; the doctors almost nonexistent. Too many hospitals closed for lack of operating funds and too little reimbursement.

It hadn't come as a surprise to many to learn the United States Health and Human Services Department had quietly stopped budgeting for the creation and implementation of the polio vaccine in

2013. They had taken responsibility for vaccines and immunizations away from parents who had long ago rejected the poisons in the makeup of the vaccines. The boards of education, no longer monitoring the children's vaccination requirements, demanded congressional investigations that went nowhere. Conspiracy advocates abounded. The most popular theory postulated that the virus, deliberately released by the government, would serve to thin the ranks of the entitlement classes. Abdicating responsibility to deadly disease; clearly far easier and more expedient than Congress risking re-election in a controversial attempt at fiscal responsibility. C'est la vie. Massive riots in the streets enabled citizens to vent, but the efforts for change advanced anemically.

Scotty grew hungry for his dinner while waiting for Germaine. If his best buddy didn't show soon, they might lose their prize to the big kids. He didn't want the big kids to spot him without Germaine for backup. The last time that had happened, they had held him down and pulled off his pants. They had jeered and taunted him, calling him 'Scotty-watty tissue paper' and, worse yet, 'ass wipe'. They had left him pantless on the pavement to slink home in disgrace. His mommy had held him and shed tears with him. His daddy had made fun of him and called him a sissy boy. He didn't think sissy boy sounded nice coming from his daddy's mouth. Now his daddy referred to both him and his big sister as parasites.

He smiled the first time he had heard it. It had sounded like a big important word. He had loved the way it rolled off his tongue and liked to repeat the word over and over, enjoying the syllables that popped out of his mouth so satisfyingly. Then he remembered his mother's face after his father had said it. It looked crumpled in. That's when he realized it was a bad word. Now, the word just slithered out of his mouth like a venomous snake looking for prey to strike.

He developed trouble sleeping, nightmares a common occurrence. He never remembered any of his dreams, but he knew they always contained a big dark murky figure who resembled his dad.

Unfortunately, Scotty had developed into a suspicious, defensive little boy, trusting only his mother and sister.

He loved his half-sister, Abby. Abby's daddy and his mom had never married. Everyone said young and foolish made a bad combination for marriage. That's what Abby said too. He didn't think his mom had ever behaved foolishly. If she had been his age, he would have made her his very best friend. Even though playing with a girl made you look like a loser.

Thirteen-year-old Abby became Scotty's strongest advocate. Whenever Scotty refused to go outside for fear of bodily harm, Abby would sit him down and spin stories of imaginary worlds, fantastic creatures and handsome, brave little boys. He loved hearing Abby's stories even more than playing with Germaine.

That's why he couldn't understand why his daddy ignored Abby. His mommy said sisters and brothers must always protect one another. But he knew his daddy didn't want to protect Abby.

Late one night when he got up to go potty, he heard his parents fighting. He heard his father shout something about Abby hanging around his neck like an anchor. He heard his daddy call Abby a bad name. His daddy said he didn't want to be responsible for a bastard kid that didn't belong to him.

Overhearing his daddy gave him a stomachache. His troubled sleep left him tired and cranky the next morning. But he still managed to promise his mommy he would always protect Abby, even if he had to stand on a chair to do it. He thought it would make his mother happy. He didn't understand why she cried instead.

Late one fall day, Scotty came home from grade school, his paperwork in his eager hands. He wanted to show his mom the smiley face the teacher had given him. His daddy was supposed to take Abby to the hospital for her weekly dialysis treatment. Mommy worked six days a week at the grocery store, so Daddy reluctantly took responsibility. When Scotty had remarked that Daddy should work so Mommy could stay home more, he claimed he had very important things to do and that a dummy like Scotty wouldn't understand. Mommy looked like her tummy hurt when Daddy said things like that.

Actually, the little boy didn't recall his daddy ever working like Mommy did. He often saw her late at night, removing her shiny leg brace to massage her tired muscles.

Scotty realized most of the dads in his building didn't work. They formulated important matters to discuss in the rec room. The dads wouldn't let little kids in the rec room because of the beer and smoking. So when he found Abby unconscious on the floor of her bedroom, he ran down to the basement and pounded on the door of the locked rec room.

"Hello, anyone in there? Daddy, I need you. Daddy, Daddy. Help." He knew Abby should have gone to the hospital this morning. Why hadn't Daddy taken her? But no one would open the door to a crying six year old. He tried again, banging over and over. The door suddenly opened, omitting smoke and loud raucous music.

"Kid, what cha doing screaming out here? Get lost." The big man wore an old stained shirt, the sleeves rolled up over his fat hairy arms. He exuded an unfamiliar bad smell.

"Is my daddy here? I need him to come home. Abby's on the floor." Scotty danced nervously, his voice small and frightened, his wandering eye floating erratically.

"I'm not gonna say it again. Don't be bangin' on this door." The big man burped, sending a gust of rancid beer breath in Scotty's face. He cringed, the door slamming in his face.

Scotty knew saving Abby by himself would require some bravery.

He ran outside into the dirty street, his heart pounding so hard he thought the bullies in the neighborhood might hear him.

Choking back his sobs, he ran up and down the street, dodging cars and screaming for the police. He glimpsed the old grannies from the neighborhood who congregated at the corner, lounging in cheap plastic chairs, holding court on the sidewalks. He scrambled out of the street, hurrying toward them.

"Abby's going to die. She's on the floor. Please, we need help."

Unable to hold back the tears overflowing his wild eyes, he dragged the grannies to his family's apartment. A nice Muslim lady sat with him while two other black grannies made a few cellphone calls.

Soon, three strapping black men entered the apartment. Scotty, positive they would rob his family, stuck to them like glue. Relieved, he watched them lift Abby in their arms and carry her out of the apartment. He tried to follow.

"Hey kiddo, you stay here until your mom comes home. Your sister's very sick. You need to hold down the fort. This nice lady will stay with you." One of the black men, his eyes soft and moist, ran his hand along Scotty's shoulder giving him a reassuring stroke, and softly shut the door behind him.

The nice Muslim lady stayed with him until his mommy came home from work. He hoped Abby didn't die. Fear made him pray.

He didn't know much about what happened after that. His mommy asked him to stay in his room. He heard lots of crying and silences. Then his daddy came home and the screaming started. He didn't know what it meant, but he felt terror-stricken anyway. He began to relax when the cops took his daddy away. Abby came home a week later, alive but painfully thin. Scotty began to sleep much, much better.

A few days later, his mother silently handed him a cardboard box, telling him to pack his toys. She folded all their clothes except for Daddy's, the brace on her afflicted leg clanking around the apartment as she packed up their little lives.

The night before the move, his mother sat them both down for a talk.

"Scotty, do you understand we're moving far away?" She pulled her light-brown hair back in a ponytail, long wisps escaping to frame her thin stressed face, her voice low and tired.

"Yes, Mommy," he assured her, not understanding the meaning of far away. But he loved and trusted his mom. He knew every line on her wonderful face. A smile failed to appear as he scrutinized her expression. Somehow, he realized, she needed him to be okay with the move.

Abby picked him up and sat him on her lap.

"Honey, you shouldn't strain yourself like that. The nurse said—"

"Mom, it's okay. Let me help." She rocked Scotty on her lap. Her pretty face lit up, her affection for Scotty giving him confidence as he looked into her eyes, laughing. "You're our big guy aren't you, Scotty? It's going to be you, me and Mom. What a great team. We can do anything, right?"

"Right." Shouting and laughing, he looked at his mom. "Right, Mommy?"

"Right, baby, a great team." She finally joined in the laughter, her children's optimism infectious.

Chapter 2

The scary move to Sussex County brought about many changes; not the least of which was Scotty never again seeing his only playmate, Germaine. Germaine said he would beg his mom to bring him for a visit, but Germaine didn't have a daddy to drive him there.

Luckily, Abby recovered from her sickness. Her physician assistant (she never actually saw a doctor, ever, not in her whole life) determined her kidney would have no lasting damage. Maybe. From now on, they must watch very carefully to make sure Abby got to her dialysis on time. It was critical. Mom told them about the cute little neighborhood not far from their new home that offered a health clinic with the services Abby needed. Relief washed over Scotty. He didn't want to have to save Abby again. The traumatic event reverberated in his memory, too much for a six-year-old boy.

Their sad little three-bedroomed ranch in Sussex County looked as lonely and forlorn as Scotty felt. The roof desperately needed repairs. When it rained, they ran around, laughing and bumping into one another with pots in their hands, collecting the drips. When they took showers, the water didn't stay hot for long; the last one in froze. They learned they must accept the landlord's response to their complaints. He gave them two choices, suck it up or get out.

They did their best to make it a home, and Mrs. Preston made sure she kept it spotless and full of love. Scotty screamed with happiness, thrilled to find it included a tiny backyard with his very own tree. The air smelled clean and fragrant. But, best of all, it didn't have his daddy. His nightmares stopped. Whenever his mother mentioned he could visit his dad, his heart raced with panic. On those occasions, he usually pottied in his bed while he slept. The next day, when his mommy changed his bed, he would tell her all about his nightmare. Her face slipped into such a haggard and defeated bearing that he felt swamped with guilt, convinced his father's pronouncements about him might come true.

Sadly, the little boy found no playmates in his hilly little neighborhood. The homes were mostly occupied by black and Spanish families, along with the usual separate enclave of Muslims. The children in the neighborhood took one look at his bald spots and disfiguring scars, and refused to play with him, turning up their noses. They made fun of his wandering eye, calling him cootie head, dick wad, faggot and douche bag. The older boys would jeer at him, enjoying his hurt. The most aggressive pushed him to the ground, kicking dirt and gravel at him to cover his cootie bugs.

Scotty wandered around and around the neighborhood, looking for someone to play with. His loneliness made him long to grow up quickly. Then he could do anything he wanted, not needing the attention or approval of kids who felt it necessary to call him ass wipe. His memories tasted nasty, festering like an infected wound.

One day, he found the top of the hill behind his neighborhood. He discovered a curious path that tempted him into the woods. The dead leaves from tall, thick grandfather oaks, dried and crinkled, disintegrated underfoot as he explored. Over time, he learned to entertain himself in the woods, fighting imaginary wars with imaginary magical creatures. The woods became an enchanting place for him. He felt peace. He felt safe. He loved the small clearings drizzled with dappled sunlight, the occasional sighting of little creatures. He never felt lonely but was seduced by the magic of timid rabbits, quarreling squirrels, hyperactive chipmunks and the silent family of deer; all his unwitting playmates, enchanting him with their innocence and acceptance.

Today he turned seven. He looked forward to the scrumptious cake his mother always baked for his birthday. He knew Abby planned to have a special gift for him from the meager money she earned from the Muslim family she babysat for. He could hardly contain his excitement during the school day, which passed too slowly. He thought he would age another year while he waited. The usual snubs from his classmates mattered not, his mind focused on the happy party waiting for him at home.

Running up to his now familiar door after the school bus dropped him off, he jerked in surprise, seeing his father's car in the drive, hearing shouts and angry voices.

Letting himself in, he trembled at the sight of his father. His heartbeat ratcheted up, thumping hard as his breathing came fast and shallow, his stomach starting a slow roil. He witnessed his father's arms looped around his mother's neck as he tried to force her to kiss him. She fought back, trying to slip out of his grip with little success, her balance a hindrance because of her brace.

His father's expression hardened: angry and ugly. A sneer deformed his thin lips as he slowly strangled her while Scotty beat on his father's legs, vainly trying to protect his mother. She screamed, fighting him off until a desperate shove sent her falling back on the kitchen table where Scotty's birthday cake sat, waiting to have the candles lit for his party. Seven beautiful blue candles on top of rich chocolate icing. His mom caught her balance on the kitchen table, sending his beautiful birthday cake flying.

Everyone froze as the cake landed upside down, splattering on the hardwood floor. Staring at his ruined birthday cake, Scotty felt his stomach turn inside out, queasiness ready to explode. And a little something new: anger. The kind of anger that festers and simmers beneath the surface, cooking in its own poison while it twists the mind with bitterness. Picking up the remains of the cake, he threw it at his father who just laughed at him, calling him a crybaby and a little turd.

"I'm not a little turd!"

Sobbing, he ran out the door, up the hill and into the trees. He just kept running, past all his favorite spots, into the deep woods, his sobs turning to anger, magnified by the resentment of his afflictions.

Slowing down, he dropped to the ground, leaning up against a hillside unfamiliar to him. He tried to block the memory of his daddy's belittling taunting tone, and the damaged look on his mom's face. Restlessly, he wandered along the hillside until he turned a corner, stepping back in surprise.

Before him stood a massive granite boulder. He eyeballed the immense rock, wondering how he dare claim it for his own. He noticed handholds seemingly carved into the side of the rock. *Hmm, can I pull myself up?* Approaching the rock, he struggled with the handholds, finally reaching the top. What a great spot for a fort. Curling up in a depression, he felt the warmth from the sun seep from the rock into his body. His drowsy eyes slowly closed over his tear-stained cheeks and he drifted off into an uneasy sleep.

The creature roused herself from a deep slumber, feeling the presence of a large life form. She sensed its closeness, but noted it was not yet in the deep quiet cavern of the Hive. She called the Hive home, and her safety had been well assured for over a century. Sadly, she coped with constant loneliness: her only companions the occasional woodland creature that found its way into the cavern. Periodically she would venture out to observe the behavior of the human creatures of this planet, caution an imperative.

The trauma witnessed over a century ago still smoldered sharply in her mind; the guilt just as fresh. She could have intervened when she became suspicious of her birth Brother's mental and physical damage during her emergence.

Or perhaps it had happened during the Womb's entry into the Earth's atmosphere. Maybe the Womb had failed to properly care for Brother, although it had certainly cared for her without complaint. She often suspected the Womb had deliberately allowed the incident to escalate just so it could study the outcome. How else could the Womb learn how to interpret the actions of the humans?

She agreed they merited study, but her sensibilities had cringed as the slaughter had transpired. Most of the time, the Womb took a hands-off policy, not wanting to interfere with the culture of any species, unless the species became catastrophically aggressive to others, of course. But this was a minion, the Womb's chosen.

She remembered back a full century to the time she had last laid eyes on the doomed Sister. She had considered making contact without her Brother's knowledge when the Sister had suddenly appeared one day at the rock that disguised the entrance to the cavern.

She had watched from her hidden position in the forest as the Sister had first discovered her birth Brother and carried him away from the Hive. She didn't understand why Brother had not objected. Confusion ruled as she had tried to puzzle out why her birth Brother had neglected to begin his mission. Instead he had involved himself intimately in the Sister's life, apparently satisfied with the tiny part of his mission that he did manage to accomplish: creating two new Elders to assist him.

As it had turned out, an evil human Brother stalked the Sister. He had captured her and participated in a brutal murder. She knew how bloodthirsty the evil species behaved on this planet, observing firsthand what had happened to the Sister, her birth Brother, and his own little furry pet from the safety of the hilltop near the forest edge. She remembered with pain her birth Brother's golden life force splashing on the unyielding ground. She bitterly remembered the look of astonishment then disgust as the evil Brother that had murdered him wiped the sacred life force off the heels of his boots.

The shock had numbed her as the mesmerizing golden light and vital thought projections had faded from Brother's disfigured eyes. She had actually felt the genetic mental connection shared by all of her species being brutally severed. Running back through the woods, she had vowed to never leave the Hive until she could assure her own safety.

It was incomprehensible to believe the bloodthirsty human Brothers would reject the very gifts meant to rescue them and justify the complex energy expended long ago on their behalf. But they had, making the unfortunate choice that had pronounced their death sentence. She wondered if the humans had rejected Sister's new tail. The humans must realize by now that a tail was nothing new to their species. The success of the mission had demanded complex alterations of their physical and biological systems. It was a good thing that only the tail had manifested, not the antlers. That would have been a disaster.

Determination coursed through her solar veins. Her job rested on her ability to ensure the Elder's grand plan, offering salvation for both species, not failure. Success would ensure the redemption from the Womb that minions had sought for hundreds of thousands of years. Perhaps the humans needed a different type of manifestation. She would have to ponder. If she could alter a few of her own cells and enzymes, a solution might be available. Maybe the Womb would help her. But her intention would never include getting rid of her own beautiful tail. The engineering for that would be too complex to attempt without help. She felt comforted by her tail, even as she knew it had a life of its own.

She curiously wondered why her Brother had not tried to contact her. She would have been willing to complete the mission in his stead. As things stood, now that Brother had expired, her honor (and genetic programming) obligated her to eventually complete the mission for him anyway.

But she remained hesitant. Over the last century she had observed the savage violence that this species perpetrated on itself. She understood why the Womb had authorized the mission. And, just like the Womb, she now saw little reason to save this species. She suspected the Elders truly had made a tragic mistake. They had offered excuse after excuse for this life form, hoping evolution would tame them. Then, with influence from the Elders no longer a factor, the Womb had passed judgment, ordering the mission. But the possibility existed that her decision might abet an error. She decided to take her time. This planet needed much more observation: direct observation. She hoped the Womb would allow her the time. Maybe if she could just find *The One*.

It would truly be a tragedy if she decided to let this species self-destruct, along with Brother's newly obtained Elder state—now tragically lost. What a surprising discovery that had been. Her species had said goodbye to Elders long ago. In anger at their hubris, the Womb had altered the minions' ability to become Elders after discovering their fateful mistake, forever preventing healing of humans, but not other life forms. Now, minion expiration came through old age or the birth process. It appeared that, for some reason, Brother's own genetic instructions, meant to prevent the conversion, had failed. She could not know for sure without a laboratory at her disposal. Her mind, distracted by the biology, pondered the complexity of their enzymes.

She wondered if she could achieve that lofty state of Elder herself. Had she already? She had easily surpassed her normal life span long ago. She would never know until the first opportunity to heal a Brother or Sister presented itself. Yet she refused to try until she decided that this species deserved it. As of yet, her doubts remained strong.

She could stay in the Hive as long as it took, but she was in doubt as to the amount of time the Womb would allow her. She wanted to wait until she had received a sign of worthiness. But she was terribly lonely. Her species thrived on close contact. They lived in communal groups—hives. Similar to what were called families here on Earth, only much larger. She had noticed that most of the other species of this planet also lived in families. Of course, she had expected human life on this planet to have evolved similar habits. Sighing, she worried about the damage perpetual isolation would do to her mental state.

The Hive, under supervision of the Womb, would always take care of all the needs a carbon-based life form required to survive, irrespective of their metabolism. The Womb, being indestructible, easily accomplished all tasks in the pursuit of creating life. But she remained alone, unable to stop the toll her isolation undeniably looked to extract. Surely her own iridescent eyes dimmed? Maybe the time to do something about her dilemma neared.

The creature planned to take an excursion to the surface sometime soon. She needed to check on the various groups that clustered in the small buildings on land that had previously grown stunning fruit orchards.

Her monumental shock when she had witnessed the fruit trees ripped from the earth, destroying a unique gift to the humans, shook her to her core. Gone the orchards that would feed so many, for so long. Within a decade, the miracle seeds from those trees and the crops would have spread naturally all over the world, feeding everyone. The wanton waste was unforgivable. As a result, the Womb angrily intensified its plan for revenge. This species clearly refused to learn. How they had become programmed for self-destruction, she did not know. Perhaps if the Elders had acquiesced differently to the Womb after the discovery of their forbidden experiment, they could have intervened, guiding evolution to a more satisfactory outcome—the very guidance that the Womb had enjoyed exerting everywhere else, feeling no planet too insignificant. But the Womb had forbidden the guidance. The humans were on their own, a punishment they were unaware of.

The creature disconnected from the Hive wall, her tail dry as it withdrew from the thick membrane. Leaving her private chamber, she shuffled and bobbed her way up the long lonely trail to the outside world.

Arriving at the end of the underground trail, the creature reached her hand into the cavern wall, asking it to part. When the wall split, she squeezed and contorted her way around the rocks and boulders blocking and disguising the Hive. Glancing back, she made sure the Hive closed behind her.

She remembered that the blame for the catastrophic events of a century ago belonged partially to her. After her Emergence, she had left her Brother behind in his helpless hibernation state in her zeal to explore topside. If her Emergence had occurred back on Oolaha, surrounded by all the help her Brother had needed to emerge from hibernation and begin transition, his eventual expiration would have been successful. She herself would have received proper guidance, allowing the time for her awareness to digest all the stimuli being transmitted to her mind from her own transcription cells. She would not have run off halfcocked and uninformed, failing to ensure the Hive closed behind her, making the fatal mistake that had allowed the Sister to enter and discover her birth Brother.

Having reached maturity, she realized her birth Brother must have called the human to use for his own recovery, but she doubted her Brother's powers had been strong enough.

The Womb created the energy she and Brother needed to survive as a by-product of its slow feeding on the organic material it rested on. It was an inexhaustible source of the energy she needed to feed on as long as she remained underground. Once above ground, she took all she needed from the sun. She could also use a human Brother or Sister, but she strongly intended to stay far away for now. Besides, she much preferred the slower absorption from the sun. It reacted more efficiently with her metabolism. Taking nourishment from a human left her species confused and disoriented. Perhaps the very reason Brother had left the Hive with the Sister. Maybe confusion had reigned.

The occasional animal which wandered near could obviously smell the membrane and knew the Womb lived. They usually entered out of curiosity and perhaps hunger, causing little damage. But she knew the Sister had entered because of her own carelessness.

Not only did she carry overwhelming guilt and barely tolerable loneliness, but she knew her species probably did not know she existed. They monitored the energy outflow from the Womb membrane to determine if Brother still lived, but the Womb could not make a distinction between its minions. They undoubtedly thought she was Brother. The Womb had never registered any simultaneous energy draws, cluing them into her existence back home. Over the last century, they had recorded her withdrawal, mistakenly believing it to be that of Brother's.

At some point, Brother would have died. They would not know that he had an offspring or that he had become an Elder. They would expect the humans to carry out the mission of their own volition after her Brother's death. Monitoring this planet would provide few answers. Only an Elder could communicate through the Womb to Oolaha. But the Womb knew. That's all that really mattered. Oh well, she could only do her best. When she thought the humans were ready, she would begin.

Pushing all the unanswerable questions from her rambling mind, she stepped around the cairn of rocks that helped protect the Hive and stretched up to the sun. Sensing the life form she detected earlier, she peered around the rocks, unable to locate it. She decided she would scramble up her favorite rock to get closer to the sun where she would be unobserved. She loved to curl up in the depression at the top. It soaked up the sun and warmed her fat belly when she nestled in.

Reaching out with her long slender fingers, she touched the rock. Her suction-like pads helped pull her body up as she climbed, creeping up the side of the rock. Her head swiveled up and down as she gauged the distance from the top to the bottom. Pulling herself up and over the top, she made an unexpected discovery. There, in her depression, lay the life form: a small human Brother. He wore the coverings humans liked to swaddle themselves in, measuring almost twice her size, yet appearing harmless enough as he slept. Quivering with anticipation, she decided to quietly sit and watch, wrapping her golden tail around herself.

As she observed, she weighed the attraction her birth Brother had felt for his human Sister. She longed to reach out and touch the long fibers on the young Brother's head, very different from the fuzz and fur on her own body. She wondered if it felt softer. It certainly did not keep him warm in the way her pelt did. She guessed that explained the swaddling. They would not be so vulnerable to heat fluctuations if their metabolisms evolved closer to that of her species; so much simpler. She sniffed, knowing that if she was consulted on the design she would certainly make improvements. Her puzzled eyes drifted over the strange markings on his head and the scars on his skin, shaking her head at his obvious signs of disease; the poor human Brother.

It was no wonder the Womb had decided they must be revisited for intervention. Perhaps the time should have come much sooner, before they had started to live inside caves instead of out in the open like herds. Before they had learned to practice wanton bloodlust, employed so often for reasons other than survival. They were a lost cause. Banishing all her troubling thoughts, she concentrated on the little Brother. Without realizing what she was doing, she let her probing aura coalesce in his mind. And suddenly his eyes flew open.

Chapter 3

What the—? Scrambling quickly up on his butt, Scotty scooted out of the depression, edging to the back of the rock. There he sat and stared at the funny looking creature, eh no, elf. No, fairy. Yeah, it must be a fairy. Wow. He had found an actual golden fairy. Hopping up, he made a grab for it. The fairy unwound his long tail and disappeared over the side of the rock. Scotty leaned over the edge, the fairy nowhere to be seen.

Carefully, he lowered himself down the rock, slipping on the sharp footholds as he descended. Desperately, he looked around, trying to discover where the fairy had disappeared to. *Gee, Mom will never believe this.* He wasn't sure he could convince her unless he brought the fairy home. *Holy mackerel, no one will believe this!* Excitement gripped him; a touch of something special in his life for the first time.

He knew he must find the hiding place where the fairy lived. Stumbling over the loose pile of rock heaped near the hillside, he discovered an enormous rip in his pant leg. Squatting down, he examined it. *Mom won't be happy about this.* And he didn't even have the fairy to show her. Straightening up, something caught his eye. A golden glint, just like the fairy.

He tripped over the rocks, his footing unsteady until he located the place the glint had come from. Digging down between the rocks, his fingers withdrew an object. A coin. He rubbed it on his jeans, removing some of the crusted dirt so deeply embedded. He stared, his wandering eye refusing to focus.

Turning it around and over in his little fingers, the heavy coin finally revealed more of the golden sheen and a date, 1702. *Hmm, It's not even new.* He wondered if the fairy had left it for him.

Maybe the fairy knew of his birthday and had left it as a gift to make up for his dad ruining his day, hurting his mom and calling him bad names. If it did, Scotty wished the fairy could have made the coin a new shiny one. But at least he could show some kind of proof to his mom. Glancing around for the last time, he brushed off his pants and started home.

The creature stood inside the Hive. She felt full of furious agitation, yet oddly exhilarated. She wished the little Brother had not run off. She supposed she could have followed him, but wondered if he might return. If he did, she should figure out a better way to handle the situation. Even though the encounter had gone badly, she felt different, hopeful. She wasn't sure why, but she had a feeling about this little human Brother. Maybe he could be *The One*.

The little boy hurried down the path that took him out of his magical woods, the golden coin tucked safely in his pocket. Running down the hill past his neighbors' homes, he could see his house. He noted with relief that his father's car no longer sat in the driveway. Bursting breathlessly through the front door, he beheld his mom and Abby waiting for him.

"Oh, baby, we were so worried. Where did you go? We called and called. Didn't you hear us? We even went up to the woods." His frazzled mom hurried over as fast as she could, her brace clinking at her side. She sat awkwardly on the floor in front of him, holding out her arms to sweep him to her chest. Tears coursed down her face, the worry lines standing out in relief as she softly ran her fingers over the bald spots on his head.

"It's okay, Mom. I'm okay. Please don't cry, I'm sorry I ran away." He hugged her tight, his young head fitting under her neck for comfort.

"Hi, sport," Abby said. "Glad you came home—got'cha something." Joining her brother and mom on the floor, she gave Scotty a kiss and put a brightly wrapped slender gift in his lap. He fingered the ribbon with wonder. The bow was bright gold. Unwrapping the gift, he grinned in amazement at the book about fairies. *Wow, did this mean they knew?* Leafing through the book, he located a whole chapter on wood fairies. He would study that chapter first. He knew he would learn everything he needed to know about his fairy in the book.

"Gee, thanks, Ab. Mom, I met a fairy in the woods today. He left me a present. Did you tell him it was my birthday?" His face shined with unconcealed innocence.

"Sweetie, I'm sure you met your very own birthday fairy. But what do you mean, he gave you a present?"

Scotty sighed, knowing his mom worried about child molesters. Though it was unlikely any lived in the neighborhood, she monitored everything, knowing they had to be extra careful ever since they had abolished the sexual predator register (declared unconstitutional—they have rights you know).

"Mom, he did leave me a present. He's a golden fairy. Abby, do fairies usually have a tail? His tail glowed. And he left me this." Pulling out the coin from his pocket, he proudly held it up for his sister and mom. Taking it from him to examine, his mother carefully scrutinized the coin.

"This coin is very old, sweetie, old is good. That's what makes it valuable."

"Is it a special coin, Mom? It must be special because I got it from the golden fairy, and he knew about my birthday." Scotty's chest inflated, his wandering eye unexpectedly centered in his eyeball.

Looking over to the kitchen table, a new birthday cake winked at him. He could tell his mom had purchased it at the bakery. He wondered where she had got the money from, but the moment contained so much joy he pushed away his guilt. Jumping up, he tugged on both of them.

"Mom, let's have cake. I want to blow out my candles and make a wish." Hurrying over to the table, she lit the candles as she sang to him. While they blazed with flame, he made a wish and blew them all out. Smiling happily to himself, he realized that, this time, his birthday wish would come true, absolutely convinced his golden fairy would grant it. He couldn't wait to wake up the next morning to hear of his father's death.

When bedtime came, his mother tucked him in. Noticing his gold coin and his new book in bed with him, she removed them, placing both on his dresser.

"Sweetie, I think we'll put your coin someplace safe, it's probably very valuable. I'll look into it and see what I can find out. Good night, birthday boy." As his mother shut off the light, his last thoughts filled his head with images of the fairy and the most fantastic birthday ever. Scotty slumbered fitfully, unaware of the probing flashes of residual rainbow light that sent fingers to tumble around in his brain.

Going off to school the next morning, he took his new book with him. Reading the chapter on wood fairies, he found no mention of golden ones with long glowing tails. As a matter of fact, he didn't see any fairies with tails. They all wore wings of some kind. Certainly none of them with horns like his golden fairy. His disappointment acute, excitement dimmed, he slowly grasped that he might be wrong about his fairy. No, he knew a fairy when he saw one. What else could it have been?

Riding home on the school bus his spirits flagged with disappointment to find the rain pouring down. He wanted to return to the big rock and wait for the fairy, afraid that if he didn't show up, the fairy might give up on him and find a new little boy to spend time with. His mom waited for him at the bus stop. Taking her hand, he scooted under her umbrella. Smiling gently, she smoothed back the wisps of hair that refused to cover his ringworm scars no matter how she brushed them.

"Sweetie, your father called. He would like to visit this weekend and apologize for his behavior. Would you like to see him?"

"No, no!" Scotty screamed, his face turning white. His father was still alive? The fairy hadn't come through for him. Something had gone wrong with his wish. Maybe he needed to tell it directly to the fairy.

"Mommy, I need to go to the woods today." His voice frantic, he begged for her permission.

"Don't be silly. You'll get soaked. You're not going anywhere except home with me."

Arriving at their front door, she closed the umbrella and scooted him into the house.

Hanging up his jacket, he ran to Abby's bedroom where he found her studying. She was in high school now, her time no longer as available to him. He climbed up onto her bed, trying to fit in her lap the way he used to as a tot.

"Come on, little dude, I need to get my homework done." Abby laughingly rained kisses down on his sad face, signs of his infant impetigo less of a beacon now that a growth spurt looked to be in play. Stroking his patchy fine hair back from his face, she pushed her books aside, cuddling up with her brother on her pillows. "What's wrong, Scotty?"

Tears slowly leaked down his chubby cheeks as he snuggled up to his sister. "Abby, I love you."

"I love you too, champ. What's going on?"

He put his ear up to his sister's to whisper. "I think Daddy's going to move back in with us." He quickly looked to his sister's face to gauge her reaction. Abby looked grim, but she hugged him tightly.

"No, Scotty, that will never happen. Mom promised he would never get the chance to hurt her or demean us again. So put a smile on your face and get ready for dinner."

"Okay, but if he does, I'm going to make a magic sword to protect us with. I'll always protect you and Mommy." Scrambling off Abby's bed, he ran to his own room. He took out his book of fairies from his backpack and slid it into a drawer. He would solve his fairy dilemma on his own and in secrecy. That's probably what his fairy wanted anyway.

Sitting down to dinner, he noticed his mom serving mac and cheese again on the fancy blue and white plastic plates she'd been given as a wedding gift before his birth. The aroma of hot gooey cheese tantalized him. Mom made it almost every other day because he loved it, naturally. Chowing down, he noticed Abby and Mommy talking in low voices about the welfare money. They needed the welfare money. Everyone got welfare money.

"Kids, I have some important news for you." He looked closer at his mom's face, her lips tightly pursed, her eyes tense. Not with anger, more like scary disappointment. Did he see fear on his mom's face? What was going on? Looking at Abby, he could tell she already knew.

"We're going to have some new house guests."

"No, not Daddy, please." His stomach started to ache. His mommy reached over to stroke his arm, calming him.

"No, baby, it won't be your father. He's gone for good. I don't even know where he's going, but I do know he'll leave New Jersey. We're going to share the house and expenses with another family. It's all arranged. You know the Diaz family, doesn't Jose go to your school, Abby?"

"Yes, Mom, he does, he's okay. Is the whole family coming?"

"Yes, except for Mr. Diaz. He'll be heading to Mexico to try to jump the fence. If he's successful, he stands a good chance of nabbing a job, and they'll probably move out if that happens. If he gets caught, he'll go to prison. It's a felony in Mexico, they're very serious about protecting jobs for their own people. Then we'll have to think about a more permanent solution."

"Solution to what, Mom?" Abby asked.

"Honey, anyone with a job is being removed from the welfare rolls. We can keep our housing stipend and our energy assistance, thank God. And the food stamps will help until they cut them out. My paycheck won't cover the rest of our expenses. Not with the co-pays for Abby's dialysis. The Diaz family is losing their welfare check, too.

"But, Mom—why? Why is the check going to stop? Can we talk to the mailman? Is this the week he comes, or is it next week?" Scotty's voice faltered with fright.

"Don't worry, sweetie, everything will work out if we all pull together. The government is just finding it difficult to collect the money from the rich people. They can't give it to us unless they collect it first. I know it's not fair, the rich have so much compared to us. It's not the government's fault. The rich people are just getting better at hiding the money. We'll learn to make do. That's why the Diaz family is moving in.

"All the boys will sleep together in your room, Scotty. The three of us will sleep together in Abby's room. I'm going to move my bed in there. The Diaz family will have two rooms for six people. Most importantly, they'll pay us rent. That'll make up for most of the loss of the welfare." Grinning, his mom tried to put a smile on her face, but Scotty could see her struggle.

"Mom, as long as we're together, that's all that matters." Abby got up and put her arms around her mother. "Hey, champ, since we're going to be roomies, why don't we do the dishes and give Mom a break?"

Scotty understood that many changes loomed large in his life. As he cleared the table, he thought about Jose Diaz, the only one in the family he recognized. Jose, an older kid on his bus a couple of years ago, didn't speak English very well. He kept to himself, never horsing around with the other kids, although he had nodded now and then as Scotty boarded the bus. Rumors said he had grown up in another country.

Helping his mother up from her chair, he glanced out the window, hoping the sun had finished chasing away the rain. The thunderclouds covered most of the sun as it began its nightly disappearance below the horizon. Oh well, maybe tomorrow.

Sunny skies greeted Scotty as he rose to get ready for school. Unexpectedly returning home after being dismissed early when his teacher had failed to show up, he changed into his old jeans and ran up the hill to find the path to the woods.

The ground under his feet felt spongy from all the rain. Small puddles collected in layers of dead leaves, turning the clear water to tannin. He took a deep breath, smelling organic matter rotting; a contribution to the cycle of life. He soon found himself approaching the path that led up to the rock. He crept slowly, not wanting to scare the fairy. Scotty's eyes scanned the area, coming up empty. Struggling with the handholds in the rock, he pulled himself up, grunting loudly in the silence. *Well*, he thought, *I hope that didn't scare the fairy away*. Scaling the top of the rock, he discovered an empty surface.

Dejectedly, he surveyed the surrounding area from his perch. Reaching into his pocket, he pulled out a plastic-wrapped piece of birthday cake. A bit stale, but he didn't think the fairy would notice. Smoothing out the plastic wrap, he pushed the squashed cake toward the edge of the rock. No, he had better put the cake closer to him. Standing, he eyeballed the position of the cake. Still not liking it, he stood to move it again, a bit more to the middle. Turning, he glanced at his seat and gasped, doing a double take. There was his fairy, sitting in the spot he had just vacated.

Thumping down hard on the rock, he stared at the fairy's eyes. They made him dizzy with their pulsing golden rainbows leaving him speechless and mesmerized. Neither one moved.

"Are you a fairy?" Scotty finally demanded an answer, getting no response. "The fairies in my fairy book don't have tails. How come you do?"

He felt pressure, his mind filling with a strange aura. He stared at the fairy, who just stared back. "I am an Oolahan." Scotty heard the words whispered in his mind, the aura bright with color.

"Did you say your name was Lula?" Scotty wondered why the creature, um, Lula, hadn't moved its mouth. He'd heard it speak quite clearly. The aura and colors had formed mind words; weird.

"Do I get a wish?"

"What do you mean, young Brother?"

"My wish. Everyone gets a wish from a fairy." Scotty grew agitated. If everyone got a wish from a fairy, he wanted to make sure he got his before it disappeared again.

"Brother, I do not have a wish for you. I am here for a mission. I have chosen you. You will be The One."

Huh? The boy scratched his head. He stared at Lula.

"I want to pet you, Lula." Standing, Scotty walked toward his new friend. Walking past the cake, he bent down to pick it up to give to Lula. Being the clumsy little boy he was, he tripped. Caught off balance, he crashed down, head first, rolling near the edge. Dazed, he sat up, perilously close to the drop. Still maintaining a hold on his gift to Lula, he stepped back and fell straight over the edge, landing in a broken heap on the sharp pile of rocks at the base.

The Oolahan scurried over to the edge and looked down. She saw blood, lots of blood. The boy's head sat at an unnatural angle, but she could tell he still lived. Unbidden, her tail shot up in the air, directed down at the boy. The air filled with pressure and the smell of sulfur as her tail extruded its membrane to do its miraculous work.

Unfortunately, the meeting had failed to produce the results she had hoped for. The unexpected disaster had changed everything. Sighing, the creature spun her head in frustration, trying to contain her disappointment. Lamenting the frailty of human offspring, she realized her mission must wait. Even though the boy had appeared to be a good choice, at the moment his youth disqualified him. She should measure her expectations carefully next time. Remembering the young of humans took twenty two years for their brains to mature, her mistake shamed her.

Life worked more efficiently for her species as all young were born with their birth parent's genetic memory. The fact that humans had not evolved this necessary trait was a severe disadvantage. She would love to know what the Elders had thought they were accomplishing when they handicapped this life form. A simple adjustment to their enzymes during evolution would have turned the trait on. She knew the Elders rarely made mistakes. Perhaps they had done it deliberately. She promised herself to ask the Womb.

Now, forced to rectify the situation the only way she knew, even though it might cause more problems, she must leave the boy alone. Sadly, she climbed down the rock, wobbling over to the boy. She watched his eyes flutter, bringing him back to consciousness. Hurrying, she reached out to grab the cake, still remarkably intact, clutching it tightly under her arm. She wobbled over to the cairn of rocks that marked the way to the Hive and disappeared.

Scotty sat up slowly. *What am I doing on the ground?* He could feel the rough edges of the cold rocks digging into his tender skin. He picked himself up off the chilly rocks and made his way back to the glen he usually played in. Looking around, confusion made him dizzy. Shaking it off, he stretched and yawned, freakishly feeling vigorous. Deciding to return home, he wondered if Abby was back from the doctors. She was so tired of late and he needed to help move Mom's stuff from her bedroom to get ready for the Diaz family. Trudging back down the hill, he wondered what had happened to the piece of birthday cake he had taken to the woods with him.

Deep inside the cavern, the creature blinked her golden eyes, curled up in her chamber, golden tail wrapped protectively around her furry body as she contemplated the shrinking piece of cake in front of her. She did not take it to eat, not having that capability. Curiosity had compelled her; it had belonged to the human Brother. Maybe it would help with the sadness she felt, knowing he could have been The One. The only reason the Womb had allowed the healing was because she had caused the incident. The humane solution called for the creature to have let him die in the fall. Sadly, even though he now lived, the human would confront a troublesome road.

She ached with the knowledge that the only thing she envisioned for herself was the unremitting loneliness of passing years. Reaching out with one of her long golden leathery fingers, she stroked the tiny piece of cake and closed her eyes.

Chapter 4

Jose hardly remembered his birthplace. At fifteen years old, his height outstripped the average teen from Costa Rica, a lush country known for its riches, lovely people and diverse topography: mountains, volcanoes, wet rainforests, dry rainforest, hot springs, mud baths, coastlines on two different oceans and rich fabulous wildlife. Unfortunately, he now lived in New Jersey with his adoptive family. A singularly ugly state of cement, asphalt, exhaust-filled highways, billboards, high security prisons, massive tenements and poverty.

He couldn't bear to think about his beautiful mother, yet he continued to torture himself with the pain, knowing he would never forget. She was found in the garden of their home in San Jose, where his father worked as a police officer.

His father had been found that morning, in his car in front of his favorite breakfast place. He stopped there every morning, without fail, on his way to the station. He just loved what they could do with a few leftovers and some fresh eggs. He knew they were fresh because he personally knew the names of the chickens in the back of the restaurant. He liked to stick his head in the backyard and say hello to the old mama that fed them. That morning, his head had been found sitting in his bloody lap, neatly detached. No one confessed to witnessing a thing.

The town, ruled by the Para Militar who had merged with the FARC from Columbia, knew survival meant silence. They used to have a mayor and a police force which enforced the law. Now, everyone answered to the drug cartels—cartels who had created their own army, the Sicario, the assassins. They wore snappy green and black uniforms and applied the laws the police used to enforce.

Of course, now the laws were full of a few kickers. And they frequently changed depending on the whims of the cartels. The country belonged to them. They controlled much of Mexico, all of

Central America and most of Northern South America. Life moved on even with the cartels in charge; the mass murders of fifteen years ago well in the past. Citizens were weary of the blood spilt in almost every family. But once the cartels stepped into the breach and took power they, unsurprisingly, started to resemble the previous corrupt politicians and leaders. Some ruled through democracy, some through intimidation.

The people learned to complain in whispers and behind closed doors. The cartels never gave up their infamous habit of silencing detractors with a well-placed bullet or the more soundless stiletto. The occasional rape of a detractor's spouse or youngest daughter was also a very effective tool.

Jose wondered what had brought the Garcia family to the attention of the cartels. His poor papa knew to keep his mouth shut. His law enforcement job had evolved over the years to traffic enforcement only. He didn't even carry a gun. His parents were renowned for their generosity and well-bred gentility. They had made a very striking couple.

The hot afternoon drew to a close as he made his daily after-school stop at Senor Brooks' house. Senor Brooks lived in what used to be his best friend, Juan Bastida's, family home.

A year ago, Juan's father had mysteriously disappeared, leaving the house available for Senor Brooks to lease. He was a fine retired military man; a gringo who loved the wildlife of Jose's country. He had lived near the Garcia family for about a year, getting to know Jose very well and enjoying his company. He never minded whenever Jose stopped after school to play with his small collection of primates. In fact, he encouraged it.

Senor Brooks' collection consisted of two African vervet monkeys, a pair of howler monkeys, and a pair of white-faced monkeys. Jose loved them all. He could not get enough of their tiny wise furry faces; so vulnerable, so human and so capricious. Senor Brooks often sat and took tea with Jose as he played with the primates, asking him questions about school and sometimes commenting on Senor Brooks' past life in the United States. He told

Jose how lucky he was to grow up in a country filled with such natural beauty, not spoiled and paved over as in the States. He talked of the great slums and poverty in the U.S. He often inquired into the health of his parents, noting how they never seemed to be ill—*an odd remark*, Jose thought in retrospect. His parents were blessed with excellent health, except for the polio his mother had contracted while pregnant with Cara.

Senor Brooks always perked up when he mentioned Jose's baby sister. At nine months old, Jose loved her desperately. From the top of her head all the way down to her tiny feet with the purple half-moon on her tiny big toe. He would actually have nightmares about their house catching on fire and his desperation to save her. The nightmares haunted him, magnifying his subconscious anxiety for her safety.

He did not go directly home that day. He hurried from school, walking quickly down the unpaved stone street, the burning sun sucking the moisture from anything touched by its withering rays. He turned off the intersection to the country road leading to his home.

Normally, he tried very hard to help his mama with Cara, but Senor Brooks had asked him if he wanted to hold the monkeys while he cleaned their cages; always an ordeal. But it was a nice chance to hold the monkeys and distract them with play while Senor Brooks cleaned the big ornamental metal cages. Helping Senor Brooks with the monkeys left him feeling special. He liked knowing the monkeys needed him. They were significant to him. He knew they waited for him after school. He didn't ever want to let them down. Mama and Cara would still be there when he eventually got home.

Leaving Senor Brooks' house, he arrived home about sixty minutes later than normal. He walked along the red dirt road, three houses away, scuffing his feet in the hot dust, when he saw two men emerge from the metal gate in the front yard of his home. Their demeanor appeared suspicious. One of them carried a bundle in his arms. Jose noticed black and green pants under the man's serape. Glancing up at the sun, he wondered who in their right minds would wear a serape in this weather. It could only be the black and green uniform of the dreaded Sicario.

Jose noticed they stared intently in his direction. He quickly ducked his head and looked down at his sandals, managing to observe the bundle, clearly wrapped in an afghan with a maize design and a bright turquoise border; the design original to and crafted by his mama. Jose continued walking past his house until he could no longer see the two men.

Doubling back to his home, he let himself in by the gate. He ran through the house in a panic, calling for his mama. Stepping out to the terrace, he saw his mama fast asleep on her chaise longue. Her leg, encased in the ever-present metal brace, had fallen off in the lounge, her hand draped inside Cara's baby carriage. He relaxed, relief instantly flooding his small body.

Running over to his mama he called her name, laughing and chattering on about Senor Brooks and his monkeys. Rounding his mama's chair he stopped in his tracks, his stunned eyes unable to comprehend the meaning of the thick bib of blood congealing down the front of his beautiful mama's chest, or the drying crimson slash across her throat. The same chest he remembered cuddling up to as a toddler. He would be seven years old tomorrow.

Things happened quickly after he began screaming. He remembered Senor Brooks lifting him up in his strong comforting arms. His screaming abated as he was carried into Senor Brooks' garden where the monkeys lived. Reduced to whimpering, he felt himself carried upstairs and tucked into a bed in a strange room. Senor Brooks stretched out Jose's vulnerable arm, inserting a needle. He tried to open his mouth to ask for his papa, but couldn't make his thick, sluggish tongue work. Gently, he slipped off to another universe, where his beautiful mama and Cara waited with incandescent smiles, his mama's ugly brace gone; her leg straight and healthy, alongside his handsome papa who called to him.

He heard his papa call his name again, sounding far away. He struggled to wake up, his eyelids felt loaded down with sludge. He could feel Papa helping him out of bed. He dressed slowly, his limbs insisting they belonged to someone else. Papa told him they must go to a funeral. He felt himself being carried down a staircase. He must not be at home; they had no stairs in the house. Coming to a stop, he forced his eyes to open. He recognized the garden where the monkeys lived, their cages open and the monkeys gone. *I must find Senor Brooks*, he thought to himself, sluggishly. *Someone made off with his monkeys.* He struggled to keep his eyes open, but failed.

Helpless and unaware, hands tucked him into a car and drove off. Unable to stop himself, he slept. Feeling the car halt, he woke; his sight wavy and indistinct, objects faraway as if underwater. The car door opened, a hand assisted him out. Dozens of eyes pinned him down as he struggled to stand. A priest appeared, his silent mouth moving, hands gesticulating. Jose shrank back, confused and disoriented. His eyes tried to focus on the big hole in the ground and the coffins sitting nearby. Two coffins.

He wondered who had died. Where had his papa gone? He cast his eyes down, searching for his papa's big feet in the crowd. His drooping lids identified the men that papa worked with, all tall and somber in their official uniforms, his neighbors grouped behind. He spotted Mama's lady friends, many sobbing. The urge to lie down fought with his rising panic. Noticing a coffin being lowered into the hole, he looked around for his family. Faltering, he slipped. Struggling to his feet, he screamed for his mama and papa. Hands reached out, trying to restrain him. Hope flared as Senor Brooks stepped before him, arms opened wide. He hardly felt the sudden pinprick on his neck. Gratefully, his eyes rolled back in his head as he was sucked into a deep soundless sleep.

Jose woke on an airplane with Senor Brooks and a splitting headache. By commercial standards, the plane looked like a mosquito, but to Jose it felt like a monstrous metal creature sporting a cold steel stomach that had somehow swallowed him up. Scanning the empty seats, he wondered where everybody was.

Turning to Senor Brooks, his sleepy voice begged to know the whereabouts of his papa. Senor Brooks calmly revealed the horror, his voice tinged with impatience.

"Jose, you know your papa and mama died in an accident. Remember the funeral? Everyone attended. Your parents' honor turned out quite a crowd. Yes, yes. So tragic, Cara too. Now we must move on and meet your new family."

"I don't want a new family. I want to go home, please." His quivery voice made no dent in the recitation of the plans Senor Brooks had made for him. As the words washed over the sound of the engines, they began to sink in. His heart tripped with panic. "I think I need to go home now, I don't feel too good."

"My boy . . . let me get you something. This will help." Passing Jose a cola, he inquired if he cared for something to eat. Jose gratefully nodded. The pretty lady who stood next to his seat returned with a wonderful lunch for them both. Jose couldn't remember the last time he had eaten.

Sipping his cola, he thought it was unusually sweet. Maybe it was a different brand then the one he usually drank. Finishing his lunch he turned to his friend. "Can we please go home now?"

Senor Brooks put his arm around Jose, squeezing his shoulders. "Come on now, champ, you need to make your papa proud. He would only want the best for you. He wanted me to take you to the best place I thought you would be safe, be happy and excel. Do you know what he told me before he died? He made me promise to take you to the U.S.A. And that is exactly where we are going."

"But the U.S.A. is a bad place. You told me yourself. Bad people live there. Everyone is poor. I want to go home."

Senor Brooks didn't hear him. He picked up a magazine and began reading as if the short conversation was over.

Jose sat, silent with confusion. He was happy to be with Senor Brooks, but too much change frightened him. Where were his mama and papa? He did not believe they were dead. Had he remembered to tell Senor Brooks that someone had made off with his monkeys?

Everything confused him. *The United States—why would Papa want me to go so far from everything I know?*

His translucent eyelids slipped heavily down. That's all he seemed to do, sleep. As he drifted off, he thought he heard the cry of an infant. It seemed to be coming from the back of the plane. Or maybe it was just an old memory. He slept soundly the rest of the way, immersed in the happy memory of Cara spitting up all over his papa as he tossed her in the air, making him and his mama laugh hysterically.

Jose did not adjust well to his new family. His sorrow for his own family turned to anger, leaving him a bitter shell, just going through the motions. It was especially difficult as he did not fully understand English. He had learned a little in grade school in Costa Rica, but not enough to blend in. Even though his new family was Hispanic, they did not speak the language. Spanish used to be taught in American schools, but, like most things, it had fallen to the absolute knife of budget cuts. As a result, he felt foreign and different; just what a child recovering from severe trauma did *not* want. He became the strange new kid in school. No friends, no *real* family.

In time, the shock and confusion of the days after the death of his family receded to a manageable simmer. He changed quickly from a secure happy little boy to a resentful disobedient delinquent. He refused to interact with the Diaz family, unable to establish any sort of bond with them. He ran away from their home many times. Each time, Senor Brooks tracked him down and returned him. Whenever he saw Senor Brooks, he deluged him with questions and entreaties to let him go home. Senor Brooks became less and less communicative, closing the door on any of the hope Jose had managed to hold on to.

He began to wonder at the unusual coincidence of Senor Brooks finding him every time he ran away. What about the coincidence of Senor Brooks living in the U.S. now, just like him? Jose had never received answers to any of his questions. He stopped asking to go home. Finally, the time came when Jose no longer burned with the desire to run away, and Senor Brooks disappeared from his life altogether.

Sometimes being very young has its advantages. Mother Nature gave youth an astonishing ability to heal; physically and mentally. Slowly, the traumatized young boy's natural curiosity helped draw him out of his bitter shell. He began to take comfort from the unrelenting warmth of Mama Diaz and her clan.

The Diaz family welcomed him warmly. They even agreed to adopt him. He later learned that Senor Brooks had moved the whole family to the country as a result of their agreement to take him in. Their previous home, a tenement city fraught with danger and dead end opportunity for the kids, became merely a distant memory.

It had been overwhelming at first, of course. The Diaz children treated him like a new house pet. The two girls, Emma and chubby little Bonita, aggressively staked their claim. They loved to dress him in their ragged finery, forcing him to play house. He became their prime choice, always the reluctant victim, coercing him to try their latest recipe of dirt cakes and sand scones.

The two boys, Tomas and Hiro loved having him be their third against the blacks and Muslims when they teamed up to play kick the can, touch football or water tag down at the neighborhood swimming hole. Tomas always seemed to get a bit of extra pleasure whenever Jose took some extra hard lumps, though.

Jose's life took a turn for the better when Papa Diaz brought home a surprise from his job at the fabric mill, one of the few manufacturing concerns in the county. A plum job and only achieved through the intervention of Senor Brooks, which had caused quite a bit of resentment from other disgruntled applicants on the waiting list for the next opening. Papa Diaz was an outsider, after all.

The puppy wandered onto the mill's property during a lunch break. He reeked: a sad and dirty little guy. Tight, possibly white, curly hair all but obscured his intelligent needy eyes. His long tail wagged so much and so hard it sported bald spots and painful bruises. Attracted by the smells and crumbs from the lunch crowd, he ran from person to person, begging for food. His starving body shivered with malnutrition, his ribs ready to pop through his paper-thin skin. Sores surfaced through his fur where fleabites tortured him.

At the end of the day, when the mill workers headed home from their shift, the pup lingered, trotting behind the exodus to the parking lot, his frantic tail crying, *take me home, take me home.* But no one responded.

By the time Papa Diaz left for home, the deserted parking lot echoed the pup's loneliness. He sat in the corner of the brick building in the weeds, shivering and discarded. As Papa Diaz came out the door he froze, desperation written on his demoralized face. Hope rose like a feather caught in the breeze, long ago discarded, now wafting forward. He sat frozen, only the hesitant motion of his eyes speaking of life as he watched Papa Diaz walk toward him. Papa Diaz stood in front of the pup as it silently looked up at him, too defeated even to beg. Bending down, he picked up the scrawny little guy, tucked him inside his overcoat and resolutely took him home.

They named him Barney. It was love at first sight for Jose. The abandoned pup's story reflected his own. He found in Barney the one thing that provided medicine to draw the poison from his psychological wounds. No longer alone, their damaged souls began to heal as they found comfort and security in each other's raw love.

The years passed. Jose grew, surprising everyone with his tall, lanky good looks. He became reasonably popular in school, good grades coming easily to him. But he remained shy, confiding in no one, Barney his constant companion to the exclusion of other kids. He knew Mama Diaz loved him fiercely, but worried about what she sensed at the back of his eyes. Just a small something at the end of the day as fatigue overwhelmed him. She said it looked like a hurt, or was it distrust? She made him sit with her so they could pray. With Barney at his feet, they sat at the kitchen table. With the Virgin Mary hanging on the wall, they prayed that life would be kind to him.

Late one Friday evening, after dinner, everyone gathered in the small but cozy living room. No one noticed the peeling walls or stained hardwood floors. The girls fought to sit next to Jose and

Barney, and the boys pounded on each other until Mama Diaz silenced them.

"Papa Diaz has a serious announcement." Her calm voice betrayed a hitch of tension that demanded their attention better than words could hope to. In a low calm voice, eyes cast to the floor, Papa Diaz broke the news fated to change Jose's life again.

The fabric mill had announced layoffs, their margins slipping. He had received his termination papers last week. With decent paying jobs nonexistent, Papa Diaz had decided to try to jump the fence, the possibility of getting caught the only drawback. It was a felony and would mean a long jail sentence. The government and cartels of Mexico were determined to protect their jobs for their own citizens, and who could blame them?

Mama and Papa had decided to merge the family with another fatherless family in the neighborhood, and the Diaz's arranged to move into the Preston home down the hill—two families banding together to help each other so they might all survive. The thought of moving in with a new family didn't really disturb anyone. They all understood the economics. Yes, it would be a bit unusual, two different ethnic backgrounds. But in the country, far from the urban centers, that factor took on a lesser significance.

Jose knew of the family. He vaguely knew Abby Preston from school. And everyone knew her twerpy younger brother, Scotty. He could be found anywhere, lurking all over the neighborhood like the ugly unwanted kid, shut out of the candy store while everyone else lived it up on the inside; kinda sad. Not too many white kids in the neighborhood; no one for him to play with. And what the heck had happened to his head? Ick. Maybe things would change for him now that they would be moving in together. He shrugged to himself. It wasn't really his concern.

Now Abby was a different story. A little older than him, they really never spoke. A slender pretty girl, he admired her thick cinnamon hair. He remembered something about her being sick. She sure looked healthy to him; probably a rumor.

That night, as Jose lay in bed, he realized that when Papa Diaz headed back to Mexico, he would be without a male authority figure in his life again. First Papa, then Senor Brooks, then Papa Diaz. The Preston kids lacked a father too. Guess they had something in common.

Drifting off to sleep, he fought the disturbing fragments of memory following the hazy death of his family. In his dream, he tried fruitlessly to outrun the ache and insecurity of his turbulent nightmares. He cuddled Barney desperately in his sleep.

Barney woke with a whine, his own doggy dreams just as frightening. His rough sloppy tongue reached up to Jose's familiar face for reassurance. Waking, Jose gave Barney a tender kiss on his muzzle and drifted back to sleep.

Chapter 5
2055 AD

Moving day had come and gone; so had Papa Diaz. The layoffs never materialized, but the dominant faction at the mill pushed him out anyway, never forgiving him for getting preferential treatment during his hiring. Since they no longer enjoyed the benevolent attention of Senor Brooks, the family knew they would sink or swim on their own. Hopefully, Papa Diaz would not get caught crossing the border.

When Mrs. Preston lost her welfare, she knew she must find a way to supplement her income or move back to public housing. The Diaz family faced the same options. Both mothers refused to do that to their kids. They all flourished in Sussex County and that was where everyone intended to stay, including Barney.

Barney made a big splash with the two Preston kids, quite the slobbering icebreaker. The Prestons had never had a pet before, only some imaginary golden fairy which the kid yakked on and on about to anyone who would listen.

They all attended the same school system. The little ones went on the school bus and Abby, Jose, Tomas and Hiro now walked to the regional high school. Abby was ready to graduate this spring. Tomas and Jose were both in their sophomore year, Hiro a freshman.

As it turned out, Abby truly was sick. It took a lot out of her family to make sure she got her dialysis every week. The whisper around the neighborhood said she would never be able to have her own family. It was a well-known fact that unless the Prestons managed to buy one of the Chinese kidneys, she would probably not make it past thirty. You couldn't tell from knowing her, though. She might be a little too slender, but she sported one of the widest smiles in school. And her generosity was just as inclusive. She made time for everyone: a smile here, a word of encouragement there; always the one to sort out disagreements at home and the first to pass on dessert if they came up short. She treated Jose like a kid brother, no more, no less.

*

Time passed uneventfully, the kids all doing fairly well in school. Abby graduated and was lucky to find a job with an Internet company doing web processing. Before long, Tomas and Jose graduated, both finding local work: Jose learning how to weld and Tomas driving a long haul truck. Hiro still needed to complete his last year of high school.

Papa Diaz found a job in Mexico. He sent home money and letters, making a big difference to the family. The letters tapered off after a few years, then so did the money. Mama Diaz confided to Mrs. Preston her suspicions about a new family. Men who had left home were well known for womanizing, even the best of them. But to reject the responsibilities of supporting the family you'd left behind in a poor country while you took off for a rich one with better opportunity? It cut deeply.

Tomas and Hiro were profoundly affected. Hiro closed down, keeping his emotions bottled up, confiding in no one. He dropped out of school, joining Mrs. Preston at her job in the grocery store. But Tomas became a hard case. He developed a real nasty edge, dissing Jose every chance he got. He started stealing supplies from the school, then disappearing for days after Mama Diaz or Mrs. Preston confronted him. He stopped contributing to the household. Everyone tried to give him the benefit of the doubt, but he sarcastically rejected every attempt to reach out.

Jose felt closer and closer to Abby and Scotty. The three of them all harbored insecurities; being self-described outsiders created a natural bond: Abby, because of her medical needs draining the family's resources, and Scotty, because of his secret disability. Oh, yes, Scotty hid a secret.

Tomas and Jose eventually moved out. Each had found girlfriends, Tomas moving in with his. Mama Diaz sorely missed their financial contribution, but she found a job in a local restaurant. Things were not too God awful. Emma and chubby Bonita, who now insisted on being called Bonnie, grew up; ready for high school. Life had actually been kind to the blended family, everyone growing up safely with a decent roof over their heads. Now that Tomas no longer lived with them, they found the tension in the house over his antics evaporate and laughter crept back into their lives.

The only problem now, was sixteen-year-old Scotty. The last few years found him developing some unusual behaviors. He became very withdrawn and secretive, although a miracle manifested in his lazy eye and skin conditions. The bald spots on his ringworm scars began to grow hair in an unusual glowing blond. His lazy eye stopped wandering and his impetigo scars disappeared. Under the circumstances, he should have been wild with joy. Tragically, he hardly noticed.

Scotty moved into the bedroom with Hiro after Tomas and Jose moved out. He currently suffered his misery alone; face down on his messy bed, waiting for Hiro to return from work with Scotty's mother. He rolled over onto his back, wracked with the apprehension and distress that had become his constant companions since the beginning of the growth of his tail. Yeah, that's right. *A tail*. Not a small one either. At the same time as his tail had begun to grow, he started his growth spurt; so sudden and remarkable that his bones constantly ached, especially the back of his shoulder blades. Now, he measured a full six feet tall. And his tail? The same length: six feet of golden muscle and fur. *Fur*. He balled his fists tightly, anger and fear fighting to overwhelm him.

He concealed his new tail by winding it around his torso under his shirt, the expanding bulbous end presenting little problem as he forced it to flatten against his abdomen. The gold sheen developing in his eyes presented a dicey dilemma. The danger of intrusive questions was the most pronounced when he stood in the sun. As a result, he stayed inside during the day. He only went outside when he was sure he would be alone, which, by the way, was most of the time. Strangely, he often felt compelled to go outside. He yearned for the sun, a new effect that energized him.

He no longer ate food like the rest of the family. His mom noticed but let it go, not commenting. He pretended the concern in her eyes wasn't for him. Hopefully, she chalked up his behavior to normal teenage angst. He covered by pushing his food around on his plate, feeding his dinner to his new bud, Barney. When Jose moved out, he left the poor dog behind, making Scotty promise to take care of him. Funny how much comfort Barney brought him.

He missed Jose immensely. Jose had eventually told Scotty most of his family history over the years. It made Scotty feel small as he compared his own nasty problems with his father who had disappeared, *thankfully*, nine years ago, to Jose's story of tragedy. They grew very close. Jose took on a big brother role with Scotty, inadvertently enabling him to better weather the physiological shock when his tail began to grow.

It had started with constant soreness, then swelling and finally breakthrough growth. He didn't mention it to his mom because he knew they didn't have money for doctors anyway, Abby's treatments were only barely affordable. He hoped it would resolve itself on its own. When it became clear that something was actually growing, he thought it might develop into cancer—a scary fatal cancer. He watched fearfully as it developed quickly into its present form, finally fascinating him. He became very secretive. Even though clearly a freak, he didn't want to be labeled again, still smarting from childhood taunts that had left psychological scabs on his vanished scars, too easily picked open.

What disturbed him the most? The big *why. Why him? Why now?* Maybe an infection? Was it evolution run amok? And shock of all shocks, he couldn't get over the fact that the tail felt *completely natural*. He could move it at will. He liked it. And that scared him the most.

Chapter 6
2056 AD

As time moved on, Scotty ached to confide in someone. His life felt like an emotional roller coaster. He vacillated between fear and depression, frustration and insecurity. And pride, can't forget that. If he outed himself, someone might tell him his tail must be removed or put him on display. He felt like a freak; the kind of freak that might send the authorities slobbering to get a chance to study him and steal his paltry life with its insignificant pleasures.

So he decided to keep secret the horrific changes his body continued to produce. Even the hair that grew back through his ringworm scars looked different. Abby teased him, saying the bleached blond look didn't really work with his dark hair color. He tried to pass it off as the latest style at school, although it was more blond now than anything else. He almost didn't recognize himself in the mirror.

The kids at school sure noticed. He couldn't fail to notice the whispers behind his back, the fingers pointing in the hallways, the garbage dumped in his locker or the crude comments written on the blackboards; probably because of his eye. It no longer wandered. It stayed centered just like his other eye. Abby and his mom were stumped but very happy for him. Maybe in time the kids would stop singling him out and want to be friends. Sighing, he prayed that when he got older, maybe then he could confess and seek help without fear.

He did have another thought, totally ridiculous of course, lodged in the back of his mind, gnawing away like a wolf cub cutting its baby teeth on its first bone. As a child, he had played in the woods constantly. He vaguely remembered an incident involving some kind of traumatic experience in the woods. Mostly because his mother laughingly told him something must have happened.

His seventh birthday; the day he wished his father dead. He remembered that part clearly. He remembered running off to the woods and falling asleep on top of a huge rock. Things got fuzzy from there, but he knew he had left the woods with a very valuable gold coin. Abby remembered a fanciful story of meeting a golden fairy. He cringed when he thought about how much of an idiot he had sounded. He knew he hadn't met a fairy, duh. Just the mention of it embarrassed him. God knew what he might have said as a kid. Nonetheless, he did have an impression of talking to someone. And he remembered having dreams about a golden glow, perhaps eyes? All very nebulous and confusing. His changes had begun sometime after that.

He sighed. Sliding off the bed, he pulled open his bottom dresser drawer where he kept his treasures. Taking out a tiny wooden box, he opened the lock and pulled out the gold coin. His mother had decided they would save it for Scotty's college studies. The coin would provide more than enough money to give him an education; almost unheard of for the likes of him. His mama understandably put all her hopes for a better life on Scotty. She thought he stood a good chance of succeeding. No one dared to fantasize about Abby's future. They all knew the chances of her living a normal lifespan. Slim to none.

Scotty wanted to use the coin to buy a new kidney for Abby, but they discovered on the Internet that a kidney could cost over $200,000. The coin was only worth a little over half that. Abby cried over Scotty's generosity, refusing to take anything from him that would compromise his own chance for a future. He remembered the pitiful look on her face. Abby wouldn't be in such a jam if he or his mom were a tissue match. They'd learned a long time ago how to deal with that disappointment.

The clock said it was time for his mother and Hiro to come home from the grocery. He liked to put the kettle on for them so she could relax her legs and catch up with Scotty about his day. When he was a kid, he liked to rub the leg with the brace, hoping he could make it all better. The memories were silly, he knew, but he loved his mom, so there you have it.

He put on his shoes and walked out to the living room where Barney lay relaxing his old bones. He tipped his head off the floor in greeting, his tail thumping its own special hello. Scotty slid down to the worn green carpet, wrapping Barney up in a big hug, always a loyal and happy-go-lucky member of their extended family.

He had never caused a lick of trouble, except for one odd day a couple of years back. Barney had come home from his morning run to show Scotty his underbelly cut open and leaking blood. Somehow, he had walked over something sharp which had slit him open. His mom rushed Barney to the front porch to stop him bleeding everywhere. While she ran to find Jose to drive her to the vet, Barney took off. Discovering him missing, Jose reassured everyone that he would find their injured mutt and raced after him, following his bloody trail.

Jose and Barney were gone for hours. Emma and Bonnie refused to go to school until Barney returned home. So Scotty stayed home to wait while his mom went off to work with Mama Diaz, leaving her old Dodge behind so Jose could get to the vet's office. Finally, after four hours, they both returned. Jose looked kinda weird, a blank expression in his eyes. Barney acted like he had just discovered he was the sole dog in bunny rabbit heaven. And there was no blood, no sign of a cut, nothing; only blissful Barney wanting to jump in everyone's lap and demanding his share of doggy love.

Without explanation, Jose yelled at them to get their schoolbooks and off they went, even though only two hours remained of the school day. One look at Jose's stormy face shut everyone up. No mention of the incident ever came up again. No one cared anyway, since Barney behaved better than ever and that's all that mattered. And not having a big vet's bill to pay, of course.

Scotty looked again at the clock which relentlessly proclaimed it to be past his bedtime. Where was his mother? She was really late now. He decided not to wait up. Taking Barney out for a potty break, he glanced balefully up the hill toward the enigmatic woods from his childhood. Could he find a clue in the woods to this strange transformation that had gripped him? *Just rocks and trees and creatures*, he thought, *nothing sinister*. Although in the dark, the woods looked unwelcoming and dangerous. He didn't lack for imagination.

Whistling for Barney, he took him back inside the house. Shaking off a premonition, he gave the woods a last glance. Peeking in the kitchen, he noticed everyone had gone to bed. There was still no sign of his mother or Hiro. *He probably got stuck late stocking shelves. Mom would have to wait for him, unfortunately.*

Scotty slept the deep sleep of youth, dreaming of the soapbox derby car Jose had built for him when he turned ten. A well-known klutz with tools, Jose had taught him how to use a hammer. He could still hear the two of them banging on the car while Tomas and Hiro mocked them, threatening to tear it apart. And banging and banging.

The noise jerked him from his slumber. Annoyed and groggy, he opened his eyes, realizing someone was banging on his bedroom door. Throwing back the blanket, he glanced over at Hiro's bed; still empty. His alarm said 3 a.m.

"Scotty, wake up."

More pounding; it sounded like Abby. Yawning, he pulled open the door and rubbed the sleep from his eyes, grumbling. Abby stood there with a frayed sweater thrown over her pajamas. She was wearing her worn sneakers and held her ratty blue jacket in her hands, her face colorless and tear stained. Scotty grabbed her hands.

"Abby, what's wrong? Abby."

She looked beseechingly into his eyes, silently begging for help. "Hiro . . . he's dead," she whispered.

"What?" Shaking Abby hard, his heart thudding, he screamed, "Where's Mom?"

"She's at the hospital. They said she's hurt. They haven't even checked her in yet. She's been there since last night. We have to get over there."

"What happened? What happened to Hiro? Where is he?"

"It was an accident. I don't know any more than that. Let's go."

Grabbing a pair of jeans, Scotty slipped them on over his pajamas, pulling a shirt down over his top. Grabbing his smelly sneakers, he ran barefoot out the door behind Abby. Mama Diaz waited in the driveway, trembling. Her fingers danced wildly over her rosary, uncombed hair streaming down her back, bedroom slippers still on her feet. Abby coaxed her into her old Ford, the agonizing drive to the hospital a nightmare of desperate prayers and anguished promises to God from the back seat.

Arriving at the hospital, they parked, maneuvering around the crowd congregating near the emergency room. The line snaked out the door. Lucky 'emergencies' with appointments used the exclusive door. Scanning the crowd, they spotted Jose running toward them. He took his mama in his arms. She broke down completely, emotionally debilitated.

"My baby boy, my Hiro," she sobbed. "God, why did you rip out my heart?"

"She shouldn't have come." Jose softly kissed the top of his grieving mama's head. "There is nothing she can do. Hiro was killed instantly. A tractor trailer—it clipped their car and kept on going. They ran off the road into a tree, head on." Glancing over at Abby, he evasively refused to meet her eyes. Kissing his mama again, he hesitantly took Abby's hands in his.

"Jose, where's Mom?" Abby looked up into his eyes, hope slowly shredding. Jose shook his head, hot tears spilling over. Abby whimpered.

"Jose, where is she?" Scotty's voice crackled with knowing pain. Jose folded them both into his big arms. They understood what he couldn't say.

Shocked, dazed and in denial, they returned to the Ford. Jose handled the minutiae of paperwork while they waited, silently railing at God's unfairness.

Mama Diaz took care of breaking the news to Bonnie and Emma. They squirmed incessantly, scared and not too young to wonder how the deaths would affect their lives.

Jose called Tomas and broke the news to him. He came to the house as soon as possible, bringing his girlfriend Kelly and unnecessary tension with him. Tomas sat in the living room, conferring with his mother in whispers. Jose, Abby and Scotty sat at the kitchen table looking glumly at one other. From time to time, Jose answered the phone, pausing to ask Abby a question, updating Mama Diaz.

Eventually, all the funeral details fell into place and quiet blanketed the house. Scotty sat in a fog, picking at a sandwich, feeding pieces to Barney. He absently noticed Bonnie surreptitiously feeding Barney under the table and made a note to cut down on Barney's chow. He already looked like a giant white sausage ready to explode.

Looking up, he noticed the whispering. Jose and Abby were in the corner, his arms around her, her tearful face pressed into his shoulder as he whispered in her ear. Emma and Bonnie sat curled up on the sofa, fearful eyes darting from one adult to another.

Finally, everyone gathered around the table. Mama Diaz cleared her throat. She looked first at Jose, then Tomas, giving him a slow sad nod. Tomas stood, looking around the table.

"We've all been together for years. And they've been good years, but we need to make some changes now." Looking at Abby and Scotty, he lowered his voice. "Mama will be taking the girls and moving in with Kelly and me. We were thinking of getting married anyway. Mama's job at the restaurant and the money Abby makes would not be enough to support all of you. Abby's money has to go for her treatments anyway."

"So, Scotty and I will be here alone?" asked Abby.

"No, Abby, I'm moving in. I can pay for the house and anything else that we need," said Jose.

Abby flushed as Jose looked at her.

Scotty looked from face to face. They all looked tense and stressed. There was nothing worse than the death of a family member, but *two* members? Catastrophic. He pounded on the table, jumped up and ran into his bedroom, returning with his little wooden box.

Slapping the box on the table he shouted, "No. We are not splitting up! Mom and Hiro wouldn't want that." He blew his nose as

Jose picked up the box and took out the gold coin. His face looked grim and determined.

"Scotty, that coin is for your education. We can take care of this without cashing it in. It's time for some changes anyway. Come on, kid, let's you and I take Barney out for a walk. We can talk."

"No," he mumbled, gruffly. "I want Mom back. You can't try to take her place." Throwing his coin across the room, he burst into tears and ran out of the front door. Abby got up from her seat to go to him and then thought better of it, wearily sitting back down.

"Scotty's just reverting to little boy behavior because he's lost Mom and Hiro. Better to leave him alone for a while. He's running off just like he used to as a kid. He'll come home when he's ready." Slipping her arm around Mama Diaz, she looked up at Jose. "Maybe you should go after him if he's not back before dark. Take Barney with you, okay?"

Nodding his agreement, Jose watched as she went to the sofa to hug Emma and Bonnie. She stood, looking at Tomas who hovered, sending loaded glances her way. He held out his arms for a hug, expectation on his face. Abby ignored him and slipped off to bed, her exhaustion weighing her down. Tomas started after her but, realizing everyone was staring, sat back down.

Chapter 7

Scotty ran blindly into the wood, his eyes swollen with tears and anger, instinct taking him through the magic glens of his childhood to the big granite rock that played a role in the fragmented memories of his past. He recognized the toeholds on the side of the rock that he had struggled with as a child. Ruefully, he realized he now need only give himself a big boost and he would be on top. The shallow depression in the top of the rock beckoned. It was only large enough for his butt now, though. Sitting in the depression, he crossed his arms on his knees and lowered his head. His tears fell warm and silent as he tried to come to grips with his loss.

As his tears slowed, he felt a numbness protectively insinuate itself throughout his body. His tears dried. He knew nothing could change what had happened, it was just another thing to live with. His bitterness accentuated the lack of control in his life.

Like his preposterous tail. Letting it unfurl from underneath his shirt, he flexed. It felt good to give it a little exercise. He looked at it critically. His guilty feeling of pride mystified him. How could he feel this way when he knew it made him a freak? He wished he had been able to talk to his mother about it. Nah—that would have just messed with her head. Sighing, he turned his face up to the waning sun as it peeked through the branches of oak and elm trees. His eyes caught a sunbeam as it unexpectedly exploded with golden rainbows. He blinked, lowering his head to find himself staring into the same rainbow eyes of his boyhood fairy creature.

Scotty froze, so shocked he couldn't move. He just stared. Then carefully he inched on his butt to the edge of the rock. The creature just stood there, silent, staring back at him. Scotty's nerves spasmed convulsively—the silence incendiary. Watching the creature, he awkwardly lifted his hand and broke the silence.

"Hi."

No reaction. Maybe the creature couldn't talk. Maybe he barked or mewed. *He did kinda resemble a cat or something. No, on second thought . . . not with those long leathery fingers and horns, definitely not a cat.* To be sure, Scotty said, "Meow?" Nothing. What if he tried barking? The creature's fragile horns resembled cut glass, sending mesmerizing refracted rainbows, generated by sunlight, spinning and tumbling off the tree trunks as it breathed.

"I see you found Echo."

Startled, Scotty looked down, surprised by none other than Jose and Barney. Barney stood wagging his tail so hard it looked like his tail was wagging his head. The creature turned and took an amazing flying leap, landing in Jose's arms.

"What the heck is going on here?" Scotty demanded angrily. He stood with his tail swirling around him. He quickly turned away in embarrassment while it tucked itself away under his shirt. Turning back, his jaw dropped as Jose lifted his own shirt, unfurling a glimmering golden tail of his own.

"I don't . . ." Scotty paused, confounded. "I don't get it. What's going on here?" His voice cracked, on the verge of hysteria. Unexpectedly, his mind sensed a foreign pressure, a hovering aura.

"You are both my Brothers now." A calming disembodied whisper hung somewhere in the air. Scotty looked around, bewildered.

"That's Echo. She doesn't talk the way we do. I named her Echo because I hear her in my mind, just like you do." Jose's matter-of-fact statement grabbed Scotty's attention, holding him back from freaking out. Placing Echo back on the rock, Jose boosted himself up and called to Barney to join them. Leaping up, Barney snuggled up to Echo who promptly climbed onto his back and sat there.

"Are you kidding me, dude? I cannot be seeing this." Incredulous, Scotty looked from Jose to Barney to Echo. "She? It's real?"

"Yes, Scotty, she's real." Flicking his tail toward Scotty, he added, "And this is real, just like yours."

"We're the same?" Breaking down, he climbed down from the rock and flung himself into Jose's arms, crying the healing tears which would say goodbye to his childhood and start him on the path to manhood. He no longer felt alone. He didn't know what the heck had happened to him years ago, but now he knew he could count on Jose's support and guidance.

Once Scotty had calmed down, Jose related the details of the first time he had met Echo.

"I'm sure you've gathered that I'm too old to be playing in the woods. Well, I can thank good old Barney here. He decided he needed to be in the woods. Here at this rock as a matter of fact.

"Do you remember a few years back when Barney came home with his stomach split open and he got away from us before we could get him to the vet? That's the day. I tracked Barney up the hill fairly easily. When he cut into the woods I almost lost him. He still dripped blood, but I was losing the light. With all his blood loss, I couldn't see how he kept going. I finally tracked him here, but I couldn't find him. See over there?" Jose pointed to a cairn of stone that Scotty recognized as where he had found his gold coin so long ago.

"I found some spots of blood over there, but couldn't see where Barney had disappeared to. Then I noticed a spot of blood up against this wall, hidden around back of all the stones. It looked like Barney had just disappeared into the wall. Not only that, but the spot of blood looked like it had been cut in half by the positioning of the wall. So I took my hand—and you are not going to believe this, but I touched the stone and my hand went right through it. It felt all wet and gooey. When I pulled my hand back out, damn if it wasn't completely dry."

"Brother, I could feel you when you touched the Womb." Scotty heard Echo's whisper to Jose, the now golden aura still evident.

"Uh, Echo, what do you mean, the Womb?" Scotty asked timidly.

"We always have a portion of the Womb to travel with. It is part of the Exalted Womb that remains back home on Oolaha. We cannot live without it. It is like your mother and father on this planet. It feeds us, maintains us, protects us, and informs us. I was plugged into the Womb when you put your hand through it. I felt you when you walked through, just like my Barney did." Echo reached down to stroke Barney's head. She wrapped her leathery golden hands around Barney's neck. If Barney could purr, he would purr. If Echo could purr, for that matter, it appeared she would do so, too.

"Your Barney?" Scotty questioned with raised eyebrows.

"Yeah, they have a thing going." Jose laughed—a joyful sound to Scotty.

"But what happened after you entered the uh, womb? And what about our tails? What do they mean? And what—?"

"Hold on, hold on. I know you have a hundred questions. And I know what you've been going through. I've dealt with the same thing. I just had the advantage of knowing more about the situation than you, so I didn't go through the panic you probably did. It's amazing you were able to keep this quiet for so long. Weren't you just a little boy? I sure wish I'd known, champ, I could've helped. Some of the info I'm going to give you will knock your socks off. I don't know everything, but I'll fill you in as much as I can."

Jose related his adventure, crossing through the Womb, finding himself in an enormous cavern. Walking to one side, he had examined the wall, his hand feeling warmth and pliancy. It too, had felt wet and gooey as his hand sank into it. And, no surprise, bone dry after he withdrew it. The cavern reflected illumination, although Jose couldn't see how.

As he had walked deeper into the cavern, he felt himself descend, although the temperature remained a constant mild coolness. The occasional drop of blood marked Barney's path. Jose had walked for about an hour, beginning to get nervous. Pathways opened, shooting off in all directions. The thought of becoming lost raised goosebumps on his arms, but his love and concern for Barney had forced him to press on.

He had soon come to a chamber carved out of the cavern wall, like a private room. Entering the chamber, he had finally located Barney, lying on his side, in a corner. Looking closely, he had been able to see that Barney's intestines protruded from his stomach, the wound now deep and profound.

In shock and sorrow, he had bent down to pick up his dog. Barney had flinched, finding enough energy to clamp down on Jose's fingers, out of his mind with pain, severing the thumb. Jose dropped the fatally injured Barney, scooting away on his butt, cursing himself. Any idiot knows not to touch a severely injured dog when it's in pain. *Damn, did it ever hurt.* Tears sprang to his eyes from the agonizing pain, blood spurting like a faucet, his head swimming with fogginess. Barney had laid his head back down, as if waiting for death, sorrowful guilty eyes awash in shock.

Out of nowhere, he had felt pressure and noticed a new smell. Sulfur? Looking around, he had seen the most bewitching sight on a ledge, overlooked in his concern for Barney. Yup—Echo—mind blowing, even as his pain had overwhelmed him. He had watched as her glorious tail lingered up in the air over her head. From the end of the tail had come the weirdest mother-effing blob of something. He had felt pressure and tingling in his hand and held it up, doing a double-take as he realized his thumb was no longer missing. A flash of rainbow color had seared his vision, briefly blinding him. As his vision had cleared, a barking Barney stood up on all fours. *Yes;* on all fours, his tail swinging wildly.

Barney had padded over to Jose, jumping up and putting his paws on his shoulders. He had licked Jose's face, and then loped over to the ledge where Echo sat. His face had turned up to Echo, whining softly. Echo had stood and scaled down the wall, her skinny body with its fat stomach strikingly graceful. She had approached Barney, tentatively touching his muzzle with a long skinny finger as Barney's tongue had reached out to give Echo's finger an exploratory slurp. Together, they had promptly flopped down on the floor and curled up together, kinship clearly established. The pressure and aura had intruded into his mind, whispering the first words from Echo.

"Hello, Brother, I am Sister and I am so happy to see you."

Jose took a break from his story. Scotty noticed he absently stroked his tail.

"Echo neglected to tell me about the tail on our first meeting. I discovered it on my own, just as you did. Quite a shock, huh?"

Continuing the story, he acknowledged the many meetings he had held with Echo. He had planned to make this meeting the last one, desperate to introduce Echo to Abby. If Echo could heal her, all their problems would be solved. But the discovery of Scotty and his tail changed everything, and he wanted Echo to come and live with them. As soon as the funerals were over and they moved Mama Diaz to Tomas and Kelly's house, they would come back to the cavern and bring her home. Auras enveloped their minds.

"Sister will live with her Brothers. My Barney will live with us too?"

"Yes, Echo," Jose said, laughing. "We'll all live together. Once we get settled, we'll talk again. We need to know all there is to know about our tails. Scotty, can you wait until we bring Echo home to deal with this?"

Yawning, Scotty agreed. They had come this far, a few days more wouldn't kill them. A seventeen-year-old boy needs lots of sleep and he wanted to crash. Now that Jose was on the job, most of his anxieties simply disappeared, just like krill at a whale convention. Looking over at Echo, he marveled at the fact that his boyhood *fairy* was wilder than he could possibly dream. It occurred to him that no one would ever believe this. He noticed Echo poking her leathery finger around inside Barney's ear, who turned around and wiped Echo's face with his sloppy tongue. Echo spun her head around a hundred and eighty degrees before it snapped back, then Echo's feet and hands flew up in the air, rocking her back on her bottom. Auras flashed with gold and rainbow colors as Scotty wondered if Echo could communicate with Barney. He watched as the leathery arms snaked around the delirious dog's neck, holding tight. *Yup, I guess Echo's right. Barney belongs to her. An interesting development.* Echo sure appeared as harmless as a house pet.

Their trek back home proceeded uneventfully, although it cost them extra time to explain to Echo why Barney couldn't stay with her in the cavern. Her answer to all of their objections: *The Womb will provide.* Ick. The guys decided they didn't want to know more about the Womb just yet. Telling Echo they needed Barney for guard-dog duty satisfied her, although she quickly pointed out that the Womb would guard them too. *Lovely,* Scotty thought. *Yup, time to go.*

Chapter 8

Organized chaos reigned at Lily Pond Road. The whole neighborhood turned out with cakes, deviled eggs, casseroles and sandwiches. Even neighbors who had never said boo once in the many years they had lived there, brought goodies to the house. The Preston and Diaz families felt honored and grateful, knowing full well their neighbors had little to spare.

The turnout for the funerals impressed everyone. Abby hadn't realized her mama's life had touched so many others. Of course, when a youth is lost, many turn out to lament the sadness. And the whole grocery showed up, having lost two popular employees.

The demands on Abby were extraordinary, having missed a vital treatment so she could attend the funeral. She played the gracious hostess, compassionate nursemaid and proficient housekeeper as she tried to mourn her mother's passing.

Her harried tasks didn't prevent her from noticing the strange behavior of Scotty and Jose. She frequently noticed their heads together, speaking in cryptic whispers, hushing as she passed to clean around them. What could possibly merit this show of male skullduggery?

Abby supported anything that helped Scotty out of the adolescent sulking that dominated his personality these days, but their behavior irritated her. And what the heck was with the sunglasses—a new fad perhaps?

She wasn't worried though. She knew the quiet responsible Jose would be a good influence. God knew she could use the help with Scotty. Her eyes lingered on Jose's wide shoulders as his hand reached up to rake back his unruly black and gold hair with masculine fingers. Gold? Not an attractive combo. Why the strange hairdo? It almost looked like he wanted to follow in Scotty's footsteps. Someone should tell him the color combination just made him look older.

She knew nothing about seventeen-year-old boys, especially her own secretive brother. She didn't date at all and had very little exposure as to how the male of the species worked romantically. *Gee, where did that come from? Why think about that now?*

Unable to stop this train of thought, she reflected on how most guys shied away from her when they found out about her kidney disease. Her classmates had labeled her 'the sick girl', not intentionally meaning to be cruel. By the time most girls reached their late twenties, falling in and out of love had become a habit. Unfortunately, Abby's experience in the romance department sucked. She longed to have an innocent flirtation with a boy. Or a not so innocent one.

The only guys that had ever paid attention to her were Jose, Tomas and Hiro. But they hardly counted. Sighing, she pulled her thick reddish-brown hair back, securing it with an elastic band. Sinking her hands into hot soapy water, she began to wash the dishes.

The guests finally departed. Mama Diaz fussed, almost ready to leave with Tomas and the girls. They had gathered their things last night and laboriously trucked them over to Tomas and Kelly's house. When they returned, Mama Diaz looked stern and tight-lipped. When Abby tried to question her, she raised her hand to her head, cutting her off. A puzzled Abby, distracted by the funeral preparations, decided to let it go.

Coming up behind her at the sink, Mama Diaz rested her tired head on Abby's shoulder. Abby's sudsy hands slipped around the older woman's waist.

"Please don't go, I don't think it's necessary. The girls should stay here until they finish school."

Mama Diaz reluctantly shook her head. "I don't know, Abby. Tomas's mind is made up. He's the man of the family now. He insists. Kelly is a bit intense, maybe, don't you think?" She began to whisper as she spoke. "Have you met her brother, Armoni? Oh, my dear, he's a troubled young man." She made the sign of the cross.

"What do you mean, Mama? What's wrong with Kelly's brother?"

Tomas walked into the room, his hand clapping down heavily on his mother's arm. "Let's go, Ma." Turning, he gave Abby a suggestive wink. Freezing him with a cool gaze, she deliberately turned back to Mama Diaz.

"Please call me when you get settled." Abby sounded frantic. Mama Diaz placed her worn hands on Abby's face, dabbing her fingers at the lonely tears that tumbled from her desolate eyes. Turning, she reached for her shopworn handbag, fraying at the seams from years of containing the minutia of growing children. She kissed Abby goodbye and allowed Tomas to lead her to the door.

Leaving everyone to settle themselves in the car, Tomas slipped back to the front door, oddly loitering. Abby stood holding the door, waiting for him to leave. He hesitated, then wrapped an arm around her, pulling her close, placing the other on her butt and roughly kissing her. She couldn't breathe as she struggled in his embrace. Squirming away, she slapped him. They both looked shocked and speechless. Tomas stared at her, saying nothing. His lips twisted into a sneer and a disturbing glint crept into his eyes. Leaving, he gave her breast a rough brush and sauntered out the door.

Two seconds later, Jose and Scotty entered, conspiratorial faces shining. Scotty held something protectively in his arms, wrapped in a shaggy yellow blanket. He went right to his room with the bundle, leaving her alone with Jose who eyed her suspiciously. He took a deeper look at her and knew something was wrong.

"Abby?" He eyed her disheveled appearance, the look on his face unexpectedly tender.

She turned to him, her angry eyes fighting back tears. She just couldn't find the words to explain. Shaking her head slowly, a few tired tears trickled down her angry face. Flopping down on the sofa that had sheltered a thousand tantrums and childish battles, she collapsed.

"Abby, are you going to answer me?" Jose moved to the sofa and picked up her hands. Her face fell. Softly, Jose rubbed her temples, gently massaging as he turned her face up.

"Abby, tell me," he whispered, his eyes searching her face. Making up her mind, she haltingly related what had happened, omitting Tomas's name.

"What? You've got to be kidding me." Jose jumped to his feet and paced. "He had the balls to do this to you in our house, after a funeral? *I don't believe it.*" He pounded the palm of his hand with his fist. Angrily, he asked, "Who is the bastard? Just tell me. I'll take care of this." Looking up, he saw Scotty return from his bedroom.

"Hey, what's going on?" Looking from face to face, Scotty waited for an answer. Jose glanced up.

"Is Echo okay?"

"Yeah, she'll stay put until we need her."

Abby looked from one to the other. "What? Who's Echo?"

"Never mind. Abby, you have something you need to tell me."

Looking into each other's eyes, she nodded her head and whispered, "Tomas."

"*What*—that bastard?" He jumped to his feet. "I'm not surprised."

Startled, Abby put her hands out to catch him. "What do you mean you're not surprised, Jose?" Charging to the door, he slammed out of the house and noisily tore down the road, the exhaust on his old red truck pouring gray-white smoke. Shaking her head and sighing sadly, Abby shut the door and returned to the sofa. She pulled her feet up under her, feeling as broken and limp as the sofa looked.

"We don't need this right now." Abby rested her head on the sofa, her eyes bruised from fatigue. Scotty joined her, flopping down softly.

"Holy mackerel, what's that all about? Does it have anything to do with Tomas?"

"Scotty, do you know something about Tomas that I should know?"

"Uh, not really Abby. Although I've heard a few things. I never mentioned anything because it didn't affect us, not now that he lives with Kelly and her weirdo brother."

"Her brother? This is the first I've heard anything about a brother. How come? Does Mama Diaz know about him? Is her brother this Armoni? And what does that have to do with Tomas's inappropriate behavior?"

"I don't know, Abby, what'd he do?" Abby could not tell her little brother the particulars of the incident. Changing the subject, she asked him about the blanket he had brought into the house.

Abby laughed as Scotty jumped up, dancing from foot to foot. His eyes flashed, his face shinning.

"Abs, we have the most amazing surprise for you, but we have to wait for Jose."

"Okay, champ, but maybe it can wait for tomorrow. I'm very happy about anything that'll put a smile on your face, but . . ." Her voice fading, she rose unsteadily to her feet. "I don't think I have the strength. Tomorrow, I need to get to the dialysis center first thing in the morning." Her voice trailed off to a hoarse whisper. Her head throbbing, she walked toward the bedrooms and promptly fainted.

"*Abby!*" Scotty screamed. Without noticing or even thinking, his tail unfurled from underneath his shirt. It stood straight up in the air like a recently promoted soldier, arching over the top of his head and pointing toward Abby. From the bulbous end of his tail came a monstrous, disgusting, membranous, *thing* that opened up to exude the smell of sulfur. He could feel a numbing pressure. Then, suddenly, it stopped. He started to shake as his tail tucked itself back under his shirt. Praying for Jose to come home, he closed his eyes.

Hearing a small whine, he opened his eyes to see Barney standing in front of him, happily wagging his tail. Astride his back sat Echo, calmly behaving as if she owned the place. Her long leathery fingers locked tight around Barney, her little swivel neck bobbing up and down.

"Oh boy, Jose better get home. There's going to be fireworks." Seeing Abby move on the floor, a dead rag doll come to life, he ran to her side. Rubbing her hands, he tried to get her blood moving faster. He needed her to get up and tell him what to do.

The front door rattled open. Relieved, Scotty turned to see Jose, anxiety written all over his face. He took in the scene, starting at Echo's presence on top of Barney with Abby crumpled and wilted on the floor. He sniffed, catching the left over scent of sulfur.

"You did it—without me? Echo—I thought we would do this together?" Swirling rainbows coalesced, an aura in their minds.

"We have a new Sister. Now there are four of us. Is this what you call a family, Brother?"

Jose and Scotty answered together, "Yes, Echo."

Jose grimaced, bracing Abby from behind to get her head off the scuffed floor. "Echo, are you speaking to all of us at the same time?"

"Yes, Brother."

"It would be so much easier if you would use our names. Could you do this?"

"Yes, Brother. Brother Jose, Brother Scotty, Sister Abby. Oh, I like that. Can I call myself Sister Echo, Brother Jose? Should we call my Barney, Brother Barney? No, Barney is not our Brother, he is just my Barney. My Barney. I like that. I will call him My Barney."

"Echo," Jose tried to interrupt. The rainbow aura kept going on and on about My Barney, who sat on the sofa with Echo clinging tightly.

"*Echo.*" He tried again. The rainbows stopped. Echo stared at Abby, who rose unsteadily from the floor. With her hand to her mouth, she stared at Echo, then at Scotty and Jose and back to Echo.

"Am I going out of my mind? I don't think I can take much more." She sniffed the air, noticing the scent. "Someone had better start making sense real soon or I'm going to go mad." Rainbows swirled.

"Hello, Sister Abby. I am Sister Echo."

Shrinking back, Abby stared at the little golden creature and trembled.

"What is this?" The look on her face was one of stark disbelief. *She's going to blow if we don't do some explaining fast,* Scotty realized.

"It's all okay." Stroking Abby's arms softly, Jose tried to keep her calm. Turning to Scotty, he said, "Look guys, we have some explaining to do. This is not how we planned this, Echo, so let me handle it. Abby . . . look at me." She stared blankly into his eyes, as if he wasn't there.

"Abby." Jose shook her. "How do you feel?" He spoke more softly, an expectant smile on his face.

"I feel perfectly fine, thank you." She still looked confused and frightened. Slowly, the significance of her words sank in. Jose grabbed her, lifting her off her feet in a hug, a happy tear tracing down his face.

"You're healed, Abby. It's a gift from Echo." Scotty jumped up, joining them in the hug. Barney flopped off the sofa, dumping Echo from his back. His joyful barking added to the celebration. Then little Echo righted herself and wobbled her way over to the huddle, trying to squeeze her way in.

Joyfully, Scotty grabbed Echo and tossed her in the air, catching her in a bear hug. All Abby could do was sit back down dumbly on the floor.

When the laughter settled down and everyone sobered up, they gathered around their cheap kitchen table to talk. There was so much to talk about, so much to explain to Abby.

Lifting Echo up onto the table, Jose stroked her golden head.

"You're amazing, girl."

Echo's gleaming antlers reflected light from the ceiling fixture, making them sparkle like crystal. Scotty wondered when Echo might trust them enough to tell them more of her history. And this mystery mission she was on. But Echo was not the kind of creature you could ask questions of, head on. Sometimes speaking to Echo was like speaking to a child. They were on different wavelengths. Maybe Abby could do better over time. Females bonded differently; maybe it would make a difference.

"Okay, handling the nastiest first, I would like to explain the problem with Tomas. Abby, Tomas has this thing for you. He's had it since we were kids. I don't think his relationship with Kelly is much more than a convenience. The real relationship is with Kelly's oddball brother, Armoni. A real nasty S.O.B, Armoni has Tomas under his thumb. Kelly is just cover. They use each other for kicks. She's meant to keep an eye on Tomas for Armoni."

"What does that have to do with me? Since when does he have this so called *thing?*" Abby asked with complete mystification. Jose squirmed. Scotty knew the next part would not be easy for Jose to explain.

"Well, uh, Tomas has always had a problem with me—a little jealousy thing. I guess it started with his mama's attention to me when I was first adopted. We were just children. As we grew, I noticed he always had to have whatever I was interested in."

"But Jose, I still don't see what this has to do with me. How do you explain his behavior?" Jose flushed, his fine dark features turning beet red. Abby looked from Scotty to Jose, perplexed. Suddenly, a golden aura flashed into their minds, a whisper infusing their consciousness.

"Sister, I think Brother Jose wants to mate with you."

"Ew," Scotty said with a laugh.

"Damn, Echo!" Jose said pounding his fist on the table. "It's not like that at all, Abby, I mean—Scotty, help me out here."

"I know nothing." Scotty could not contain his laughter. Jose jumped up from the table, pacing nervously. "Maybe we can talk, you and I, and uh, gee Echo, sometimes you have to think before you speak. Abby can we discuss this later?" Jose swallowed his begging voice, embarrassment plastered like a short-circuiting neon sign on his face. Abby put her hand out, drawing him to the table, her expression unreadable.

"Jose, please sit down. The Tomas issue is not important right now. I think you know it's time to answer my questions."

"Okay, yes, saving the best, the very, very best for last." Jose exhaled with relief. Grabbing Scotty, goofing at him like a fool, he clapped him on the back to share a macho moment of male bonding.

Jose shook his head. "I can't believe we were able to keep this secret for so many years."

"What secret? Who's we? Come on, what the heck is going on? I'm too tired for games, guys."

"Scotty, make sure the drapes are all shut for me, just in case."

"In case of what? Come on now, guys, this is weird enough without you trying to scare me."

"It's not about pumping the story," Scotty said, getting up, "It's about being safe."

"Yeah, Abby, what we're going to tell you will sound unbelievable. More unbelievable than what's already happened to you tonight," Jose said, stroking Echo.

"But, Jose." Abby sighed, her frustration and growing impatience clear as a bell. She rubbed her bleary eyes. "I don't even know what happened here tonight. Something happened to me? You mean with Tomas?" Scotty came back to the table and hugged Abby.

"Sis, this is going to be very hard to believe. Jose, I think there's only one way to do it. We need to show her." Raising his eyebrows to Jose, he got a nod. Slowly, both he and Jose let their tails unwind from under their shirts, standing bravely and waiting to be judged. They watched Abby and held their breath.

"Is this some kind of joke?" Abby appeared stunned and angry.

"No, Abby," Jose said softly. "This is who we are now, both of us. Please don't be upset, but this is a side effect of being healed by Echo. We've all been healed by her, even Barney. We've been hiding this for years. Scotty, since he was a boy."

Abby looked over to see Scotty, the pain of isolation clear on his pale face, his freckles straining with the struggle to hold his emotions in, fighting back the tears. He had been so young, and so alone.

"It was hard, Ab. But now I have Jose and Echo, it's so much easier. I don't feel alone anymore. How do you think my eye straightened out and my scars disappeared? And now we have you."

"What do you mean, you have me? Why do you say I'm healed? Am I going to grow a tail too?" Her voice was rising, faint hints of hysteria hiding behind her eyes.

Calming golden auras spoke. "Sister Abby, I am pleased you are healed. You are special now. We have chosen you. You will be a survivor now. This will help make my mission easier. Soon, I must make a decision. But now we are a family and always will be."

"Jose, what is she talking about? I don't understand any of this! Where in the world did this . . . creature . . . come from?"

"That's just it, Abby, she's from another world; another planet. She's been here for a very long time. And she chose us to live with. I know she talks about mission stuff, but who knows? She's ours. Isn't that cool? And she cured you, Abby. That's a great thing! She doesn't seem to eat either, so she won't cost us anything." Jose tried hard, pulling out all the stops to sell Abby the idea of keeping Echo.

"Well now, Jose, I need you to know just a little thing," Scotty spoke slowly. All eyes turned to him.

"It wasn't Echo that healed Abby. I did it."

"What do you mean you, Scotty? How would you know how to do it?"

"I don't know, Jose, my tail just popped out without me thinking. It healed her on its own. I guess that means you can probably do it too. And maybe Abby will be able to do it."

"Echo, can you please tell us what's happening to us?" Jose glanced around, not seeing the creature. Barney appeared to have slipped away too. The three of them hurriedly searched the house. No Echo or Barney.

"Hey, guys, out here." Abby peered out the back window into their miniature yard, its lone maple tree doing a proud job. Echo lay stretched out on her back with her face up to the sun, a waft of air ruffling her golden fur. Steadfast Barney crouched next to her, a faithful guard.

Scotty slipped outside to scoot them back in. Looking around, Scotty spotted a vintage white Volkswagen parked up the hill on the side of the road. He didn't recognize the car. *Is that someone sitting inside? Can they see into the back yard?* Dismissing his paranoia, he closed the back door and returned to the living room with the two wanderers.

Jose knelt down in front of Echo, slipping his arm around Barney's soft curly neck. Echo's head bobbed around, turning in all directions. Jose waited patiently until she settled down.

"Echo, it's dangerous to walk outside without one of us with you. Someone might want to steal you. Do you want to leave us?" Golden rainbows flashed madly.

"No, Brother Jose, I need you. I need Brother Scotty and Sister Abby. You are very, very important to me and my mission. And I would never leave My Barney, would I, My Barney?" Echo's round furry face bobbled up and down as she rubbed her golden fur against Barney's chest. Barney just sat there with big doggy insouciance, his sloppy tongue hanging over his mouth, dripping slobber onto Echo's shining head.

"Brother Jose, if I am to live with you, I must be able to access the sun to do what you refer to as *eating*. I cannot survive without it. Otherwise, I must return to the Womb in the woods."

"Okay, Echo, I have an idea. Tomorrow is Saturday. We'll all be home. Scotty and I are going to build you a private tree house. You can get the exposure to the sun that you need without anyone spotting you. Can you climb a tree?" The golden auras swirled and then stopped.

Before anyone could speak, Echo broke away from Barney, ran to the living room wall and placed one foot in front of the other as she climbed. She walked upside down across the ceiling, swiveling her head to watch them, then walked back down the opposite wall. Wobbling over to Barney, she pulled herself up, plopped down on his back and curled up. Speechless, Scotty, Abby and Jose just stared.

"Well, I guess she showed us. Okay then." Abby laughed. And it felt good. Many questions remained unanswered, but she felt giddy with the new possibilities. Could it really be true she was healthy now?

Glancing over at Jose, who was planning the tree house with Scotty, she gave him a long pensive appraisal. He had certainly taken the reins here. It made her feel secure. Her face flushed with other thoughts. Was she completely oblivious or what? Things might be looking up a lot more than anyone expected.

Abby said goodnight, pleading exhaustion. At their quick questioning looks, she reassured them that she felt great. She just wanted some time to be alone. She needed to think about so much. This would dramatically change how she thought about herself and her life. And she needed to think about the loss of her mother. She pressed her hand to her stomach, her emotions in a free-for-all. She needed to take time to say goodbye to her mom in private and have a healing cry.

She pushed back the small seed of bitterness that surfaced. With all of this mystical healing stuff, how come it hadn't been used to save Mom? Irrationally, she refused to admit that they hadn't known of her mother's accident until it was too late. *Gee, wouldn't Mom be happy to see me cured?* As she shut the door to her bedroom, she sighed mournfully, realizing the old adage was correct. *Timing is everything.*

Back in the living room, hilarity sounded as Jose collected his tools for the tree house. Echo steered Barney over to the toolbox so she could examine them. Taking the tools out, she lined them up in the hopes of discovering their purpose. Picking up the hammer, she remembered why it looked familiar. Brother's two humans: Sister Netty and Brother Wil.

Now that Echo no longer worried about her loneliness, they had completely slipped from her mind. She remembered watching Brother Wil from the woods. He had often used this primitive tool called a hammer. Echo wondered why Brother had not called on the Womb to make their lives better. Had Brother forgotten who he was? And now Brother Jose planned to use the same tool. Perhaps Echo should show him the easy way. Well, maybe she should first see what he planned to use the tool for. Echo remembered that sometimes, when she volunteered information, someone got upset. *Sister Abby clearly needs a little looking after, she gets upset easily. I better keep an eye on her.* She refused to let any trauma or upset come to her new family. *Fam-i-ly.* She decided she liked the way the word sounded.

Studying Echo, Jose wondered what the rascal was up to. She obviously didn't know what to make of his tools. Well, tomorrow he and Scotty would show her a thing or two. They would have her tree house up in no time. Motioning to Scotty, they decided to sit at the table and draw up some rough plans. As they sketched, Jose filled Scotty in about Tomas, Kelly and Armoni.

"The news is not good, kiddo, Armoni pulled a blade on me when I confronted Tomas. Armoni's quite the knife freak. I didn't get inside, but when I knocked at the door I could hear some girl screaming for help. I had Kelly and Armoni in my eyesight, so it wasn't them. God knows what freaky stuff happened in there. I got out of there while the getting was good. I gave the cops a quick call—concerned citizen and all. I hope they were able to get in. Tomas will know it was me who called, though. We've got to be ultra-careful. I'm afraid to leave Echo alone during the day. I think we're going to have to invest in a good security system. Hope we can swing it."

"By the way, Mama Diaz and the girls didn't move in with Tomas. He said Armoni put his foot down. Mama Diaz didn't have a choice. Tomas is going to drive her back to the projects in Short Hills. Isn't that where you used to live?"

"Yeah, I can't believe he'd do that to his mother and his sisters. Should we bring them back here?"

"I don't think so. We have Echo now. And how do we explain Abby's recovery? And our tails? I don't know how you kept it hidden. Give me some time to think about what we can do for them. Don't worry, I won't let Mama and the girls be dumped like this. What do you say, time to hit the sack? We can start this in the morning. We'll pick up lumber at the lumberyard and price out security systems. We start building after lunch, okay?"

"Yeah, I need to hit the sack. Echo? Barney? You guys want to bunk with me?" Barney jumped to his feet, following Scotty to his bedroom with Echo shuffling quickly behind, her tiny leather feet trying their best to keep up with Barney. Jose turned out the lights and followed them all to bed.

The house on Lily Pond Road finally settled down for the night. Sleep came to the occupants of all their neighbor's homes. The night's creatures woke up, starting their nocturnal foraging. And the predators; oh yes, the predators were afoot. Slowly, ever so slowly, the white Volkswagen on the hillside turned on its headlights, quietly rolled down the hill and silently glided past one particular home on Lily Pond Road, before disappearing into the night.

Chapter 9

The next morning, Scotty woke to a harsh pounding on his door. Recognizing urgency when it woke him up, he slipped into his jeans and shirt, not bothering to tuck in his tail. Glancing around, he noticed that Barney and Echo were nowhere to be seen. Dashing to the living room, he searched for Abby and Jose, finding them hunched over the back window. Joining them, they silently made room for him.

"Holy Mother of God," he whispered with awe in his voice. There, up in the maple tree, sat the furry twosome: Echo, stretched out doing her *eating,* and Barney keeping watch, happily slobbering all over the new tree house. Looking at Jose, Scotty asked, "Did you?"

Shaking his head, Jose said, "Not me."

Looking back at the tree house, Scotty saw how it gleamed like gold in the sunlight. He couldn't see any joints or supports. *No. It couldn't be, could it?* He noticed the trunk of the tree encased in the same substance the tree house was made of, giving it a solid support. *Could it be? And how had Barney got up there?*

Running into the garage, he returned with a couple of cans of black spray paint. Hollering to Jose to get a ladder, he ran into the backyard, starting to spray. Jose dragged the ladder up to the tree house and begged Barney to come to him. Echo sat up, motioning to Barney. Golden rainbows flashed in their heads.

"My Barney, please let Brother Jose take you down to the ground. Brother Jose, Brother Scotty, Sister Abby, do you not like my surprise? Now you do not have all of that difficult manual labor to do."

"Echo, will you please come into the house? We would like to talk to you. Oh, and yes, we do love your surprise." Lifting the squirming Barney, Jose eased him down the ladder. Scotty watched, tapping on the mysterious metal. The tree house felt like solid gold.

Watching Echo walk down the gold-encased tree, he grabbed a spray can to add more camouflage.

Abby gathered up the wayward buddies and scooted them into the house, with Scotty and Jose not far behind. Gathering at the kitchen table, Echo climbed up unaided. Abby couldn't squash a laugh as she watched Echo make herself comfortable on the table. Looking up at her family, Echo stared into their faces, her beautiful golden eyes flashing rainbows.

"I guess you were very busy last night, Echo," Jose commented softly.

"Oh no, Brother, I slept very soundly last night, and so did My Barney."

"Well, how did the tree house get built? And is it actually made out of gold?"

"Yes, my Brother, I hope you don't mind the gold. I realize it is a soft metal, but the Womb found it the most plentiful metal in the earth near the Hive. Since it was only going to be used for my eating and, of course, the occasional company of My Barney, we thought it would be strong enough. Do you approve?" Jose looked at Abby and Scotty, amazement leaving him speechless. It was clear Echo had no idea of the value of gold. And it was just sitting in their backyard.

"*Oh-my-God.*" Abby's eyes were popping as she looked at Jose. "We have to get that tree house out of there."

"I am sorry, Sister Abby. I did not realize what I did was bad. I will have the Womb take it back," Echo flashed her auras wildly.

"No!" everyone shouted in unison. "That's okay, Echo, we can handle this. Guys, we will need to discuss this again later. I guess we all realize we have some new developments on our hands. But right now, we have to get that hunk of gorgeous gold cut up and stowed away, fast."

Grabbing Echo, Jose picked her up and gave her a huge kiss on the mouth. Scotty did the same. Abby smiled and patted her on the head. Barney put his paws on the table and, standing as tall on his tippy toes as he possibly could, gave Echo a very happy, very sloppy kiss. That one made Echo smile.

Scotty and Jose took off for the local hardware store with Abby staying home to keep an eye on Echo and Barney. They all agreed that Jose and Abby should quit their jobs. Even without the specter of independent wealth sitting in their back yard, the complexity of Echo, the Womb and their own changes forced them to re-evaluate their schedules, their jobs and their public exposure.

They made a note to pick up a good pair of sunglasses for Abby. She would need them soon enough. Scotty and Jose both noticed that direct proximity to Echo seemed to accelerate the changes. Jose's eyes had deepened their golden color since they had brought Echo from the woods. And Scotty's golden eyes had developed a distinct rainbow shimmer.

They both agreed they needed a wraparound style of sunglasses for more complete coverage. And how goofy would that look—the three of them walking around in wraparound sunglasses? That would only serve to draw more unwanted attention. For the glasses to protect them more effectively they should only appear in public separately or maybe just two of them together. With that agreement, Scotty and Jose took off for the local hardware store.

Arriving at the huge store, they quickly loaded their cart. They needed a lot more paint to cover the gold. Green and black would do—it would likely take them all day to cover the gold completely.

Then they faced a daunting task—cutting up the gold and figuring out how to hide it from the neighbors. They couldn't do it in the dark. The light from the blowtorch would be more noticeable. And where to start? Jose decided the top would be best. They couldn't allow the whole structure to collapse by starting at the bottom. Eyeing the equipment they would need, he realized they probably didn't have the skills to do the job properly. Glancing in the cart, he hoped his money would cover everything. Abby had been reluctant to pool their money. She just couldn't get over the idea that it was no longer necessary to save every penny for her medical treatments.

Jose smacked himself in the head as he thought of their money shortage; *duh*. He only needed to blowtorch off a couple pounds of the gold and they would be rich. He could stop sweating. At $5,500 an ounce, even two pounds would be worth over $176,000. He estimated the gold tree house must weigh over two thousand pounds, maybe more. *Holy shit.* After doing the rough math, he thought he would wet his pants from shock, and a sizable amount of fright.

Could they get into trouble with the government? Would they try to take the gold away from them? Did they need to explain where they got the gold? Maybe they should just sell a little at a time. But even a little would be noticeable. The government would take their half, no matter what. Maybe they wouldn't question where it came from as long as they got their share.

Jose realized he needed to talk to Abby about this. But they already had a lot on their plate dealing with Echo and the changes. He didn't want to flip her out and push her over the edge with more problems. After all, he and Scotty had had years to get used to the idea. Jose took a deep breath. His head spun with exciting possibilities and confusing ramifications.

In the back of his mind . . . way, way back, a small nagging worry began to grow: Tomas and Armoni. He still couldn't figure out if they would develop into a problem. He hoped Abby wouldn't become an issue with Tomas. And what about Mama Diaz and the girls? He knew he must go after them and bring them back. *Hmm, bring them back.*

A fabulous idea occurred to him. The more he thought about his idea, the more he realized what a super solution it could be. But they must accomplish so much before he could even broach his idea to Scotty and Abby. And of course Echo. That could be his biggest stumbling block right there. Sighing, he pushed their shopping cart up to the register. He helped Scotty unload their purchases, grimacing at the pile of equipment. But behind his sunglasses, a tiny pinprick of rainbow light pulsed, giving his mouth the suggestion of a smile.

*

As Jose and Scotty wheeled their purchases out of the store, they passed by a huge heap of bagged garden soil stacked halfway up the wall.

They failed to notice a stubby bandy-legged man with a dirty plaid cap pulled down over his face. He leaned with his back on one of the bags of garden soil, seemingly in a doze. As Jose and Scotty passed by, he twitched.

A minute passed. He slowly rose and pushed his cap to the back of his head, his eyes following the backs of Jose and Scotty as they made their way to Jose's car and loaded their purchases. He slowly chewed a tobacco wad, his teeth stained with the vile juices which leaked out the corners of his mouth, dripping onto his shirt.

Casually, he made his way to a parked white Volkswagen, spitting a wad on the pavement. He slid behind the wheel and pulled out in front of Jose and Scotty as they continued to stack their purchases. With a salute in his rear view mirror, he calmly pulled out of the parking lot and sped down the road.

Jose finished loading the equipment, his anxious mind already on painting the tree house. Jose paused as he pulled up behind a white Volkswagen blocking his way. The driver made a gesture then pulled away. Jose turned the car in the other direction and hurried home.

Chapter 10

Katie had just finished celebrating her seventeenth birthday. She knew she rated about a four on the pretty girl meter. Her tree-trunk legs and round, plain Irish face accentuated her stout figure. Not surprisingly, the young teen longed to be kissed by a boy. She used to worry about that fact, all the time. But that was in the past. Ironically, it was the very reason she now hovered on the verge of death.

Her weakness debilitated her to the extent she no longer registered her surroundings. She couldn't summon the strength to fight her captors. Time in the basement had passed in a confused kaleidoscope of pain and abuse for over a month; possibly longer. She found herself still strapped to the same table they had strapped her to so long ago. The day she fell like a foolish eager moth into their psychotic flame.

Six months ago, she had felt flattered when Kelly and Tomas started to pay attention to her. Kelly was a few years older and so pretty. They worked together in a popular seafood diner downtown. She made a few bucks bussing tables for the cocktail waitresses after school. She knew Tomas liked to watch her from the bar as he mixed drinks for Kelly and her customers.

She had thought Tomas liked her. His sexiness had made her heart race as he cornered her in the kitchen, pressing his leg into her hips, brushing his lips against her ears, telling her how much he wanted to be with her. She dreamed about the first time she would let him kiss her. She would fantasize about it all day in class while she neglected her assignment. Her face would burn with shame as she remembered Tomas's insistence that they keep their feelings a secret. All the time, he and Kelly had laughed behind her back.

When Tomas had asked her into his house the night he offered to give her a lift home after work, she had almost dropped the tray she carried. After work, she had flown to his little white car, flopping eagerly into the front seat. Her excitement had risen when he had induced her into stopping by his house before taking her home. Her enthusiasm had slipped as he pulled up to little more than a shack in the woods outside town. He had swept her inside before she could protest, passing through the tiny living room to a filthy kitchen. He had pointed to a scuffed chipboard door in front of him, claiming his apartment was in the basement. Katie had felt a stirring of anticipation as he took her arm, stroking it softly. He had opened the door and turned on the light.

Descending, he had told her to shut her eyes, a surprise awaited her. Carefully helping her navigate the stairs, he had murmured in her ear, telling her how long he had spent dreaming of this moment. He had led her over to the table she was now chained to. He had told her to sit, but not to open her eyes. Slowly his hand had caressed her flat and undefined breast. She had blushed, so giddy with excitement that she hadn't even felt the pinprick of the needle as Kelly, who had been hiding in the dark basement shadows, plunged a disabling chemical into her bloodstream.

When she woke, she had found she couldn't move. She had felt groggy and her vision had fought in vain to focus. Where the heck was she? She hadn't recognized the ceiling tiles over her head. Or the exposed pipes that ran under the tiles. *Huh?* She had run her tongue around her mouth, feeling the gummy dryness catch in her throat, preventing her from swallowing. Gagging, she had tried to identify the strange taste in her mouth. It tasted like she imagined a bad oyster would taste. Like dog shit. Slowly, the realization she was restrained had sunk in. Straining her eyes, she had tried harder to focus, softy calling for Tomas. Was he tied up too?

Little by little her vision had started to clear. An image had appeared at the end of the table near her feet. She tried, but couldn't make it out. Pushing her bleary eyes to focus, she had realized her restraints were actually chains, spreading her feet wide. She couldn't look down, but it had felt like she was no longer wearing her skirt and panties. Her bottom felt exposed from underneath, as if positioned over a cutout in the hard table, edges cutting into the substantial flesh of her wide ass.

"Well, hello there." A voice . . . hard and rasping, trying at sweetness. Her bleary eyes had identified a figure at the end of the table; an oddly shaped man. She hadn't been able to see his lower body, but she could easily ascertain his diminutive stature and large head. He had leered at her with stained ugly teeth, moving closer to her head. Close enough for her to smell a heavy stench of body odor rolling off him.

"My name is Lover. We're all here ta play a game, a game that you'll come ta love. After we've finished the game, Kelly will take ya home, right, Kelly?"

"Yes, Lover," Kelly had said, emerging from the shadows of the basement. As she approached the table, Katie had spotted a knife in her hands. Kelly had languidly caressed the knife, her attention focused on Katie. Katie's heart had thumped wildly.

"What the hell is going on here? Let me up, right now. Where's Tomas?" She had felt the panic rising in her throat. Her voice had cracked, her lips looking for moisture.

"Here ya are, babe." The man had inched closer, a bottle of water held in his hand. She had eyed it gratefully, her hands straining in her chains, trying to reach out for the water.

"Not so fast, babe, let me." Slipping his hands under her neck he had poured water into her mouth. She had choked and gagged. The odor of the man had overwhelmed her, yet she needed the water. Gasping for breath, she had glanced at Kelly, who stood unmoving, seemingly riveted by the scene playing out in front of her.

"Okay, little girl, it's time to reward me for my generosity." She had looked at the little man, noticing his inordinately large muscular arms. Kelly had stepped forward, handing the shiny knife to the little man. Her adrenalin had shot through her head, paralyzing her with fear.

The man had taken the knife and delicately slit the front of her shirt down the front, exposing her bra. He had slit the front of her bra, the ends folding to the side, exposing her flat breasts.

"Please, I need to go home now," she had managed to squeak out. "Kelly, can you take me home?" Kelly had let out a tinny laugh that had frozen Katie to her core. Suddenly, the room had crackled with silence. Breaking the ominous quietude, she had clearly heard the sound of a zipper slowly moving down its track, followed by the sound of pants dropping to the floor. She had glanced again at Kelly, her face beseeching her for help. Her voice had died meekly on her cracked lips as Kelly's eager look, eyes glassy with anticipation, left her with little hope.

Events had happened quickly. The little man had straddled her with his stubby hairy legs, his penis erect and angry, forcing its way into her tender virgin flesh. She had screamed in shock and pain. Kelly had reached over, slapping her face. The little man had pumped up and down, his face contorted with pleasure, his cock a devouring branding iron on her innocent flesh.

"Call my name, little girl. Call my name." He had shouted in ecstasy. Kelly slapped her again.

"Call his name, you stupid bitch," she said.

"His name . . . I don't know his name," she had screamed, her childish voice breaking, tears flowing down her flushed cheeks. "Lover, yes Lover," she had suddenly remembered.

"That's my girl. You know this game, don't you? I bet Tomas slipped it to you, didn't he? You love this, don't you? You're just a slut like all the others, aren't you? Answer me!"

"Yes, Lover, yes, Lover," she had said after another slap from Kelly. It had gone on and on: a slap from Kelly and the required words to the little man. Kelly's slaps had soon changed to punches, her required words to whispers and slurring. Her lips had turned black and blue; her thighs slippery with blood. And yet the little man had not stopped, he had kept banging away and Kelly had kept punching her.

And right before she had passed out, there . . . yes, there in the shadows, she had just made out Tomas; his nakedness glowing in the dim light. His engorged penis had glistened, fully erect as he watched the rape, his hand fondling his treasure as his greasy face reflected a picture of exquisite pleasure. Katie's eyes had rolled back in her head and she was gone.

Waking the next day, she had noticed her body was still shackled and protesting, her muscles screaming in pain. She had ignored the terror from her rape, not willing to think about it. If she had, she might have started to cry and she felt bad enough. Hunger pangs had consumed her. Maybe she would be able to convince one of them to give her some food. Then she could concentrate on trying to get out of here. They could not keep her forever. She would make sure they paid for this after she told her mother.

Maybe Tomas would come to regret his part in what happened. He had originally liked her, after all. Straining, she had noticed the basement door at the top of the stairs was cracked open. The quiet was pierced by the sound of murmuring as she noticed a sliver of light. Suddenly, she had heard shouting. Another voice, quite angry; an unfamiliar voice.

Maybe this was her chance. She had screamed for help.

"Help me, please help me. *Help!* Please someone, help me," she had screamed over and over. Her voice had grown weaker and weaker. She had soon given up as the angry voices receded. Trembling, she had wondered if they had heard her or if she had made her situation worse.

Time ticked slowly. Before long, the basement door opened wider and the three of them came down the steps, Kelly holding some kind of cage. She lifted it up over Katie's table bed, hooking it to the ceiling, leaving it covered.

The little man came over to Katie and dumped some water on her face. Frantically, she tried to catch some of the moisture with her tongue. She noticed Tomas stayed in the background, silent and watching. The inevitable sound of the descending zipper drew her attention back to the little man.

"Noooo, please not again. I'll do anything," she whimpered as the man climbed on top of her.

"Shut your trap, bitch. Did ya think your screaming was gonna git by us? I think ya need ta be taught how ta behave, don't ya?" Plunging into her agonizing swollen flesh he raped her again. Pulling his penis out of her, he saw she was non-responsive. Slapping her face until her eyes focused from the sharp bite of pain, he bent down to her face, his breath reeking of garlic and tobacco. Katie couldn't help it, she heaved all over herself, her vomit spraying the little man, almost choking her. He pulled back in disgust, nodding to Kelly.

Kelly stepped over to Katie's table, a shiny meat cleaver in her hand.

"Nooo, please, why are you doing this to me?" she whimpered, losing control of her urine, her eyes following every move of the meat cleaver. She was so engrossed, she completely missed Kelly's other hand shooting out with the syringe until she felt the sting, prompting her to fall mercifully asleep.

"Hey, Kelso. What little trinket ya after this time?" Armoni giggled, his eyes eager. When she ignored him in her absorption of the task in front of her, he started to whine. "Why don't ya bring me one a those skinny stuck-up bitches. Why's it always gotta be a fat ugly one? Takes all the fun out'a it."

"All the fun? I doubt it," Tomas said disgustedly. Swift as a jack rabbit, Armoni snared Tomas's throat in his meaty hand, backing him up against the wall.

"What'd you say there, boy? Ya got somethin' ta complain 'bout? Any time you want out, you jis say so. Me an Kelso here can handle this on our own. Jis like we can handle lil ole Miss Abby on our own. I sure would like to put it to her." Tomas squirmed in Armoni's hand, trying to speak. Armoni farted and released him just as suddenly. Slapping Tomas on the back, he laughed.

"Come on boy, I'm jis jiving with ya. When the time comes, she's all yours. I'll even keep Kelly off a her for ya. You know I'm jis after the kid's gold coin ya say he's got in the house. I'm jis waitin for the right time. Now shut yer mouth and let's have some fun until then."

Slapping Tomas up alongside the head, he moved back to the table to monitor how far along Kelly was.

He could see she was making nice progress. Her work truly was a talent, her results artwork. How many people could make these savage cuts without the victim bleeding to death? She collected her trophies in a wooden bowl and took them upstairs. Armoni knew what she planned, but it would have to wait for tomorrow. He felt exhausted; all that fancy detective work he'd undertaken over the last few days.

He wondered what those three on Lily Pond Road were up to. Well, he would find out soon enough. If he couldn't discover it on his own, he would let Kelly employ her favorite knife, after he had his own fun with the stuck-up bitch first. He laughed to himself, thinking of his promise to Tomas. Oh well, he would make it up to him. *Or not.* He cackled to himself, climbing up the stairs, Tomas following close behind.

Katie's body flamed with pain. So did her throat. She needed something to drink, her discomfort acute. And she was faint from hunger. She just lay there on the table, suffering.

She tried to think about her mother and father. They must be frantic with worry. Tears trickled down her face as she thought of how she must have disappointed them. Her pain screamed for her attention. She wondered what time it was. As much as she needed her captors to feed her, she knew their presence would mean more pain. She tried to distract herself and failed. She tried to doze. The pain took over again. It was a vicious circle. No matter what she thought about, she felt only the pain.

Finally. Was someone stirring overhead? She heard pots and pans. Dare she hope? In passing, she realized they hadn't beaten her completely down, yet. Would that time come? Would they let her go home? Was she ready to die? No. She just wanted to eat and have the pain stop. The kitchen door cracked open. She heard steps descending down the stairs. She could smell food! Opening her eyes, she saw Kelly standing over her, a frying pan in her hands.

"I have something for you to eat. I am going to lift your head and feed you."

"Can't you unlock my hand?" Katie whispered painfully. Kelly ignored the question and spooned the food in, occasionally giving her a sip of water. Katie tried to place the flavor of the food, but gave up. Who cared? She was just grateful to Kelly for feeding her.

She noticed a very bad smell of feces. Remembering the cutout in the table she realized what it was for. It was her; her own feces. She felt her stomach rebel. She tried to keep it down, but up it came. Kelly furiously pounded the side of the table with the frying pan.

"Oh, you don't like my cooking? You have no one to blame but yourself." And she dumped the rest of the food on Katie's face. "What, you don't like toe jam?" Laughing loudly, she picked up one of Katie's arms showing her the end of her hand. She dropped the arm and picked up her leg. A leg that was taped but clearly missing its toes just as her hand was missing her fingers. Not comprehending, Katie's face remained blank. Kelly picked up some of the food on Katie's neck with the spoon and pretended to munch on it, making sloppy noises. As Katie's face showed a slow dawning of horror, Kelly scampered up the staircase to the sound of more vomiting and choking.

The days passed in a haze of pain, but Katie didn't suffer any more rapes. The smell in the basement had become so unbearable, they left her alone most of the time. Thank God for that. She suspected her hands and feet were infected. She couldn't feel anything from the waist down, but she could feel the swollen state of her hands, the pain excruciating. They gave her water once a day. No food. She could tell she had lost a massive amount of weight. She finally admitted to herself that they wanted her to die, it was just a matter of time.

One day, Tomas came into the basement with something in his hand. He reached up to the cage hanging over her table and dropped something in. She idly wondered if he was feeding something. Occasionally she would look up and see the cage in motion. But it wasn't enough to hold her attention for long. Her pain and misery overwhelmed her most of the time.

Kelly never spoke when she brought water. Katie tried to engage her in conversation, but found the effort too difficult. Her feelings of hopelessness intensified and she constantly slipped in and out of consciousness. Days passed. Katie vaguely noticed a change in Kelly's behavior. She fed her extra water. The slop bucket that sat under the cut out in the table to catch her feces and urine was taken out and emptied. Kelly actually washed the crusted gunk off Katie's face and neck. The smell in the room noticeably improved. Something was definitely up. The extra water allowed Katie to maintain consciousness more often, but she felt so weak, she could no longer move her head.

Katie dozed off, not hearing the three of them enter. They fanned out around her table, their voices coming from far away.

"Wake her up, Kelso baby. I got places ta go. I wanna git the grand finale over with." Armoni rubbed his hands together, dancing with glee. Kelly slapped the side of Katie's face, forcing her eyes to stay open. Kelly's hands held a short black rubber tube. While she watched, her heart beating wildly, she saw Tomas reach up and unhook the cage that hung over her table. He set the cage down, right on top of her stomach and lifted the covering. She could see the cage was covered by a fine mesh screen. The faint whispered rattling that came from inside the cage increased as Armoni slapped the mesh sides.

"Hey there, babies. Wake up! Duty calls!" Katie could see a writhing mess of baby eastern diamondback rattlesnakes inside the cage. They were only about a foot long, their rattles very faint. They were beautiful snakes, more than happy to bite, their venom stronger than an adult: They were not yet mature enough to have learned their venom must be used judiciously for actual prey. Stunned, Katie wondered what the heck they planned to do with the snakes. Looking into their excited faces, dread descended in waves, paralyzing her thoughts.

With a jab in the ribs from Armoni, Kelly took the hose and connected it to a covered round opening in the cage. She slid the cover of the hole up, allowing the snakes to bolt for the tube. The men grabbed the sides of Katie's face. As her eyes popped, Kelly quickly secured the other end of the rubber tube to Katie's mouth; sliding it in as far as it would go, opening a direct pathway down her gurgling throat.

Katie's face turned purple. Kelly quickly secured the tube with duct tape around Katie's mouth. She tapped the sides of the tube until she was convinced all of the snakes had descended to the end around Katie's mouth where she prevented access back up the tube with a clamp. There was only one way for the skinny buggers to go now.

Armoni watched with delight as Katie stopped her feeble struggles. *Is she even conscious anymore?* He knew she was still alive. He wished he could hang around to see what killed her off first: the snakes or a heart attack. Probably, the heart attack. It wasn't like this was the first time he had tried this, after all. But duty called.

Slapping Tomas and Kelly on the back, he declared, "Time ta saddle up, gang." And with that, they climbed the basement stairs, walked out to the little white Volkswagen and drove off to Lily Pond Road. Not even a casual glance back to see the last death twitch of a young seventeen-year-old girl who had just wanted to be kissed by a boy.

Chapter 11

Scotty and Jose pulled into their driveway. Opening the garage door, they unloaded all the equipment and supplies they had purchased at the hardware store. They each took a can of paint and paintbrushes and headed for the back yard where they found the rest of the family. Yes, they were clearly a family. It felt right.

Looking over at Abby as she lay sprawled on the ground with Echo and Barney, Jose kept his feelings for her hidden. He knew she couldn't deal with a relationship right now with her world so turned upside down. He needed her to see the merits of what was happening on her own. He delightedly watched the three of them romp on the ground as if they didn't have a care in the world. Abby looked up.

"Oh, you guys are home. Anyone feel like something to eat?" No one was hungry; except Barney, that is. Abby got up to get some dog chow from the kitchen, while Scotty and Jose studied the magnificent structure in the tree.

"Brothers, why do you stare at the tree house? You look unhappy. Do you need to go up in the tree house to eat?" The aura wafted in their minds, golden color swirling.

"No, Echo," Jose answered. "We need to figure out how we're going to dismantle it and hide it in the garage. Otherwise, someone will steal it from us. But for now, we're just going to paint it so it doesn't draw any unwanted attention."

Echo stared as Jose and Scotty did their best to cover the tree house with paint. It didn't have to be perfect. As a matter of fact, the more haphazard the better. The job took them quite a while; dusk was descending by the time they finished. Scotty went in to clean up while Echo and Barney stayed with Jose as he finished the job, stashing the tools in the garage.

Moving from the garage to the back yard, Jose happened to glance up the hill and noticed the white car again parked in the same place. It looked occupied. The thought occurred to him that the car looked just like Tomas's white Volkswagen. It couldn't be. What would Tomas be doing spying on them? He wouldn't dare. Dismissing thoughts of the car, he shooed Barney and Echo into the house.

"Abby, we're done for now," he called. "Where's Scotty? I'd like to make some plans and I think he should be in on this." Abby came into the room, laundry in her hands. Jose looked at her and stared. *Gosh, she's so pretty*. He sure had it bad.

"What are you staring at?" Abby set the laundry on the table, snapping her fingers.

"Scotty ran out to get the mail. He should be back by now."

"Just look out the window and see if you can see him."

Jose went to the window and reported Scotty squatting on the ground. He noticed a young boy with him.

"That's Kimir. Scotty used to follow his brother around when he was little. I don't even think Kimir was born then," Abby said coming up behind Jose and joining him at the window.

"What are they looking at?" She peered out the window.

"I'm not sure. It looks like a box turtle. *Holy shit, no*." He grabbed his sunglasses and tore out the door as Scotty's tail unwound itself from under his shirt, standing up, high over his head, then pointed at the turtle and unleashed its magnificent power.

Too late, Jose stopped at the mailbox and was soon joined by Abby, who had also thought to grab her new sunglasses. Little Kimir sat on the ground. He cradled his arm which sported a nasty gash. His tearstained face held a stupefied expression of astonishment. He picked up his turtle, rubbing a spot on its back. He tapped the turtle's shell and glanced up at Scotty with confusion. Scotty's tail was just retracting its membrane and winding itself back under his shirt. Snapping out of it, Kimir stood up and screamed at the top of his lungs. Picking up his turtle, he ran across the neighbor's lawn screaming, "Mama, Mama," as if pursued by demons.

"Oops!" Scotty displayed a guilty look on his face. Looking over to an angry Jose and a bemused Abby, he confessed. "Believe it or not, it was an accident. I couldn't help myself. My tail has a mind of its own. I couldn't control it. Gosh, I'm so sorry." He looked into their faces, looking for forgiveness, but seeing only alarm.

Peering in the direction Kimir had run, Jose scanned the area to see if anyone else had observed them. Seeing nothing but the annoying white Volkswagen, he hustled them into the house. Scotty flopped down on the sofa, his head bowed in consternation. Barney padded over, his tongue offering sloppy succor, making Scotty feel better. Wiping Barney's saliva from his face, he turned to Abby, innocent guilt in his wretched posture.

"Ab, I know I made a mistake. Maybe nothing will happen. Kimir's only a kid. Who's going to believe anything he says?" Taking a chair from the kitchen table, Jose carried it over to the deformed sofa, setting it down in front of Scotty. He took another chair and brought it over for Abby, indicating she should sit down.

"Okay, champ, why don't you tell us exactly what happened. Don't worry, no matter what, we'll work this out. We're a family. Just give it to us straight." Taking Abby's hand, he gave it a squeeze. She rewarded him with a tentative smile.

"Okay, I was going out to get the mail. On the side of the road, I saw a bunch of big kids. They were picking on Kimir. I could see he had some kind of an injury on his arm. He was jumping up and down, trying to retrieve his pet turtle which the boys were holding over his head. One ass in the group took the turtle and set it down on the ground, ramming a walking stick down on the shell. It split the shell through, blood and guts, geee-ross. Kimir went bonkers. The turtle probably wasn't going to survive. I chased the big kids away. Honestly, I absolutely didn't plan to do anything else. Before I knew what was happening, my tail was having a field day, the turtle was healed and you guys were glowering at me."

"I noticed the bad cut on Kimir's arm. Why didn't you heal that?" Abby asked.

"Don't know, Ab. I had no control over anything." While they were talking, Echo climbed up on Jose's lap, showing interest in their conversation. Jose looked pensive.

"Abby, did you have any desire to heal the boy after we got to the mailbox?"

"No, I didn't. Did you?"

"No, I didn't. Don't you find that a bit strange? Echo, I think it's time to fill us in on a few things." Echo remained silent. Abby and Jose looked at each other, wary and a little fearful. Tipping Echo's soft golden head up so he could gaze straight into her eyes, he just glared. The golden rainbow swirls were hypnotizing but unreadable. Jose felt Echo's presence in his mind.

"My Brothers and Sister will not understand." Echo sounded tentative. "It is against the law to heal a human. But it is compulsory to heal a creature."

"But you healed us. And Scotty healed Abby. Are you trying to say God's creatures come before humans?"

"My Brothers, my Sister. The creatures do not belong to God. They belong to themselves and to the Womb."

Jose felt bewildered. Unconsciously, the creeping wariness began to worm its insecure way under his skin.

"What the heck does that mean? The creatures belong to the Womb? You have got to be kidding me! And what about us, Echo? You're part of our family now. We love you! Barney loves you," cried Abby, her passion taking everyone by surprise. Echo turned her face down. She leaned back against Jose, crushing her tiny wings and snuggling in as if to ask for protection. The now very familiar auras flashed pressure. They could feel emotions warring in their minds: human emotions from Echo, frailties and imperfections.

"I am sorry to say, I have defied the Womb. But the Womb has forgiven me, just as it forgave my Brother so long ago. We are not here to heal the human population. That is not our mission. But we are a lonely species. I picked you for myself. I have been selfish. And I could not live without My Barney." Barney whined, hearing his name. "If I am able to stay part of the family, you will be very happy. I will make sure. You have been chosen."

"Of course you're going to stay, Echo. We all belong together, protecting one another. What's this mission you're talking about?" Abby appeared appeased and relieved.

Perhaps this is not the time to bring up Echo's mission, Jose thought, *Especially since Echo clearly doesn't feel inclined to answer the question.* He watched her climb down off Jose and curl up beside Barney's tummy.

Echo said a final, "Goodnight, family," then was fast asleep with Barney as her pillow.

"Well, I guess that's that. I don't think we're going to get much more out of Echo tonight," Scotty said. "I'm beat. Do you mind if I go to bed? I know we have a big day tomorrow." Scotty looked really tired. It had been an emotional day. No one really cared why Echo had healed them or what her mission was about at this point. They were just happy that they were the chosen ones. It felt good to be chosen; real good. Kissing Abby and mock-punching Jose, Scotty took off for bed.

Abby rose, looking after Scotty as he walked down the hallway.

Turning to Jose, she smiled. "Thank you. What would I do without you, Jose? He looks up to you. You make us both feel safe." She put her hand on the side of his face, patting his cheek, softly. "See you in the morning."

"Night, Ab." Jose smiled to himself as he followed her down the hall to his own bedroom. At least she regarded him as a grown man, instead of a kid. It was a start; a real good start.

In the diminutive white Volkswagen, they looked at each other with astonishment. "What the fuck was that?" Armoni jived around in his seat so fast Tomas thought he would wet his pants. *Yeah, the little fucker, Scotty revealed himself to be a freak show.*

"Things are get'n mighty interesting, my friend. I think we need to include little Scotty in our investigation, don't you? We can make a fortune off a that tail a his. This keeps get'n better and better. Can't wait ta tell my sister, she's gonna love it. Hope she got rid of the fat cow's carcass. Don't want to deal with that now, do we? I got me some strategizing ta do." Armoni removed a frayed cigarette from behind his crusty ear. Lighting it, he took a deep drag of gratification, exhaling in Tomas's submissive face, the scurvy bouquet of cheap tobacco and halitosis redolent in decay.

"Come on, boy. Maybe I'll give you a go at Kelso tonight to celebrate. I think I might have her suck my dick while she's at it." Sneering at Tomas's red face, he double-punched him playfully, "I promise I won't make you watch me and her get it on again. Now boy, let's go celebrate."

Chapter 12

Jose woke early the next morning. He had a few ideas he wanted to discuss with Abby, but he and Scotty were swamped with so much hard work to do today he doubted he would find the time. His biggest challenge was to start chopping up the gold in their back yard; if you wanted to call it a challenge. He preferred to think of it as their salvation. It would enable them to escape from Tomas and his buddy Armoni. And to escape the potential of discovery after yesterday's incident at the mailbox.

Washing up in the bathroom, he admired his tail. He loved looking at it: it gleamed and he wished he didn't have to keep it hidden. He wasn't ashamed; on the contrary, he felt proud. It made him special. He felt confronted with a destiny, and it linked him to Abby in the most special way. Wiping his face, he thought he heard raised voices in the living room. *Oh, please, it's too early.* Sighing, he hurried down the hallway to confront the newest crisis.

Entering the living room, Jose was confronted by Abby and Scotty's sickened faces. Echo and Barney were playing 'catch me' in the kitchen. *Well, it couldn't be that bad if Echo was ignoring them.*

"What's up, guys?"

"Jose, *it's gone.* Our tree house is gone. Do you believe it? Look out the back window." Scotty stamped around, angry as a honeybee caught under a horse's blanket. Looking over to Abby, Jose saw her nod with confirmation, clearly dumbfounded.

Going to the window, he confirmed the tree house was missing. It appeared as if it had never existed. Letting himself out the back door, he walked over to the tree. Looking down at the ground, he searched for signs that someone had been here in the night to steal their tree house away. Nothing. So what the heck had happened? He walked back into the house, where Abby and Scotty anxiously awaited his pronouncement.

"We are royally screwed." Jose sat, feeling as broken as the busted sofa on which he rested, bracing his head in his hands. Abby and Scotty looked at one another in consternation. Abby slipped over to the sofa, her arms wearing sympathy as she slid them around his neck.

"Jose, don't be upset, things aren't that bad. We still have each other and the house. Maybe we can get our jobs back."

"No, Abby. I had plans for us. We need to get out of here. It's too dangerous here for us to stay."

"Jose, what in the world are you talking about?" Abby demanded.

At that moment, the doorbell rang. Abby's hand rose to her throat. Shaking off her sudden fright, she stood up to go to the door, musing how she had better stop letting Jose's paranoia get to her. Opening the door, she discovered Kimir's mother standing there, with Kimir hiding timidly behind his mother's skirt. She didn't look happy, by any stretch.

Kimir's mother was a rotund Muslim woman, wearing a standard hijab. Her no-nonsense face exhibited a respectful demeanor, but she clearly had a mission on her mind.

"May I help you? Oh, hello there, Kimir, why don't you come in?" Abby held open the front door.

"No thank you, Ms. Preston. If you could be so kind to answer a few questions for me, I would be so grateful."

Although Kimir's mother looked like she would be anything but grateful, Abby said, "Of course."

"My Kimir told me how your brother chased off the bullies that were tormenting him. He told me what they did to his turtle. I would like to thank him. Is your Scotty at home?" Abby would prefer Scotty not be exposed to Kimir's mother. He was not equipped to deal with a suspicious mama, but she had been caught off guard. With Scotty lurking in the background, it was pretty clear he was inside. Moving aside, she called to Scotty, "Scotty, do you mind coming to the door? Someone is here to see you." Scotty approached the door hesitantly. He patted his tail, reassuringly flattened around and over his back, his sunglasses in place.

"Hey, kid, how's your arm doing?"

Kimir shyly held up the bandage on his arm. His mother shooed him back behind her skirts and fixed Scotty with a critical eye. She examined him thoroughly up and down. Turning to Kimir, she said, "Tell Scotty and Ms. Preston what you told me."

Kimir's eyes bulged as he haltingly described the monster he saw pop out from under Scotty's shirt. "The monster made my turtle better. The bad boys killed my turtle. The monster made my turtle come back to life, good as new. I was scared. The monster was very big." Kimir stood on his toes with his hand up in the air as high as he could reach. "Way, way up in the air. I think Scotty is a big monster, Mama."

Abby laughed nervously.

"Kimir, you simply saw the sun in your eyes and imagined a monster because you were frightened by the boys. I appreciate your mother's concern, but I am very busy and must get to work." Pushing Scotty back into the room, she said goodbye to their visitors. But not before she caught the suspicious cold stare of Kimir's mother.

"We will be back later with Kimir's father. He will ask you to explain. Goodbye." And off they went.

Abby closed the door, breathing a temporary sigh of relief. She really didn't want to be here if Kimir's father planned to show up. She could not let him anywhere near Scotty. What if he actually tried to look under Scotty's shirt? *Jose*, she thought. *He'll know how to handle it.*

She found Jose in his bedroom with Echo and Barney hiding under the bed covers, if you could call the vigorous scrambling going on 'hiding'.

"Hey, guys, I need some help. The coast is clear, for now. But they'll be back when Kimir's father gets home." Wringing her hands, she sat on the edge of the bed. "Come on, can you please stop the horsing around? We might have a problem on our hands. And what about the gold? It's still gone."

Jose popped his head up from under the covers, sobering quickly when Abby reminded him of the missing gold and how instrumental it was to his plans for their safety. Getting off the bed, he led Abby into the living room so he could include Scotty in their conversation.

As they left the bedroom, they failed to see Echo's quizzical expression and the flashing of her golden eyes. Ordering Barney off the bed, Echo clambered onto his back and quietly rode him into the hallway where they took up a comfortable position to listen in on the conversation. Echo felt disturbed. Watching her Brothers and her Sister talk quietly on the uncomfortable living room sofa, she could hear the concern about the missing gold, their safety, the need for secrecy and some disturbing information about some humans named Tomas, Armoni and Kelly.

Echo decided it was time to enlighten them about the gold as she began to realize the significance of the shiny mineral. She thought she had better learn what she could about the other three. Her mission might actually start sooner than she expected. Sliding down Barney's back, Echo entered the living room, her tiny useless wings undulating as they always did when she was disturbed.

"My family, please do not fear. I have tried to make things easier for you, with the help of the Womb, of course. Come." Sliding across the floor on her tiny leather feet, she shuffled to the door leading into the garage. "Come," she beckoned. Abby and Jose tossed questioning looks at each other.

Shrugging, they followed their enigmatic sojourner. Opening the door and switching on the light, their jaws dropped. And then they grinned, grabbing Echo up in their arms, laughing with relief. They danced into the garage where, wonderfully, all the gold was neatly stacked in small sizes, very easy to handle.

Golden auras flashed in their minds, "You are happy now, yes?"

"Yes, Echo, we are very happy. What a relief! You're such a monkey!"

"No, Brother Jose, I am not a monkey. I am an Oolahan."

Jose chuckled. He had forgotten how literal Echo could sometimes be; and how observant. Abby announced she wanted to take a shower. She gave Echo a kiss and danced down the hallway.

Jose continued to muse about Echo. She must have realized he and Scotty were complaining about the difficulty of moving the gold. So she had taken care of it on her own. Well, with the help of what Echo called the 'Womb'; whatever that was. It had never occurred to Jose to consult with Echo over the problem. Staring at Echo, he realized they knew so very little about her. His earlier trepidation dissipated, but he had better stop thinking of her as their special pet and Barney's personal playmate. There may be much more to Echo than they realized. Time for a little chat, although he admitted he usually didn't get far trying to pry information from her.

"I know you're not a monkey. That's a slang term of endearment. Actually, I don't really know what you are."

"Yes you do, Brother. I am an Oolahan, a minion of the Womb from the planet Oolaha. Did we not have this conversation already, Brother Jose?" Changing the subject, Echo demanded to know who Tomas, Kelly and Armoni were, and why they were dangerous. Were they bad humans?

"Yes, they're very bad and very dangerous. They wish to harm Abby. I'm worried they might get to her if we don't move away from here. That's why the gold is so important. We can use it to exchange for money. Then we can afford to move away."

"Gold will do that for you? I am so happy the Womb chose to make the tree house out of gold then, instead of the diamonds it was going to use. The diamonds would have been stronger, but the Womb could not find enough material to complete the task. The gold was much more plentiful."

"Diamonds? You had diamonds? This is too much. Echo, any diamonds you find are a good thing—a very good thing. A diamond is something a man gives to the lady he loves. If she accepts it, the man knows she loves him back and they get married, hopefully living happily ever after."

"Do you want a diamond to give to Sister Abby, Brother?" Echo asked innocently.

"Yes, sometime I hope to give Abby a diamond. But I must wait until I am sure she will accept it."

"Oh, I think I understand." Echo's aura splintered into a new pattern.

"Brother Jose, don't worry about Sister Abby. I will protect her." Jose looked down at the tiny two-feet high furry enigma. Echo sure did have a magic bag of tricks, but they had better rely on *him* to provide the protection. Patting Echo on the head, he decided he had better go round up Abby and Scotty so they could plan how to dispose of some of the gold. *Oh, one more question for Echo.*

"Echo, do you have any objection if our family moves away from this neighborhood? Like about a thousand miles away, to another state."

"No, Brother Jose. I will be happy to go wherever you need me to go. Will My Barney come too? I cannot leave him behind."

"Of course Barney will come. He's family. And he's special to you. We wouldn't leave any of our loved ones behind, okay?"

The aura whispered assent and Jose left to find Abby and Scotty.

Three very happy young people sat around the kitchen table, staring at a piece of gold retrieved from the garage. Abby held it in her hand, estimating the weight.

"This must be at least ten pounds." Taking out her cellphone she turned to a calculator app and figured the worth of the hunk of gold. "Current quote for gold is $5523 an ounce. I don't know what they will actually pay, but it will be less a commission. I have no idea how much that is, but it doesn't matter anyway. What matters is how many pounds they can move for us without questioning us too closely. We may need to use every dealer in the county. Spread it around. Sooner or later they'll talk to one another and realize they have the same customer trying to dump the gold. I think we should be prepared to get out of town within a month of starting to sell. And of course, we'll have to research how this is reported to the IRS. We want to be very careful about avoiding the appearance of anything illegal. We may want to consider consulting with an attorney, maybe a tax attorney. What do you guys think?"

"Sounds great, Abby. Glad you've been doing some thinking about this. Scotty, you on board? Scotty?"

Scotty scribbled furiously, very busy with a pencil and Abby's cellphone. "Well guys, at $5500 an ounce, allowing for commissions, attorney fees, bribes, etc., I estimate we have over two thousand pounds in the garage. That is almost $176 million. The government leaches will take 60 percent. That leaves us approximately $71 million." Looking up, Scotty beamed. "I'm good with figures."

Jose and Abby looked at each other with astonishment. "Do you think that's enough, babe?" Jose said to Abby.

"Babe? What do you mean, *babe*?" Scotty blurted, looking from one to the other. Abby shrugged her shoulders looking tolerant. "Hey—what's with you two?"

Jose clapped Scotty on the back and jumped up, giving him a bear hug.

"Don't mind us. We're just giddy with happiness. I'll make an appointment with an attorney. Abby, do you want to come with me? Scotty, I want you to stay here and guard the house. Have the cops on speed dial. Just in case Tomas or Armoni decide to show up. *Do not answer the door* . . . for anything, *no matter what*. Abby, I think you should call a security company and have them give us the works. Once the rumor of Scotty's *oddness* gets around, and it will, we might have more unwelcome visitors."

"Jose, I'm starting to feel nervous about the timing of all of this. Maybe we should relocate to someplace temporary as soon as we get our hands on some cash. We might be safer there because no one will know where we are. Here, we're sitting ducks. Just selling one piece of gold will give us the money to move."

Abby had a point. They decided it might take more than one day to sell even three pieces of the gold; one apiece. They realized gold shops probably didn't have the kind of money they needed on hand. The transactions might take a couple of days.

In the meantime, they could look for a decent hotel with an outside entrance. They should be safe there until they sold the rest of the gold. Of course, they were going to have to rent a very secure truck to store the gold. Maybe the security company could get them the correct truck. They should have everything done within four days. No less.

Tomorrow would be the first contact with the gold dealers. They decided Scotty would not participate at first, because of his age. They wanted to get a handle on the procedure and the possible pitfalls before they sent in a young kid who might arouse suspicion. After all, even a sixteen ounce lump of gold was worth over $88,000.

As the day drew to a close, everyone retired to their bedrooms. Echo decided to sleep with Abby after first explaining that she must guard her as she slept. So of course that meant Barney must join them in Abby's small single bed. Thank heavens she would soon be able to afford a bed large enough to get a good night's sleep. Even with unexpected furry company.

The next day, Jose woke at a knock on his bedroom door. Scotty leaned against the wall, his arms crossed, shaking his head, but grinning all the same. Crooking his finger at Jose, he said, "Follow me."

Walking into the living room, Jose knew he was in for another amazing day. And he was right. There in the middle of the floor sat a heap of what looked like dirty rocks, of all sizes. The largest looked as big as a baseball. There sat Barney looking dumb and proud, as if he had personally dug them out of the back yard. And there sat Echo, eyes big and flashing golden rainbows. She watched him with her head bowed, but make no mistake, she followed his every move. Rainbow auras pressed his mind.

"These are for my family. Do you accept them, Brothers?" Kneeling down, Jose examined the rocks. "Do you accept them, my Brothers?" Echo repeated.

Jose asked slowly. "Are these actually diamonds, uncut diamonds?" Brightly the aura whispered, "Yes. But Brother, do you accept them? Will Sister Abby accept them?"

"Holy moly, Jose. These are diamonds?" Scotty joined him on the floor. "Yes, Echo," he shouted. "Yes. We accept. Abby accepts."

Jose picked up Echo and tossed her in the air, much to her delight, auras flashing madly.

"This means you love me if you accept the diamonds, right, Brothers? I offer you the diamonds as a token of my love."

"Gee Echo, does this mean you want to marry us?" Scotty teased.

"What is *marry,* Brother Scotty?"

"It's when you give diamonds and make a commitment to be together exclusively and protect one another, forever."

"I will be happy to marry my Sister and my Brothers. I have already made that commitment when I chose you. We truly will be together forever, except for My Barney. Sadly, I do not have the power to make that happen."

"Echo," Jose asked. "What other powers do you have?" The aura dimmed.

"I am sorry, Brother, I do not know how to answer that question. I am what I am. I do not recognize what I am as having powers. I am aware that humans are not very evolved yet. It's quite a disappointment to a minion like me. And then there is the unfortunate mistake. When mistakes are made, the Womb insists we must intervene. The Elders convinced the Womb to allow the mistake to evolve, expecting the eons to smooth out the potential problems. Unfortunately, that did not happen. The Womb is patient, but now it is time to draw the line. With your help, we will do that together." The aura faded and Echo fell silent.

Whoa. What the heck does Echo mean, do what with our help? Jose couldn't imagine what Echo referred to, but he didn't want to pester her right now. He faced a ton of work. And Echo was clearly proud and excited about her gift of the diamonds. He didn't want to ruin it for her with intrusive questions. There would be time for that after they had made their escape from this town. Now he must get Abby moving and out of here with the first pieces of gold to sell.

Chapter 13

Selecting an attorney had been very simple. They just picked the firm in town with the largest ad in the Internet directory. Pulling up in front of the firm's office, they realized that *large* was a relative term.

The cedar shakes on the one-story shabby building were crying out for a coat of paint, and the law office shared space with a small neglected used car dealer. Oh well, this was a poor rural community. Even though, as the county seat, they had expected something a bit more auspicious from Newtown. They scanned up and down the street as they got out of the Chevy. It looked clear, except for the scruffy white Volkswagen that sat parked near the busy corner that most attorneys used, coming and going from the courthouse parking lot.

Slipping on their sunglasses, Abby and Jose let themselves into a basic but cheerful reception room, comprised of four yellow plastic chairs and the obligatory sofa table stacked with fairly recent magazines. They gave their name to the pretty young receptionist with a nametag that announced her name to be Tiffany. Jose asked for Mr. Gavin, and Tiffany pleasantly escorted them to Mr. Gavin's clean but cluttered office. Scanning the room for personal family photos, Abby found nothing that indicated Mr. Gavin's age.

While they waited, a man entered to rifle through Mr. Gavin's files. He appeared to be in his early thirties and a rumpled mess. His big pale moon face with round owl eyes hidden behind even rounder wire-framed glasses gave him a professorial demeanor that his rumpled exterior only enhanced. Nodding to Abby and Jose with a slight shy smile, he hurried out of the office. A few more moments passed before he returned, taking the seat at Mr. Gavin's desk.

"Mr. Gavin?" Jose inquired.

"No—oh no. Mr. Gavin is my father. I'm Peter. Peter Gavin. Please call me Peter," he invited, his tone self-effacing. "Now, how can I help you, Mr. Diaz?" He looked down to refer to a paper, glancing over to Abby. "And Ms. Preston?"

As Jose related the parts of their story they had agreed to tell, Abby noticed Peter didn't even blink when Jose spoke of needing his guidance to dispose of a considerable amount of gold bullion and untold karats of rough uncut diamonds. Abby passed photos of the items in question across Peter's desk for verification. The photos, taken by Scotty, showed both Abby and Jose in the frame. After listening for half an hour to their plans, Peter, undaunted, announced he was prepared to give his advice.

"Well, it appears you will both be coming into some sizable assets. First the gold. In all of Sussex County, there are no dealers I am aware of who can handle even one of your pieces, at ten pounds each. I suggest you melt one piece down to a more manageable eight-ounce size. The dealers will have no problem with that. It will give you more than enough cash to begin your plans. My office will file all the necessary papers to the government and make sure all applicable taxes are paid. The bulk of your gold assets will need to be sold in Manhattan and other major metro cities—I hesitate to use just one dealer. And you do not want to flood the local market all at once. I believe we should make some inquiries in India, another wonderful source of eager gold dealers. One of the problems I see here is the necessity to carry the gold personally to the dealers and negotiate a price. If, as you say, you don't want to handle the task yourself, you must hire a bonded agent to do the work for you. That can be quite expensive." Blushing, Peter looked down at his paperwork. "Of course, it appears you wouldn't have a problem with that. I beg your pardon."

"Now the diamonds are another matter. To get your best price, it would be wise to participate in an auction. You may or may not know, but diamonds are very much regulated and tightly controlled by the big diamond families out of South Africa and the cartels in South America. The provenance of a diamond is also critical."

Noting their puzzled looks, he hastened to explain. "Their history . . . their place of origination. As that seems to be a bit of a problem for you, I would like to suggest you invest more time in this part of your endeavor. I need to do a bit of research, but I am sure it would be much easier to dispose of some of the stones, if we could locate a craftsman who could cut them for you. A finished stone of a smaller size, even a few karats, will not attract the kind of scrutiny you are looking to avoid. The stones will be much easier to protect than the gold, due to their smaller mass. Again, I see the need to hire someone trustworthy to expedite the process for you."

"As to your relocation, one must think like the wealthy. In order to blend in you must live in an affluent area, an area where wealth is the expected norm. To do otherwise would draw attention, unless you plan to not spend any of the proceeds from the sales." The looks on Abby and Jose's faces clearly evidenced their intention to spend the money.

"The issue of your security is easily solved. It is only a matter of hiring the best to do the job. Much depends on where you eventually settle. Again, a location where others of wealth have settled will come with many security advantages. I know there are few of these enclaves left, but may I suggest a small city in the state of Florida? It is called Sarasota. A very lovely enclave of the rich—sensational amenities, world-class restaurants, a natural wildlife environment and full of luxury properties I would consider highly defensible. Getting you moved from here to there with the secrecy and security you have requested will be a bit more problematic. There are many loose ends to control, but it's not impossible. Clearly, this is simply a matter of the amount of investment you are looking to allocate to the endeavor."

Peter Gavin concluded his summary by outlining his attorney fees and looking up at them, again with the shy smile that appeared to be his trademark.

"Peter, we appreciate your obvious knowledge and quick grasp of what we need to do. We also appreciate the fact that you haven't intruded on our privacy. Jose and I would like a few minutes to talk. May we use another office?"

"No, no. Please, use my office. Take all the time you need to confer." Scrambling out from behind his desk, he hurried out to the hallway.

"Well, Ab, what do you make of this guy? Do you like him? Do you think he's the guy for us?" Jose looked at Abby, his eyebrows spiked, pensively rubbing his chin.

Abby looked quietly at Jose. "It's a little overwhelming to hear Peter outline what we must do. But he made it sound like we can certainly accomplish it. With someone's help, of course. That's what scares me. I don't want to be exposed to other people. My changes haven't even begun, except for some occasional aches on my tailbone. I'm sure I'll become even more hyper about exposure once my tail starts to grow."

"Do you like Peter's idea about Sarasota? It sounds good to me. I know you'll be happy wherever there's wildlife. It'll make Scotty happy too. And a sunny location will make Echo very happy."

"Yeah, that sounds fine to me. I think we'll all do better in a warm climate."

"Good. Abby, I have an idea. Do you feel really comfortable with Peter? We might have him take a larger role in our plans than we first thought. Would that be okay with you?"

"I suppose so, depending on what you have in mind. More important, I trust you and your intuition." Abby slid her hand over to Jose, squeezing it for a boost of reassurance.

Going to the hallway, Jose and Abby looked around for Peter Gavin. They found him in the reception room. Mr. Gavin appeared to be consoling his receptionist, his arm ineffectually patting her shoulder as she wildly gesticulated. They both looked up with grim expressions.

"Are you ready for me, Mr. Diaz?" Peter hurriedly escorted them back to his office where he slowly moved back behind his desk, his fingers tented and thoughtfully tapping. Abby could feel the dynamic of the room change. She decided to sit back and observe, letting Jose handle the rest of the meeting.

"Mr. Gavin—"

"Peter, please."

"Okay, Peter. I have a few odd questions for you and I ask for your patience."

Peter looked unaccountably uncomfortable. Jose and Abby glanced at each other, with Abby asking sharply, "Peter is there something you need to tell us?"

"Ms. Preston, before we continue our business relationship, I must confess to you that while we were in our meeting, two young men that I can only refer to as thugs, entered the reception room to strong-arm my receptionist into revealing the purpose of our meeting. I will not repeat the lewd threat made by one of them. We were just deciding whether we should contact the authorities to report them, when I realized that would compromise your privacy. I cannot have that. You are my clients, even though you have not yet engaged me."

Jose and Abby froze in their seats.

"I assure you, I do not judge my clients, but if you are involved in any activity that will break any laws or compromise the personal safety of anyone, I will be forced to decline to represent you." Peter made his pronouncement so softly, so gently, Jose knew they had their man. But would he agree to their proposal?

Diving in, he began, "Peter, I respect your position and I assure you, we're not involved in anything illegal. The men you mentioned are familiar to us. It's a story we'll disclose if you agree to accept our offer of employment. I *can* tell you that Abby's mother recently died in a tragic accident that may have exacerbated some inappropriate feelings from a family member who took advantage of the moment and assaulted her. He didn't get as far as he intended, but it's clear to us that he'll try again.

"As I said, I have a few questions that you'll find a bit unusual. But I do have a purpose, if you can please bear with me. Are you married by any chance, Peter?"

"No, I'm not. Nor do I have any immediate plans to marry."

"Okay, that will make things a bit easier. I'd like to propose that you become the agent you suggested we hire to accomplish our plans. We feel that your personality, professionalism and expertise are just what we need."

"But—" Peter interrupted.

"I know," Abby said reassuringly, taking over the conversation after a quick glance at Jose and a subtle nod. "Your practice. We're hoping you can wind up your affairs as you begin to organize us. I propose that you either take on another associate to handle your other clients or refer them to other attorneys. We would like you to be available to us exclusively. It will mean quite a bit of traveling in the beginning. If we're satisfied with one another, it'll mean you'll have to relocate."

"You may be happy to hear that we have decided to move to Sarasota, Florida as you suggested. We'll need you to facilitate the purchase of an estate for us. Something private, with a guesthouse if possible. We'll work out the details on the house search later. We're hoping you'll live on the property with us, or at least nearby. We'll cover the cost of any living arrangements you make for yourself, with a generous allowance, separate from your salary. We realize we're asking a lot, but as you know we'll be able to make this financially advantageous to you. If, after one year, you decide to terminate our agreement, we'll pay you a $2 million bonus and wish you well." Taking a breath, Abby looked at Peter, waiting for an answer.

"I appreciate the faith you've placed in me. And your offer is very intriguing. But I must say, Abby, I have a small problem agreeing to something like this with someone whose eyes I cannot see." Peter made his remarks with a smile, but they could hear a sticking point.

Jose made a quick decision. Abby's change wasn't nearly as far along as his. They weren't in direct sunlight. She might get away with it. So, thinking quickly, he grinned smoothly and said, "Peter, I'm so sorry, sometimes we forget. Most of my family members inherited a propensity for a form of congenital conjunctivitis. It's not contagious." He nodded at Abby, who smoothly reached up and removed her glasses. She smiled at Peter and looked him straight in the eye.

"Jose is my distant cousin and unfortunately he gets it bad, can't even open his eyes in the light. I have a much better time with the condition, but the older I get the more sensitive I seem to be. My brother, Scotty, also has the condition." As she slipped her glasses back on without batting an eye, she smiled and said, "You'll be meeting Scotty soon enough."

That's my girl, Jose thought proudly. *I think we're actually going to accomplish this.*

"Well then, Abby, I must thank you for indulging me." Standing, he held out his hand to Abby and then to Jose. "I will put some details on paper and get contracts to you by tomorrow. I further suggest that we incorporate the three of you and make me an employee of the corporation. There are some tax advantages you would enjoy. I will put my salary specifications in the contract, subject to negotiation. Is that okay with you both? Please leave your contact numbers with my receptionist and we'll be in touch."

Watching Abby and Jose from the window of his office, Peter wondered why he had agreed to work for this interesting couple. He recognized himself as a very meek-mannered professional. He didn't like chaos in his life. He liked control. Women found him nebbish and only mildly successful. This was a poor county after all. He nursed his share of resentments as he was always passed over for the sharper guys in the room. At his age, he thought he would have married and had a few children by now. He thought he could support a family, as long as his wife worked too.

His clients were mostly African American, whites and the occasional Latino. No Muslims. They engaged their own Muslim attorneys; the imams. He, himself, did not support Sharia law. And this was a large Muslim area. Sighing, he realized he would probably never do any better than he already was. Perhaps this unusual opportunity meant he might find some adventure attractive?

He thought about Abby Preston; a very lovely woman. And single. His forehead beaded with perspiration at the ridiculous thought of the two of them together. He took a handkerchief from his breast pocket and carefully dabbed the sweat from his brow. He removed his round eyeglasses leaving his owl eyes naked. Cleaning them off, he replaced them and turned his attention to the work piled up on his desk. Speculation about Ms. Preston must wait until later.

Scanning the street carefully, Abby and Jose hurried to the car, locking the doors behind them.

"You did good, Abby. We're on our way." Abby smiled and absently nodded her head, wondering how much more trouble Tomas would cause her. *What business did he have following them around town?*

"How come you haven't said anything about what happened in Peter's office?"

"I don't want you to worry. We've got it covered. Just keep the doors locked and we'll be out of here faster than you can say, *my brother has a tail.*" Jose cracked up. Abby glared. "Come on, you've got to laugh. Let's go home and break out the blowtorches." They gave each other a high five and started the car.

Arriving home, they found Scotty on the sofa with Echo and Barney, the television turned to a news story which was playing softly in the background. Appraising the sofa, Jose noticed the beaten condition. Barney and Echo could sure be hard on the furniture.

Jose wanted to start melting down the gold, but he thought Scotty would do a better job than Abby. He didn't want to risk her getting burnt.

Walking over to shut off the television, he glanced at the news story. *Just some politician. Hmm, They sure are an attractive family.* Turning up the volume, he heard the announcer say, "Senator Omar Nasir with his beautiful wife, Jane, and their charming fifteen-year-old daughter on the eve of the senator's announcement from his home in Sarasota, Florida. They are pleased to announce he will be seeking his party's nomination as the first Muslim president of the United States of America." Watching the happy family wave to the crowd, Jose caught a glimpse of someone he thought he recognized. An older man, in the crowd behind the senator's family . . . *Nah, can't be.* He didn't know anyone of note, certainly not someone in politics.

Sarasota again, a good omen. Snapping off the television, he clapped his hands.

"Come on, Scotty. Let's get cracking."

In the garage they carried a piece of gold over to a table Jose had set up and which was covered by thin metal, an ultra-fine mesh. On the mesh sat two small lead bowls. They planned to hold a piece of the gold with a pair of tongs over a bowl while holding a blow torch to the metal until it melted and dripped into the bowls. Simple but effective as gold melted easily. They could melt several eight-ounce quantities, easily selling them in the next two days.

That would give them plenty of cash to start Peter off with. Shortly after, Peter would sell a larger portion and they could leave. In the meantime, they might as well continue melting as much as time allowed. Maybe they could sell more when they hit the road— they would need a lot of cash, quickly. They needed to pay deposits before they could get the show on the road.

Leaving the melted gold to cool, the boys went to look for Abby. They found her in the kitchen, watching Echo and Barney frolic in the back yard.

"Do you see what I see?" Echo sat on the ground in the sunlight. Scotty and Jose looked out the window, not seeing anything unusual, but Jose didn't think it was a good idea for Echo to be outside any longer than necessary. Calling the buddies in, Jose noticed how the sunlight made Echo's antlers look like golden crystal.

He had noticed that phenomenon before. But today it looked like a new streaky swirly component had been added. Maybe that swirliness had attracted Abby's attention too. They took the two buddies over to the sofa. Abby turned on the overhead lights, sending Scotty to his bedroom to retrieve a flashlight he used to attract night crawlers when he needed good fishing bait.

Abby and Jose sat on each side of Echo, pushing Barney down on the floor. They turned on the flashlight, asking Echo if she minded if they take a look at her antlers. There was no response from Echo.

Abby gave Jose a questioning look. He shrugged his shoulders and shined the light on the antlers. On closer examination, they could see that the antlers actually grew in a very fine design of crisscrossing cuts, very similar to the facets on a diamond. But it was the inside that caught their attention.

Looking closely, they could see dark-red swirls inside the antlers. They seemed to be swimming in some kind of liquid. They appeared very faint, almost undetectable. Jose noticed the pattern of swirls were random . . . yet they felt some kind of familiarity with the movement.

"Hmm. Scotty, do you have a magnifying glass?"

"No, but Mama Diaz had some kind of magnifier to read with. She kept in the kitchen drawer. I'll see if it's still there." Returning with the glass and passing it to Jose, they all leaned in to gaze at the substance.

"Oh."

"Ugh."

"What the heck?" They all jumped in surprise. There, swimming inside Echo's antlers were little blood-red, almost black, creatures. They looked like they were all head and tail. Almost like a polliwog, only tiny; very, very, tiny. Jose felt a chill in the room as their attention focused on the tiny creatures.

Jose wrinkled his nose in concern. Gently, he spoke to Echo, trying to figure out a way not to offend her. He decided a direct line would be the best.

"Echo, what's that inside your antlers?"

The rainbow pressure in their minds spoke matter-of-factly. "Brother, it is I."

"What do you mean by that, Echo?"

"I am me, just like you are inside of you. Do you admire my antlers? They are very beautiful. They are very important to my mission."

"Echo," Jose said. "You speak of your mission and the fact that we'll help you. Can you tell us about your mission and exactly how do you want us to help? Has your mission started yet?"

The golden aura swirled gently and silently.

"Echo?"

"Brother Jose, there are many bad Brothers and Sisters. Your species was a mistake. Your species does not fit. I am here to make a new fit."

"Echo, what does that mean?" Abby asked, confused and a little alarmed. She knew Echo thought rather literally. But the literal interpretation of what Echo said sounded scary.

"Do not fear, Sister Abby. I told you I am here to protect you. I have chosen you all. You are my family now. You will always be happy and in time you will be an Elder. That is the greatest honor in any universe. It comes from the creator." *God*, thought Jose, *what did he have to do with this?* The aura receded and they knew Echo would say no more. Clambering off the sofa, Echo joined Barney on the floor, where she stood by his side like a faithful soldier.

"I don't think we need to be alarmed. Echo is not the one to worry about. Scotty, please be extra careful. We think Armoni and Tomas are spying on us. When they start to see the activity involved in getting us out of here, it might encourage them to pull something. As soon as we get our hands on the money from our first sale, I would like to consider hiring an armed guard to be stationed here at the house and one to accompany us on our errands. Abby, what do you think?"

"If you think so, Jose. Scotty does seem awfully vulnerable here alone at the house. And I shudder to think what they might do to Echo should they find her." Their minds flashed with a quick aura.

"Sister, you can count on me. No bad men will hurt you." Abby looked at Echo and slid down on the floor to take her in her arms. Abby rained kisses on Echo's face.

"Sweetie, I love your optimism and your generosity. But this beautiful world of ours can be an ugly place sometimes, and we need to protect you."

Auras immediately brightened. "Sister, you are so wise. I am glad you understand. We will work together." Abby looked at Scotty and Jose with raised quizzical eyebrows. Ruefully she shook her head, kissed Echo one further time and announced she felt like pancakes for dinner, any takers?

Dinner was a fun riotous affair. They'd been so busy lately they had forgotten to take time to relax and be silly, to be young, instead of responsible adults forced to handle such a bizarre situation. They did find the desire to eat had diminished; it was not as stimulating as before their change. But Barney made up for it, a true bottomless pit. Echo insisted Barney have a chair for himself so he could sit at the table. She dragged a chair to the table and tried to lift Barney up, tugging and pushing while Barney just turned to watch. They decided Echo would have better luck trying to pull a kitten off a sardine truck than getting the fat dog up on a chair. What a pair. They sure brought lots of the laughter into the house.

The three of them discussed their plans for tomorrow. They decided Scotty would go with Jose this time so he could meet Peter when Jose stopped by his office to review the contracts and answer a few more questions. They hoped Peter would have some kind of a timetable for them so they could plan their move.

One of the most important things they must do was secure the gold and the diamond rocks. They decided that half the diamonds should go into a large safety deposit box in Manhattan; especially the largest of the stones. The balance should be delivered to them in Sarasota with some of the gold. Peter himself would secure most of the gold in storage somewhere in Manhattan where it would be centrally located for buyers.

Once they agreed on the schedule for the next day, Scotty pulled out his list of demands for the new house. Of course, it included every electronic device known to man.

Abby ruffled his hair, laughing. "Make sure you put a tutor on your list. You're special, but not special enough to miss your studies. This reprieve for you won't last forever."

"I don't need to finish school, we're rich now. I can do what I want."

Abby turned, giving Scotty the stink eye. "I'm very sorry to hear you talk like that, Scotty. You sound like a spoiled brat and we don't have a dollar of the money in our hands yet. I suggest you change your tune, right now. Mom would be ashamed of you."

"Gee, Abby, relax. Can't a guy dream a little without you getting in a twist?"

Abby cleared the table, Jose jumping up to help her. She put an arm around his shoulder, guiding him back to his chair and absentmindedly kissed him on his head. Downing a glass of water, he let out a big burp, ducked the towel Abby threw at him and went off to bed.

Saying good night, Abby decided to get some sleep herself.

After washing up, Abby sat on the edge of her bed, rubbing her spine and lower back. The area now ached fulltime. As she pressed down, she could feel tender swelling. She knew what it meant. She felt nervous, yet excited. Neither Scotty nor Jose had fully displayed their tails, but what she had seen of them was magnificent. But this sure would be easier for her if she could talk to her mama.

Sometimes she felt as if a breakdown awaited her. Between the stress of all the life changes they planned to make and the inability to fully mourn her mother's death, she lacked the time to pay full attention to her changes. She knew she should. She must be prepared to understand how her new body would work. Maybe it would help if she had girlfriends. Sometimes she found her loneliness difficult to cope with. She made a very determined effort to hide her feelings from Jose and Scotty, but they wore her down.

She wondered if Echo sensed her turmoil. As exciting as their new life promised to be, it was still filled with uncertainty. She wondered if things would work out with Peter. They hardly knew him. She reasoned they needed the help and must trust someone.

She thought they really should limit their exposure in public. Glancing toward the bedroom mirror, she stared at her eyes. She could see the difference from the bed. It made her appear very exotic. It was surprising she had got away with it in Peter's office. *What the heck?*

Getting up from the bed, she went to the mirror, looking closely. Was that gray hair mixed in with her auburn? Picking through the strands of her hair, she isolated the errant strand and plucked it out. Giving it a glance before she threw it in the trash, she did a double take. It wasn't gray. It looked like a fiber of spun gold. Quickly looking through her hair she noticed more and more of the little fibers. The new growth on her head was growing in gold! Well, that was certainly not going to go unnoticed. The fibers had a faint glow to them. She would not look like an ordinary blonde, that was for sure. Now she knew the real reason behind Scotty and Jose's punky look, it was their gold hair growing in. Donning her robe, she slipped into the hall and tapped on Jose's door. Entering the room, she failed to see Echo or Barney. They must be sleeping with Scotty tonight.

"What's up, Abby?" Jose sat up, rubbing his eyes and yawning, his blanket falling down to expose his well-developed chest and strong shoulders draped by his golden tail.

Abby went right up to his bed and sat down, bending her head down to his face to show him her hair. Misunderstanding, Jose placed his hands on the side of her face. Whispering her name with a groan, he drew her lips to his without hesitation. In shock, Abby didn't resist, feeling the warmth of Jose's desire for her. His arms enfolded her in a strong embrace, pulling her down until she lay alongside him. She realized what would happen and pulled back.

"Jose, this is wrong."

"No, Abby, this is so right. I'm crazy about you, you have to know that." Stunned, she let Jose pull her back down so her head rested on his pillow. With another groan, he gathered her in his arms and their lips met. Unfamiliar feelings washed over her. Her heart beat uncontrollably. Her body responded on its own as Jose's hand parted her robe. *Oh no, this had better stop.*

But she felt so nice, his kisses overwhelming. He felt so strong. Her fingers tripped over his hard warm chest. Her legs parted as he lifted himself up over her. *Oh my gosh, is this what I want?* She felt his weight press down on her. Looking up into his gleaming gold eyes she found herself lost in the familiar beautiful lines of his face.

"Abby, baby, is this what you want?" Kissing her breast, he stuttered, lost in the unexpected moment. "Gosh, Abby, please tell me you want this, I love you so much."

Abby actually didn't know what she wanted at all. But she loved the feeling of Jose's arms around her, and his hard body pressed up to hers felt maddening. Her loneliness begged for release. Smiling and running her hands through his thick black and blond wavy hair, she drew him down into her and surrendered.

Chapter 14

Abby overslept. Waking up in Jose's room alone, she stretched, savoring the new feeling Jose had awakened in her during her delirious night with him. The depth of her feelings for Jose surprised her. She had always viewed him as an ally, a chum. She trusted him fully. She thought of him as almost a brother, even though they hadn't grown up together as infants. Good thing they weren't related. Her feelings astonished her, exploding with just a kiss. How could she have been so oblivious? What did that say about her? Was she normal? She knew for sure she felt fantastic. Grinning to herself, she made a promise not to get all dopey about this. *But it felt so good.* She didn't feel alone anymore. *Could that really change overnight?*

Sitting up in the rumpled bed, her body groaned with unusual aches, a reminder of the intimate evening. Stretching, her hand brushed a slip of paper sticking out from under her pillow. Smoothing the creased note, she read:

Good morning, sleepyhead. You looked so beautiful, I couldn't bear to wake you. I want to get Scotty out of the house before he makes an accidental discovery. We can figure out how to handle that when I get back from our errands. The security company is sending a guard for the house starting tomorrow. Keep the doors locked until we are back! I love you. J

I love you? Smiling, she held the note to her breast. How did she want to handle *it* with Scotty? Thinking it over as she dressed in a pretty teal jumper for Jose, she got a flash. Of course, Jose wanted them to be a couple. She smiled to herself; hoping she wouldn't act like a grinning fool all day.

Walking into the living room, she noted how empty and quiet it sounded, the cheap plastic clock sitting lonely on the wall, celebrating its chance to be heard as its proud ticking proclaimed the hour well past twelve noon. She spotted Barney and Echo curled up in the corner sleeping, Barney's wet nose snorting as he breathed into Echo's crinkled ear. She had certainly overslept. Blood suffused her cheeks as she remembered how they had spent their time: whispering and touching long into the early hours of the morning.

Turning into the kitchen, still filled with the dirty dishes from yesterday she had neglected, she heard the doorbell ring. *What now?* Jose and Scotty would not be back this quickly. Peering out the window, she saw Kimir's father, with the boy in tow. She had totally forgotten about Kimir's mother's threat to send her husband to talk to them. Well, she did not intend to let the happy cloud she was floating on be blown away.

She quickly donned her sunglasses and opened the door. Saying hello, she thanked Kimir and his father for coming, firmly suggesting they come back later this evening when Scotty and Jose would be home. Quickly closing the door on them, she leaned up against the frame from the inside of the house, proud of how she had handled them. Thinking of last night again, she decided to make a cup of her favorite tea and do some more daydreaming. *What the heck.*

Selecting her favorite teacup, she slipped in a tea bag, breathing in the tea's spicy fragrance, reminiscent of the weekends she had spent laughing with her mother as they chopped veggies for dinner.

Was that the front door rattling? She thought she heard a noise from the living room. As her heart started to pound, she realized she had forgotten to lock the door. She looked up with trepidation to find Tomas standing in the doorway, his face a study in malevolence. Behind him, she could see a base little man with a big blotchy weasel face and bow legs. *Could that be Armoni?* Her heart shot to her throat as she dropped her teacup, splashing tea all over her teal jumper.

"What are you doing here, Tomas? I didn't hear you knock. Hey, you . . . *just what do you think you're doing?* Get out of there." Abby spied Armoni opening the door to the garage. Marching over to him, she slammed the door. Turning back to Tomas, she opened her mouth to order them to leave when she felt something slam into her back, knocking her to the floor. Dazed, she rolled over and watched Armoni rubbing his hand, his face cratered with acne, spittle collecting in the corners of his twisted mouth. At the front door, she saw another figure. Kelly. She held something in her hands . . . chains?

"Listen, Ms. Hot Shit Bitch, shut your friggin' mouth. Kelso, get over here with my equipment." Grabbing her arms, Armoni twisted them painfully up over her head. With his other hand he grabbed her jumper and ripped it down the front, exposing her breasts. She screamed. Grabbing a breast he kneaded it painfully. Abby struggled, trying to kick him with her feet. She must get them out of the house before they discovered Echo. As Armoni held her pinned to the floor, she could hear Barney barking. *Not a good sign.* Suddenly, Tomas grabbed Armoni and hauled him off her.

"You promised, Armoni. You got all the others. This one is mine. I get her first." Belligerence turned Tomas's face a mottled purple. She struggled to her feet in time to see Barney leap up at Armoni, who reached out and gave him a vicious raving kick with his steel-toed shitkickers, catapulting him across the room. Barney's skull cracked hard on the wall where he collapsed in a lifeless heap, blood draining from his nostrils.

"Barney!" Abby screamed. Whirling around, she flew at Tomas, beating on his face with all the vengeance of the Furies. Armoni grabbed her from behind, calling to Kelly to get the needle. *Needle?* Abby panicked. As she felt a prick on her neck, she saw Echo run over to Barney.

"No, Echo honey, run." She watched Echo wrap her little arms around Barney's neck and lay her head on his. The room filled with sulfur as Echo's tail shot up over her head, directed at Barney. Echo then twirled to Kelly who stood with a syringe in her hands, her mouth open with astonishment.

"Armoni, check this out," Kelly called, a new strangled note in her voice. In unison, they turned toward Echo as her crystal antlers peeled open from the ends, omitting a dark-red stream of liquid gunk that splattered all over Kelly. As Abby sank to the floor fighting unconsciousness, she felt the flutter of a swirling aura in her mind.

"I am here, Sister. I will take care of the bad humans. Banish your fear." The last thing she remembered was the malignant sight of the black-red crud covering Kelly dissolving her face to the bone; leaving her stripped and consumed skeleton to collapse face first onto the floor. She distantly heard a raving scream and then she passed out.

Scotty and Jose headed home from Peter Gavin's inauspicious office, the contracts for Abby to review tucked in a file at Scotty's side. Peter had already started his research, proving how diligent and enthused he felt toward their new partnership.

An armored truck was on the way, scheduled to pick up the bulk of the gold and the uncut diamonds tomorrow. Peter had already obtained a commitment for thirty pounds of the gold. When he had completed the transaction, he would fly to Florida to meet with a realtor to start the search for their new home. As soon as the gold and diamonds were logged in and secured with the armored truck, they would pack and await the arrival of a hired limousine that would take them to Norristown, where they would check into a suite at the best hotel Peter could find. Abby would visit the local gold dealers to convert some more of the melted gold, then they would continue south to Florida, stopping at the occasional good hotel to rest and give Echo a chance to *eat* of course.

Pulling into the driveway, Jose whipped off his sunglasses, unbelieving. The front door flapped in the breeze, wide open. They jumped out of the car, not bothering to shut the doors, and raced up the short cement walkway, the smell of sulfur overpowering. They detected an underlying stench of rot. *Good God, no. Please, Abby, be okay.* Jose's heart thundered; his skin was clammy with dread.

Stepping through the front door, Jose and Scotty were assailed with a riotous flashing aura. Echo lay plastered to Abby, golden leathery fingers stroking her blanched face as she lay sprawled on the floor like a wooden puppet discarded by a capricious child, the front of her wrinkled jumper torn to shreds. Unbelievably, two human skeletons also lay prostrate on the floor, the bones old and dissected.

"Welcome Brothers. Sister Abby will not wake up. The vile evil humans are exterminated except for the one that ran away. He hurt Sister. I will find him and make him exterminated."

Their stunned and unbelieving minds couldn't process Echo's whispers. Horribly and undeniably, Abby lay on the floor not moving. Jose ran to her side, gently pushing Echo away. He put his hands to her fragile throat, feeling the warmth, her pulse strong. Relief flooded Jose's senses. She was alive.

"Jose, should we call for help? An ambulance?" Scotty held up his cellphone.

"No. They'll take too long to get here anyway. We can handle this, as long as she's alive. We can heal her can't we, Echo?"

"No, Brothers, she does not need to be healed. She is just sleeping and won't wake up. It has been many hours." Jose scanned the area, grabbing a handy throw pillow from the sofa to place under Abby's head. He felt a bulge under his foot and bent down to retrieve a disposable syringe, its needle bent from stepping on it. Foreboding jammed its way down his throat to lodge like a leech in the pit of his stomach.

"Echo, did you see what they used this for?"

"No, Brother Jose," The aura spiked frantically. "My Barney was dying. They did evil and hurt him. I needed to save him before he died or it would have been too late." Echo got up and ran to the back of the sofa. "My Barney hides. He will not come out to be with me. They hurt My Barney. Brother Jose, please tell My Barney it is safe now." Jose moved the sofa from the wall where Barney huddled, trickling urine over himself in fright, shivering uncontrollably.

"Hey, boy, come on out. It's okay. We're home now. Yes, that's my boy, come on," he coaxed softly. Wrapping his arms around Barney, he placed him on the sofa, where Echo could get to him. He quickly returned to Abby. It seemed to him that she had probably been injected with something meant to subdue her while a rape took place. He couldn't imagine they would want to kill her. Scotty grabbed a T-shirt from Abby's room and they pulled it down over her head. As they did so, he watched her eyes twitch and then flutter. Her consciousness surfaced and his relief was so palpable he thought he might urinate all over himself too.

Scotty flopped down next to Jose holding ugly chains in his hand, his face deceptively calm.

"I found these next to one of the skeletons. I don't know what happened here, but we need to go, now. I'm scared, Jose."

"Yeah, you got that right. Stay here with Abby. Let me make a call. Make sure the gold's still in the garage for me first, okay champ?"

Calling Peter's office while Scotty checked on the gold, he explained he wanted the armored car at his house in two hours, even if they had to fly it there. He would give the limo the same instructions. They were to be taken to Norristown where Peter would meet them sometime after work. Hanging up, he told Scotty to pack enough clothes for three days. They could buy anything else they needed on the road.

Before Scotty started to pack, Jose asked him to box up some of the diamond rocks to take with them. They also needed to box up the equipment they used to melt the gold, along with five or six of the gold pieces. That would be at least fifty pounds, more than enough to see them through, even if they got separated from the armored car.

He went to the kitchen and prepared a wet cloth to place on Abby's forehead. She appeared sluggish, but warm color in her complexion chased away her pinched and gray face. She struggled to focus her eyes, slowly realizing Jose knelt over her.

She started to sob, holding her arms out to him. He wrapped her up in a bear hug, softly kissing her head as he rocked them together, grateful they could be on their way to safety in a few hours.

As Scotty passed through to the garage, he contemplated his sister. Had he just heard Jose say, 'I love you, babe, it's okay'? The scene looked awfully intimate to him. He glanced back at the couple. Geesch, Abby was kissing Jose now. He continued on to the garage, not entirely pleased with the obvious signals they were sending. If Abby found happiness, he would be the first to celebrate, God knew she deserved it; but Jose? He was practically their brother. Well, kinda. But he was *Scotty's* go-to guy. His best bud. *His*. Not Abby's. Now they wanted each other. Echo had Barney. He had no one. He'd be eighteen soon, a tough time for any teenager on the cusp of manhood. Shaking his head in confusion, he wondered if things could get much worse.

Placing a box of the uncut rocks near the front door, he watched Echo cradling Barney's head in her arms, her head against the fur around his face as if whispering quietly to him. Barney relaxed, much calmer now. It didn't take much to make Echo happy if Barney was involved.

Glancing at the skeletons on the floor, he wondered when they would get the details on those two gems. Maybe he should pack them up too. They certainly couldn't leave them here. Glancing over to the couple, he prepared to ask Jose what he thought. He watched Jose pick up Abby and carry her toward the bedrooms. Grabbing a few more boxes, he made the decision to stuff the skeletons in, grimacing as he placed the boxes at the door with the rest of their stuff.

Scotty knocked on Abby's bedroom door. Jose motioned him in grimly, patting a spot on the bed for him to sit. Abby reached out and searched for Scotty's hand.

"It was Tomas and Kelly, and some other guy. I guess it must have been Kelly's brother, Armoni. He's a real prize. I stopped him from getting into the garage, though. I thought they killed Barney. *The fucking bastards.*" Her lips moved with no sound, her anguish robbing her of her voice. She swallowed hard, breathing deep.

"He tried to protect me. Echo saved us." Abby held her face in her hands, hiccupping as her tears leaked through her fingers to stain her comforter. They waited while she recovered her composure.

Looking up at her brother and her new love, she whispered, "They stuck me with a needle. Then I saw Echo kill Kelly. It was awful. Her antlers split open and the little things inside flew to Kelly and just ate her face off. I heard the others screaming and then I blacked out."

Jose met Scotty's eyes. Turning back to Abby, he explained what they had seen upon returning home. Abby's face drained of color. Looking to Scotty for confirmation, he nodded his head.

"Skeletons? Only two? But there were three of them. One of the guys must have gotten away. Who was it? We need to do something, Jose, he'll be back." Her voice rose, verging on hysteria.

Jose put his arms around her. "Abby, we'll be gone within two hours. The arrangements have been made. I'll pack for you. If you feel up to it, I need you to go through the house and collect any keepsakes you want to take. We'll never come back here. It won't be safe; ever. This is a permanent goodbye to Lily Pond Road."

Hearing the doorbell ring, he peeked out the window and spotted the armored truck.

"That was fast. I have to handle this. Let's get a move on now. Our car will be here any minute. We should be gone as soon as we get loaded. There's much more that we need to talk about. We'll have to do that in the car. Abby, you okay? Scotty?" When they nodded their heads, Jose left to answer the door.

"Abby, is this what you want?" Scotty asked as soon as they were alone. At the questioning look on her face, Scotty said, "You know what I mean. Jose?" Abby took a deep breath and exhaled.

"Scotty, you know I love you more than life. You've always been my baby boy. But I've learned that there needs to be more to be a whole person. That day will come for you too. I pray you'll have an easy time. I'll help do whatever it takes, under our unusual circumstances, to make that happen for you. But regarding Jose? I need to see what this is about. The three of us care deeply about one another and that will never change. Jose will always be your best buddy. It's just that my feelings for him are different now." She smiled gently. "And I'm happy. Or at least I will be if we get the heck out of here. I need some happiness to have the strength to get through this. Do you understand, kiddo?"

Scotty thought he did understand but he wasn't happy himself. Maybe that would change over time. Right now, he knew he had better support Abby and Jose and hold up his end. There would be more time to think this through once they were in Florida.

Abby shook out her hair, pulling it back to secure it with an old-fashioned scrunchie that had belonged to her mother. She stiffened her spine and got out of bed to help with the hasty packing. Returning to the living room, she noticed the skeletons were gone. She wondered what the boys had done with them. Looking out the window, she saw Jose standing with two uniformed men. They signed something and gave it to Jose.

After they drove off, she saw their limo had been parked unnoticed behind the armored car. She had better hurry now. Someone was sure to notice the unusual vehicles and come poking around. Stuffing her ruined jumper under her arms, she dumped it, along with the memories of today's events, like a curdled carton of milk into the trash.

Chapter 15

Armoni paced back and forth, muttering to himself in the dirty greasy kitchen with the basement door opened to what they used to call the fun house. No time for more of that. That uppity bitch and her fucking little nightmare gremlin had put an end to that.

He couldn't escape the image of Kelly's face covered with the funky shit that had popped out of the little nightmare's horns. He should have stomped the little shit when he had the chance. Kelly's dissolving face and her fucking screams would haunt him for a long time.

But he had a scheme. As he busily reworked it in his mind, he decided it could be sensational. He reviewed the events at Tomas's old house. When the action had got hinky, he decided to check out fast, cutting through the garage. And, on his way out, he quickly grabbed one of the big gold lumps stacked all over the place. *Holy shit, no wonder that bitch hadn't wanted us in there. Where the hell did they get all that gold?* Just a pure stroke of good luck, he mustered the good sense to grab a piece—it must be worth a fortune.

But his scheme needed refining if he didn't want to get caught. Yeah, he wanted to get back to that garage, you bet your ass. He wasn't going to let them get away with what they had done to him without getting his share of the gold.

It would be dark soon. He planned to go back for the gold as soon as he thought everyone would be soundly asleep in their beds. If he couldn't get in the front or back door, he planned to break in through the garage door. He relentlessly paced, thinking about his plans for that uppity bitch the next time he got her alone.

He pulled up to the house on Lily Pond Road in the pathetic Volkswagen, rolling down the window to let in fresh air, the sound of crickets masking the cooling tick of the old vehicle. He needed the car close by so he could load the gold quickly. A beat-up old truck sat innocently in the driveway, the house shrouded in dark silence. *They must be asleep.*

Flexing his arms, popping his knuckles, he figured the timing was perfect. Crouching and crawling to the garage door, he pulled on the lock. It moved. Curiously, it wasn't locked. Praising his good fortune, he raised the door part way and slid under. Hardly able to contain his glee, he took a flashlight out of his pocket. Shining it upward, he illuminated a very empty garage.

"What the fuck?" He ran to the connecting door to the house, ripping it open. Evidence of a hasty departure lay strewn on the floors: forlorn empty boxes still awaiting their share of possessions. Running through the hollow echoing house, he confirmed it was deserted. *Damn, too late. They've slipped out of my hands.* Well, at least he still owned one piece. That would last him a long time. He just needed to make a new plan. This wasn't the end of anything. And as soon as he figured it out, he might just start with that pissant gay-boy lawyer in Newtown he had caught them with the other day. He got psyched just thinking about having a little sit-down with the juicy Tiffany.

He didn't care how long it took to track them down. That bitch and her freaky pet hadn't seen the end of him.

Chapter 16

The dark-skinned unusually attractive man placed his foot softly on the plush apricot carpet that molded the carved mahogany stairs, stopping to admire his hand-tooled Italian leather loafers. He would have to remember to pick up another pair in Cordovan the next time he flew to Italy. He made a note to have his assistant call ahead to order them.

Leaving the carpeted treads, he mounted another set of stairs, bare and unembellished, which led to the attic tucked far away from the rest of the mansion. Standing in front of the attic door, he tried to juggle the tray in his hand while he searched for the key that would unlock the plain nondescript oak door. Locating the key in his silk-lined pocket, he carefully inserted it in the keyhole. He listened for sounds, hoping she would be sleeping. It was so much more difficult when she was awake. He found her wailing tiresome.

He adjusted the smile on his face, deepening the dimples in his seamless cheeks. Not too many people could boast a grin as famous as his. He could say anything he wanted and still be believable as long as he flashed his famous dimples. His brilliant white teeth—all caps, but worth every penny—contrasted handsomely with his dusky complexion. Turning the lock, he entered the silent room.

She rocked slowly, a handmade stuffed doll in her fragile right arm; her left arm flaccid and unmoving, was tethered to the arm of the hard wooden chair she sat in. When she looked toward him, he noticed the vacant look in her damaged eyes had not improved.

He set the tray down on the small oak dresser he allowed her to have—*no sense making her too comfortable*. He saw that her thick blond hair could use the service of a hairdresser. Drool pooled on her lovely chin and crusted there. It appeared as if she had lost more weight.

He could not have that. It would be commented on. He must have everything appear as normal as possible when she left the attic.

Taking out his cellphone, he pressed a button. Within a few minutes, two men entered the room. They both carried the kind of bulk that screamed, *"Don't even think about it."* One carried apparatus that could only be described as a feeding tube.

The screaming and begging started as soon as she recognized the tube. The men picked her up and tied her to the bed. She was trying to bite the hands that held her down, but to no avail. Shaking his head in disgust, he left the room. He would allow her one week to snap out of it, even though he knew it looked unlikely. He hoped his backup plan would show some results. He had invested almost a year in the project and time was running out.

He decided to make a call, unwilling to wait any longer. The campaign was starting to suffer without her appearance. He changed into his boat shoes and walked out the French doors to the terrace.

His panoramic view of Sarasota Bay was the best that money could buy, showcasing the boats tethered to his dock; the smaller unrecognizable thirty-eight-foot Bertram was being made ready for his trip across the bay where he would dock at Marina Jacks. It was only a short three-block walk from there to the mosque.

He hurried down the formal garden path bordered by his wife's favorite yellow tea roses and made his way to the slip, quickly boarding along with his two bodyguards. Casting off, he gave them both instructions to stay with the yacht.

Going below, he donned his disguise before emerging as an elderly gentleman of vague Middle-Eastern distinction. Nodding to his bodyguards, he hardly noticed the small school of dolphins amusing themselves in the wake of the yacht as it skimmed across the breathtaking bay in the shadow of Ringling Bridge.

The occasional wave sent cold spray back into his now lined and aged face. He glanced down at his hands, recognizing how damp his palms were. He rubbed them lightly on his baggy cotton pants. A shiver passed through him, making his stomach spasm with fear. Stoically, he shook it off. His only thoughts swirled around the bottomless power and iron fists of the important men he would soon meet.

Chapter 17

The drive to Norristown took about an hour with no traffic other than the occasional late night gin mill patron. It felt like they were on the lam, stealing away like guilty thieves in the night. Leaving the house so chock full of treasured and vibrant memories was so difficult. A feeling of deserting her mother washed over Abby as the limo sped along the highway. Scotty moodily kept to himself in the corner of the car, a dog carrier in which to hide Echo when necessary at his feet.

Echo and Barney sat next to each other, noses pressed to the smoked glass of the limo. The limo driver, if need be, communicated with them through an intercom as their compartments were segregated by an opaque partition, creating complete privacy. For the first time in days, they felt safe.

Five pieces of gold, individually wrapped in old wrinkled paper bags, sat on the seat with them. They had decided not to let the gold out of their sight until Jose had melted it down to be converted into cash, and they planned to spend a week in Norristown while he completed the task. Half the cash would be deposited in an account and safety deposit box in Norristown's largest local bank, The Doyle Farmer's Trust. The rest would remain safely with them.

Arriving at the hotel, they relied on their driver to check them in while they took the gold, Barney, his dog food, and Echo in her dog carrier up to the penthouse. There they found two well-appointed bedrooms, a deluxe gourmet kitchen, and a living room and dining room furnished with antiques. With a glance at Abby and Jose, Scotty took the smaller bedroom. Although it could hardly be called small and allowed plenty of room for Barney and Echo in the big bed with him.

After putting the *Do Not Disturb* sign out, Jose sat them all, including Echo, at the mahogany dining room table. They all felt a bit sheepish and intimidated by their surroundings, having never laid eyes on such luxury and excess. All rich jewel-tone fabrics, wainscoting and marble. The enormous hand-painted ceilings were enough on their own to make them feel intimidated. Their whole house would have fitted into the mirrored entry hall and crushed bourbon-colored velvet living room alone. Wishing circumstances were different, they realized celebrating their good fortune must wait. They must deal with the fact that two people had died; quite a dampener on things.

"Well, is anyone going to tell me what happened to the skeletons that sat in our living room just a few hours ago?" The audible tension in Abby's voice reminded the others of the problem.

"We have them," Scotty said.

"What do you mean, we have them?" Abby's face looked shocked.

Jose reached over and took her hands, trying to reassure her, wanting her to stay calm as they tried to work this out. "Abby, we couldn't leave them behind. When they were discovered, and they would have been, the authorities would have to come find us. It doesn't matter that we didn't do anything wrong or that they planned to harm you. They deserved to die. I've heard rumors about Armoni and Kelly for a long time—serious, disturbing rumors. Tomas fell under their spell, attracted to whatever fueled their psychotic behavior. There was nothing we could do to change that. If your mother and Hiro hadn't been hit by that truck, maybe we wouldn't have been a target for them. But sooner or later they would have met a similar fate. It was only a matter of time."

"Please, I don't want to know any more about them." She held up her hands, attempting to ward off the noxious information.

"Echo, do you understand what you did?"

Golden auras flashed in their minds. "Oh yes, Sister Abby, I exterminated the bad humans. It was most necessary. They were a scourge with a hate toward all other life on this planet, especially fellow humans. They were no longer in balance. They hurt you." The aura dimmed; the room filling with silence. Then the auras whispered in gray tones. "They were predators. They tried to kill My Barney.

He was dying. They did not deserve to live. That is the law and always will be." Echo said nothing further, even though they tried to get her to explain what she meant by the law. Maybe she simply meant the U.S. laws.

"Now, as you all realize, one of the guys got away." Jose's face looked harsh and determined. "I don't know what that's going to mean for us, but we'd better keep on our toes. I don't know who survived, Tomas or Armoni, but he'll be gunning for us. The good thing is, he probably won't be able to find us. What will he do without any money anyway? When it comes right down to it, they were just local scumbags," Jose said. "Why don't you take Barney to the kitchen, Echo, and get him some chow? Fill his bowl with water . . . thank you." Jose wanted to raise a new subject.

"We know Mama Diaz and the girls didn't move in with Tomas. I suspect the only reason he suggested they move out was so that we would be more vulnerable. I think they may have been after Scotty's gold coin. It's the only thing that makes sense. But that still leaves the problem of Mama Diaz's whereabouts. I'd like to suggest we put Peter on the case and have him hire a detective to find them. If they're willing, I'd like to bring them to Sarasota with us. We can't have them in the house with us, obviously." He waved his tail. "But we can get them a house on the same street. I would feel much better if I knew they were with us, okay?"

"But how would we explain our sudden wealth?" Abby asked.

"What about the truth?" Scotty proposed. They all looked at one another in surprise.

"Well, I guess we could. But without knowing how they would react, I'm not sure. Can we think that one over for a while? I don't think I'm ready for more people to know our secret or about Echo. It makes me very uncomfortable. And how would we hide our eyes from them? Won't they question the constant sunglasses?" Abby's face reflected her doubts.

"Oh yeah. I forgot about that, but I guess it wouldn't be a problem if we tell them the truth." Rubbing his eyes, Jose felt the stress overwhelm him. He felt tired; so much happened in such a short period of time. Standing up, he pulled Abby to her feet, tipped her head back and looked into her eyes. She smiled.

"Let's go to bed, babe. We can figure this out tomorrow." Saying good night to Scotty, they headed arm in arm to their bedroom. *Their* bedroom, Jose thought, beholding Abby's smile again. *Could things get any better than this?*

Chapter 18

Omar stood on the terrace, watching his lanky teenage daughter with her diving instructor as he drilled her in their Olympic-sized in-ground pool. Always a bright, sweet cooperative child, she bore no resemblance to her uncooperative mother. The fact that his heroin-addled wife had not given birth to her went unnoticed by all but his most trusted men. His loss of patience with his wife was hardly surprising as Jane slowly became more difficult to control. He had hoped that obtaining the child for her after the death of their own infant would satisfy her and she would become more malleable. No such luck.

He idly wondered when this adopted country of his would get its act together on the health front. It was inexcusable not to provide the best medical care to those who could afford it. Let the masses languish in the bureaucracy of socialized managed care; he paid plenty to avoid being lumped in with them. But even he must admit getting access to government vaccines was wishful thinking. Like the one for polio. U.S. distribution was mired in red tape, inefficiencies and incompetence. And the virus did not discriminate.

He glanced at his watch, noting the time for his wife's injection approached. She must be getting very jumpy by now. He must remember to avoid her until she got her next shot. He detested his wife, especially when she begged for her fix; her revolting behavior offended his sensibilities. He chafed at the demands his handlers required of him in their quest to ensure he became the Socialist New World Party's nominee for presidential office. He agreed with the imams, he did need a proper Anglo-Saxon wife and child for public consumption. And Jane came from a solid American family, one well known in the breadbasket of the country. Her family owned a very successful produce and cattle farm which had been passed down through the generations, keeping it in the family. Best of all, they didn't rely on government farm subsidies. That made them very popular with the common folk and good for his career.

The fact that his heritage was Middle Eastern was no longer the obstacle that it once was, thanks to the emergence of the Muslim Brotherhood Party. But the Socialist New World Party held the power and controlled the country. Some thought they always would. Which is why, decades ago, the Brotherhood had prepared for this eventual possibility; with him. Yes, the Brotherhood's Manchurian candidate. He smiled ironically.

To the world, he appeared to be the rising hope of the SNW Party; the party that had always bent over backward to their own detriment, constantly displaying their ridiculous political correctness and obvious hypocrisy. The party that believed keeping their constituency down and perpetually needy was the way to control them.

The radical Brotherhood's constituency was huge. Out of fear, the SNW decided they could do an end run around the Brotherhood by offering their own Muslim candidate. He was Muslim, but not too Muslim; dark, but not too dark. With a socially-acceptable blond American wife from the heartland of the country, it would be an easy win over the Muslim candidate who would be offered by the Brotherhood; a candidate they planned to ensure would lose the election, handing the victory to him.

But even his handlers weren't aware of his deepest commitment to the hidden agenda of the *real* power behind the Brotherhood. With his election, the SNW Party would be secretly headed by none other than The Salafis; the deepest, darkest enemy of the west and feared even by their own radical Muslim supporters. They would finally be in a position to destroy the evil in the west as they had long sworn to do, blaming another country in the process.

He heard laughter coming from the pool. The sounds diverted his attention back to the present and he watched his daughter execute a perfect dive off the board. He decided he would have lunch served out on the terrace where she could join him. He enjoyed taking more of an interest in her now that she no longer chased after her mother's skirts like a child. He actually enjoyed watching the development of the person she showed signs of becoming. Yes, he could admit it. He nurtured a deep fondness for her.

He had not expected that reaction when Brooks had delivered the infant to them over a decade ago. She had been such a good baby. Knowing they could not lose her to another polio epidemic surely helped—one of the many requirements he had given Brooks was that the mother must have survived a bout with polio while pregnant. The gestating infant would then have the antibodies to give it immunity. He had not been concerned with the details of obtaining such a child. That was up to his men. Brooks knew never to disappoint. Interestingly, the report indicated that the search for a child had reached beyond U.S. borders to countries where the incidence of the virus was more prevalent. Looking at his daughter, none would suspect she had been born anywhere but in sunny Florida.

He picked up a phone and ordered lunch for two on the terrace. He preferred his wife not join them. Their relationship had evolved over the years, and in the beginning it had been exciting. The corruption of an innocent often had its moments.

Jane had clearly been in love with him when they married. He'd had to submit to all kinds of suspicion during their courtship, but his charm, ivy-league education, and impeccable, though Muslim, family history as moderates had won her family over. And one could not negate the powerful effect of craggy good looks and irresistible dimples on the insipid American female.

Not that Jane was less insipid than others. They were all that way. He had luckily been able to put his distaste aside long enough to get Jane pregnant. Later, he determined her attachment to the baby was unseemly and unhealthy—he was concerned that she would infect the child with her western entitlement philosophy. So the baby was turned over to a nanny. He then devised a plan to get his wife addicted to heroin as a way to control her. Her incessant whining about the child distracted him.

Unfortunately, when Sarasota was hit with the polio epidemic over a decade ago, they had lost the child. By then, Jane was firmly owned by the white powder and was in no condition to handle her grief. Her mind had temporarily broken.

Had the public known what they were going through, his plans would have been ruined. No one votes for a politician with a wife in the loony bin. So he put her in the attic instead. He turned her care over to his men. They knew what had to be done. It had not been easy—they had almost lost her as she wasted away and they'd had to use the defibrillator on her, twice.

When Brooks had finally obtained a suitable baby, she had been in the attic for over a year. By then, she wasn't even sure who she was, and it had taken the slow introduction of the child to snap her out of it. But she would never again be the person she had been when he married her. She didn't even remember the wedding or her family in the Midwest for that matter.

Jane had initially been easy to handle, even taking a small interest in his political affairs. Enough so that she was more than presentable when he needed to trot out proof of his normal American family. But it was becoming more difficult to have her around. She constantly interfered in his decisions for their daughter, and she could no longer be trusted in public.

That was going to get much, much worse as his campaign heated up. He was beginning to wonder how a recently widowed senator might fair in the polls. His closest competitor was the Muslim Brotherhood candidate, and a brave widower with a young daughter was beginning to sound appealing.

He was distracted from his musings by his household staff setting up the terrace table for lunch. He changed his mind and requested that his wife join them. She knew better than to refuse. His new idea was beginning to take shape. If he wanted to go through with this new plan, he had better be seen with her as often and in as loving a light as possible, even by the household staff.

Besides, he had a special present for his daughter. Dialing his secretary, he asked her to make sure the puppy was ready. He wanted it brought to the terrace right after lunch. It would be nice if they could use this as a photo op for the campaign. He asked her to alert the press and arrange their transportation to the island. He wanted their presence to be coordinated with the conclusion of lunch, allowing refreshments to be served to them after the event. Yes, that would work out beautifully.

While the press stuffed their faces, and his wife and daughter played with the new puppy, he would excuse himself for an important conference.

The conference would necessitate him donning one of his disguises before the press left. He would mingle with the crowd as they were herded to his yacht to be taken back to the mainland, disembarking at Marina Jacks. Then he'd spin off from the crowd and walk the few blocks downtown to a waiting car driven by his mistress, who would drive them to The Oasis Club, fifteen minutes away. The exquisite home was on a private cul de sac, surrounded by palm trees and a private reserve where no one could observe their comings and goings.

Lita was a beautiful, intelligent and tempestuous Syrian woman. He had met her by chance at his mosque, had been instantly attracted to her, and was positive that she had no knowledge of his identity as a mover and shaker in U.S. politics.

Their relationship had flourished for seven years and she refused him nothing, no matter how brutal he became in his lovemaking. He had actually developed a real affection for Lita; a thoroughly genuine, likeable and very loyal young woman. He knew that positively, for he'd had his men thoroughly investigate her. He realized that by now she must know who he was, but out of respect, she had never alluded to it.

He wondered how he could continue to see her once the election was over. Perhaps, it was time for them to have a serious discussion about her future. Maybe she needed to play a more visible role in his life. Considering his plans for his wife, he thought a cushy yet prestigious job in Washington might be in her future. Giving a big smile and a thumbs up to his daughter as she checked to make sure he was still watching, he slipped down the elegant stairs to the pool to join her.

*

Omar's daughter loved her handsome daddy. She knew he was an important man, because everyone fussed over him so much. Her mother said they were going to live in the big White House in Washington D.C. She wished they didn't need to move. Her swim team needed her here. And her school friends would grow up and forget about her.

She knew that to be true because her daddy had told her she must learn to be independent and not rely on other relationships. Her mother told her that relationships were all she had to rely on. Her parents were very different. She knew she was loved by both her parents, but sometimes she felt very lonely. She wished she had a sister or brother. Everything would be so different in the big sunny house they lived in if she had a sibling to talk to instead of just her nanny or Mrs. Iskander, her father's secretary.

Her best friend, Nancy, owned a little dog named Snowball, fluffy and white. Nancy treated Snowball like her very own child. It made her long for a pet of her own. One she could sleep and cuddle with when her daddy left home or when her mother was indisposed, which was much of the time.

Her daddy waved to her from the terrace of their bay-front mansion. She loved to excel at her diving, as it pleased her daddy so. She hoped he would be able to spend some time with her once her instructor left. Glancing up, she saw her daddy coming down the staircase and walking toward the pool with a big smile on his handsome face. Oh, goody, she just knew today would be a good day.

Lita set her cellphone on the counter. She had just received instructions from Omar; she'd be seeing him this afternoon. She hastened to the lavender Jacuzzi tub in her extravagant cream-marble bathroom to prepare for the riotous lovemaking that was sure to soon follow her collecting him from downtown. She found the constant charade of pretending not to know who he was exceedingly tedious.

It was bad enough that her life had obsessively revolved around him long before she had met him. But he would never know that.

As she disrobed, she examined her lithe tapered arms and seductive hips. Faint traces of the ugly bruises, left by Omar the last time they were together, still existed. She rested her head on an Egyptian cotton pillow as she soaked in the Jacuzzi and tried to shake off her depression as she thought about how much of her life she gave to her job. She might have Syrian heritage, but Omar knew nothing of the fact that first and foremost she was an American, *a very proud American*. So proud, she had not even batted an eye when asked to undertake this undercover assignment over seven years ago.

At first, Omar Nasir had been a small potato on their radar, just another wealthy Muslim with some hazy roots and questionable sources of income. She had been part of an investigation which had followed his movements for many years.

It wasn't until he had started his fledgling political career that her superiors had become worried; his rise in politics had been nothing short of meteoric. Her superiors had decided they needed to get closer, to ascertain how much of a threat he may be. Without hesitation they had selected Lita for the assignment. Single, beautiful, intelligent and, best of all, she could pass as Middle Eastern. Her cover was exemplary, impossible to pierce, as her last seven years attested to.

The most surprising aspect of this assignment had been the discovery of what an excellent little actress she was. Who knew? She had only improved as the years passed.

Her newfound talent certainly came in handy whenever he laid his loathsome hands on her. He made her flesh crawl. In the throes of passion, his handsome face looked dissipated and repulsive. But he had slowly started to confide in her; nothing big, just the occasional tidbit that, when linked with other information in his file, led them to conclude he hid an agenda.

They were already aware that he fed his wife heroin. Unfortunately, they could not figure out why. Perhaps she had discovered something deleterious about him. Successful politicians usually tried to avoid scandals and divorces; perhaps he had chosen to control her through an introduced addiction. Whatever he was up to must be very serious to go to that length.

They had also received an unusual tip a few years ago. Omar had attended the mosque in Sarasota for many years, but on certain occasions he would appear in disguise, as an old man. He would secrete himself behind private doors, off limits for everyone except the imams. This was the same mosque that had long been suspected of secretly supporting the Salafis. She shuddered at the thought of the Salafis getting a toehold in her country. They were an ultra-conservative group who believed life must be based on Islam's past, including the worst of Sharia Law, and dedicated to the destruction of the West.

It was perfectly clear to Lita and her superiors that letting Omar Nasir win the election to become President of the United States would court disaster.

Chapter 19

Abby and Jose woke up refreshed and ready to tackle the new day. They both noticed how muted Scotty's behavior seemed to be, so they decided Jose would stay with him in the suite to melt down more gold while Abby unloaded what they currently had ready.

They hoped their budding relationship didn't make Scotty feel excluded; they needed to keep their unit tight. Who else did they have to rely on but each other? The fact that Scotty was still a teenager made it more difficult for him. Abby and Jose were each very aware of how difficult their teenage years had been, especially for Abby. And they had both enjoyed the support of other family members at the time. Scotty only had them. And Echo, of course, and Barney.

Scotty, Echo and Barney turned to watch them enter the kitchen, anxious to plan the day. They decided they would set up their equipment on the balcony, nicely secluded and private. It also gave Echo the exposure she needed for the sun. Abby would leave after lunch, when a cab would pick her up and take her where she needed to go. It was impractical to use the limo, and the less their driver knew of their affairs, the better.

The afternoon passed pleasantly. Barney and Echo sat quietly in one corner while Jose and Scotty did their work with the gold. Scotty seemed to warm up as they made progress, and soon the camaraderie they shared seemed as good as always.

"Did you know that the driving age in Florida is sixteen? You can get your permit," Jose informed Scotty.

"Sixteen? You mean I can get a car?"

"Yeah, I don't see why not. I'm sure Abby wouldn't have a problem with it, as long as you're careful." Jose smiled up at Scotty who looked simply amazed. *Problem solved*, Jose thought to himself. *Never underestimate the power of a set of wheels on a teenage boy.* Glancing at his watch, he wondered where Abby was; she should have been back by now. As soon as the thought passed through his mind, he heard the door to the suite open. Turning off their equipment and leaving the melted gold to cool on the balcony, they met Abby in the living room. She carried a recently purchased briefcase and, opening it up, she dumped out the cash.

"Time to get this to a bank. Shall we go and open an account here? A big branch of The Doyle Farmer's Trust is across the street. We can go over before it closes. There were only two gold dealers in Norristown, so if we make this deposit we can leave in the morning. We'll be way ahead of schedule and Peter's calling tonight." They had all decided that Peter should leave for Florida immediately to start house hunting whilst they made arrangements to leave Sussex County.

"Yes, he'll have an update for us. Let's get to the bank." Jose leaned down, tying his sneakers' laces.

"I'll stay here. I think I'll go online. I just want to check out what's new on the auto horizon," Scotty announced eagerly. "And these two need a babysitter, don't they?"

"Auto horizon?" Abby asked.

"I'll fill you in later." Grabbing the briefcase, Jose took Abby's arm, waved to Scotty and Echo and out they went.

Crossing the street, they entered the imposing lobby of The Doyle Farmer's Trust. Along one wall of the lobby was the history of the bank.

Strolling over to the wall they noticed a well-guarded display of old gold coins. Reading the captions, they discovered the coins had been donated to the bank by the founder, Mr. Robert Doyle himself. They were part of an important collection that had belonged to his family for decades. It went on to say that one coin had been stolen and never recovered. Alongside the collection was a photo labeled 'Mr. Robert Doyle and his first wife, Netty'. Abby studied the photo, a formal sepia-tone portrait of the husband and wife taken on their wedding day. He looked stern; she looked luminescent. For some reason, she found the face of Netty Doyle arresting. *Why would that be?* Perhaps she resembled someone Abby knew. Looking back at the coins, she did a double take. They looked just like the coin Scotty had found in the woods so long ago. *Could it be that Scotty had found the stolen coin? It's a good thing he never tried to sell it. Mr. Doyle's estate could probably make a claim on the coin.*

She would have to break the news to Scotty. It would be up to him to decide what to do with it. Turning it over to the estate would not be a good idea, as they could not afford the attention or the publicity it might bring. The loss of the potential money from the sale of the coin no longer mattered to them, thank heavens.

Dismissing the display, they continued into the bank to make their deposit. They fully expected to raise a few eyebrows with a cash deposit of the magnitude they were making, but Peter told them not to worry as they were committing no crime. The IRS would inquire about the deposit anyway, and Peter was fully prepared to handle any queries it generated. They asked the bank to forward all paperwork and their checks to Peter's office, in his care. Due to the size of the deposit, the bank bent over backwards to accommodate them.

Returning to the hotel, Abby and Jose felt an uncontainable sense of exhilaration. Maybe it had something to do with freedom. They now possessed most of the funds they needed to give them a secure base for a long time. And tomorrow, when they left Norristown, their new lives would begin, overlaid with the complexity of Echo and the changes of their bodies. They felt pretty darn confident they would learn to adjust.

Entering the suite, they found Scotty still auto shopping, and Echo and Barney curled up on the antique sofa with Barney's head resting in Echo's tiny lap, her legs curled to the side like a lady in love stroking her betrothed's brow. They filled Scotty in about his coin, agreeing they were lucky he no longer needed the money.

"I guess that means I won't have to go back to school?" Scotty looked hopeful.

"Oh no you don't. You are not going to grow up a dummy, just because we're rich. Seriously, I've wondered what we would do about Scotty's schooling. I think we run a risk, registering him in a local school. They'd need his transcripts from back home. That means we'd have to disclose where we're located. I don't think we want to do that. Do we?" Abby asked.

"No . . . absolutely not." Jose frowned. "I agree he needs to finish his education, but I think we'll have to look into having him homeschooled. We can look for tutors. If our changes become more of a problem, maybe we can do it ourselves. It's better than no education at all. It would only last a couple of years anyway. Scotty? What do you think?"

"Well, I don't think going to school will be an option. I was going to get around to telling you, but we've been so busy and things were turned so upside down."

"Tell us what, exactly?" Abby interrupted. Scotty stood up and removed his shirt. Where his shoulder blades came together he had developed two ugly swollen raised masses. When Abby carefully pressed down, she felt solid mass; nothing soft, no yielding.

"Does that hurt, Scotty?" Jose stood to look.

"Not much, more like an annoyance. It was worse in the beginning. I wonder what it means." Auras crossed into their minds.

"You will be Elders, my Brothers, and my Sister too. The change takes many years. I am surprised this change has come so soon. The Womb has plans for us. The honor is ours."

"Echo, what the heck are you talking about? What plans? What changes?" Jose demanded, stomping uselessly around the tasteful room like a lady of the evening trying to convince her john she was a virgin. No matter what he said, Echo, in what was becoming her typical fashion, would say no more.

Giving up, Abby decided it was time to place a call to Peter to check on the house hunting. Abby found the conversation productive, Peter not being one to spend much time on social chitchat.

He had previewed many houses, mostly waterfront. The homes were all exquisite yet lacked the acreage they thought they would need. That gave Jose an idea. Sticking to the waterfront would give them an additional escape route in the event it was ever needed, God forbid. It also precluded the problem of another house located behind them. They must reduce the possibility of neighborhood eyes accidentally seeing something that would cause alarm. Like funny little golden creatures which hung out with a big fat slobbering dog. Or furry golden tails seemingly attached to the new neighbors.

So they would buy the neighbors' homes too. After asking Peter to look on one of the keys off the mainland, he responded that he'd found a good possibility on Bird Key, a small island in the shadow of the Ringling Bridge which spanned the bay. The homes were exclusive and their numbers low. Docking access was also provided with the house, a rarity on Bird Key. They could look into the purchase of a yacht, if needed. Abby nodded her head, her eyes lighting up. The additional homes would provide the quarters Peter would require as well as plenty of room for other hired help.

Since everyone agreed, Peter suggested Abby catch a plane from Newark and meet him in Sarasota to approve the purchase. Abby glanced quickly at Jose, not wanting to go alone.

"We'll get her on a plane tomorrow, Peter. We'll call you back as soon as we have the flight details. Thanks, buddy." Jose ignored her protesting frown and hung up.

"Jose," she said tentatively, "I've never been on a plane before. I won't know what to do."

"I'll go," Scotty piped up, sounding pumped about the prospect.

"We can't send you. You aren't old enough to sign a contract. It must be either me or Abby. And since she's the oldest and a woman, her input on a house would be much more relevant." Abby's shoulders sagged. Breathing slowly and deeply she tried to calm her jitters. She was stuck. It was going to have to be her.

They went to bed after firming up the flight arrangements and arranging a hotel for Abby to stay in while she waited for Jose and Scotty to arrive. They thought it prudent to avoid putting Abby in the same hotel as Peter, just as a precaution. Jose was not the jealous type, he just wanted to limit Abby's exposure until he arrived to protect her.

They gathered their things the next morning, repacked their equipment, then called for their limo driver. Unable to avoid it, Jose went to the busy ceremonious lobby to pay the bill. Most people paid by credit card and found it unnecessary to pay in the lobby, but Jose could only pay in cash.

Abby and Scotty rode the elegant elevator to the quiet parking garage and deposited Barney and Echo—in her doggie carrier—in the limo. There they waited for Jose to join them. Saying a relieved goodbye to Norristown, they started for the airport.

Chapter 20

Leaving Abby at the airport made Jose heartsick. She wasn't confident about the flight, yet Jose felt powerless to make the situation better for her.

His apprehension diminished as he watched her be searched by the soldiers at the parking lot security point. The soldiers knew what they needed to do. They could spot a terrorist or nut job a mile away. Since they had taken over airport security, the hijackings and terror of a decade ago had stopped. Air travel was truly a commitment of time, as it took two hours alone to get through the off-site parking checkpoint.

No longer could you drive up to the curb to drop off passengers. It had only taken a bomb-laden SUV at a United Airlines curbside check-in at noon of Christmas Eve 2027 to kill the nine hundred and seventy five people that had been checking in for three flights and lining up for their security check to get to the gates. And that was only at Newark's Liberty International Airport. Six other airports had been hit that day, all with similar losses. There had been no loss of life or property since, which was what gave the public the confidence and nerve to get on the planes. Jose thought it was a miracle any airline had survived the chaos back then. So many lives had been lost, so many lawsuits filed.

Jose stood at the curb, waiting for the airport bus, killing time while he said goodbye to Abby. He wasn't comfortable leaving Scotty and Echo alone with the limo driver. Not that the driver was untrustworthy, just that anything could happen in a motor vehicle and he would not be there to handle the situation. He breathed a sigh of relief as he spotted the airport bus coming to pick up the next load of passengers.

He kissed Abby goodbye and slid into the back seat of the limo, giving Scotty a thumbs up, Barney a pat on the head and scooping Echo off the seat to sit on his lap.

As the limo made its way to the turnpike, he confronted the mysterious Echo.

"Come on, you rascal, we need to talk."

The golden aura fluttered in his mind. "I am happy when you talk to me, Brother. Have you an inquiry?"

"Yes. I would like you to explain to me exactly what your mission is." Jose tried to be careful with his questioning. Sometimes Echo shut down or spoke so literally that she was impossible to understand.

"The mission is not mine, Brother."

"Echo, you told me before that you had a mission to fulfill."

"Yes, Brother, but the mission was not mine, it belonged to my species Brother."

"You have another Brother here? Can we see him? Is he from your planet? And what was his mission?" Jose stopped his rapid-fire questions. No point in overwhelming Echo. He was quite surprised to learn that there was another of Echo's kind. Why had he not thought to ask Echo if she was alone? Maybe there were more of them back at the cavern.

"Echo, how big is the cavern where we met?"

"Brother, the cavern is as big as the Womb thinks it needs it to be. The Womb knows your question. I also questioned, for over a century, until you came into the woods and brought me My Barney. I have a great affection for my human Brothers and Sisters, for the few good ones. You deserve the privilege of helping me create the future. The Womb also agrees. I feel the Womb soften.

"My Brother, sadly, does not walk on this world. He was killed by violent evil humans. His death necessitated the Womb to take more time to assess human viability. We have waited a long, long time. Many chances have been given, always a disappointment.

"Humans, as a species, are detrimental to all life on this planet. This is not the first time the Womb made a mistake with a species. This has happened before. It began to disturb the Womb after humans achieved the ability to greatly change their environment. The Womb is proud and protective of all life on this planet. I am the offspring of my Brother, so the duty falls to me. If I fail, another minion will be sent to take my place. But I will not fail. The Womb will see to it. As much as the Womb softens with direct observation, it affirmed the mission after Brother's vicious death. Your future is assured. You will be Elders. For a human, there is no greater honor."

"I'm confused, Echo, some men killed your brother? When did this happen? Who exactly is the Womb? Do you answer to him, I mean to the Womb?"

Jose was deeply disturbed by Echo's words, they only invited more questions. *Assess human viability?* He needed to talk to Abby. This sounded serious.

He knew that if he probed further, Echo would only shut down. Looking over at Scotty, he could tell from his fearful look that he had also received the golden aura in his mind. With a nod to Scotty, he signaled silence.

"Echo, I hope you realize how much we love you and would protect you at all cost."

"Of course, my Brother, and I you. We are family. I am happier than I have ever been." Hopping off Jose's lap, Echo climbed up next to Barney to bury her head in his fur. Clearly the interview was over.

Jose thought about Echo's revelations. *What the heck is she talking about? Echo hails from another world, but she and the Womb—even saying the Womb sounds like a joke—seem to think they are in charge here. Why?*

Looking at the funny-looking little creature made him laugh at the thought. He wondered how to explain the changes they were all going through: his tail, and the fact that Scotty had healed Abby. *Wait a minute. How do they know that Abby was healed? Sure she felt great and had missed several treatments without any negative effect, but . . .* Jose made a note to suggest to Abby that she see a doctor. Maybe there would be a way they could do it without her doctors in New Jersey discovering her location. They didn't want to make any slips with anyone, not even her doctors. That connection could be easily traced.

Jose studied Echo. Why the obsession over a dog? Echo was obviously a highly evolved—appearances aside—creature. Yet there was much in Echo's manner that suggested she was childlike and naive. He supposed that being a different species would present some interpretive communication problem. Perhaps he simply misconstrued some of what she said. *But what about the gold and diamonds?* The acquisition of those raw materials seemed to have been done innocently, although mysteriously. Echo clearly attached no significance to the commercial value of the gold and diamonds. Discovering that they were overjoyed to be rich didn't seem to effect Echo that much either. If they were happy, then Echo was happy. He had to admit that it was all a bit overwhelming.

And then there was his tail. He had spent the last few years wondering what effect it would have on his life. His periodic visits to the woods to see Echo had never elicited any pertinent information from her. His inability to curb his awestruck feelings had forced him to spend most of the time answering Echo's questions. So he'd reluctantly managed the problem on his own. Just like always.

He had matured quickly as a boy, intimate with adversity. Emotional trauma had introduced itself to him when just a defenseless child. How did a child fill the void left by a beloved family, savaged by mysterious brutal strangers? He didn't. He was forever damaged. He was forever different.

His changes just made him even more different; nothing new to him. But his tail, not even on his radar now, a part of him just like his arm or his leg, no longer needed to be hidden from his loved ones; a huge improvement to his mental health.

Or maybe Abby had brought the improvement on. He no longer felt depressed. The hole in his psyche still left him damaged, but now he felt joy and hopefulness. He recognized that he might be part of something that portended to be an adventure of a lifetime. Slicking back an unruly shock of his curly hair, his strong capable hand slid down to absentmindedly scratch his three-day-old stubble. Sliding down in the comfortable leather seat, he shut his eyes. Tiring of the puzzle that was Echo, he cleared his mind for some snoozing.

Unbidden, Abby's face appeared in his mind. As the limo sped quickly down the busy highway, taking its strange occupants to their new life, a very special young man inside simply dreamed of his sweetheart.

Chapter 21

He sure was having a hard time unloading the hunk of gold he'd caged from the fucker's garage. Christ, he got a spot of good luck and someone still wanted to make it tough for him. The sign said, *Gold for Cash*, for Christ's sake. He should come back at night and burn the fucking place down. That would show them who they were fucking with.

Shaking his head in anger, he realized he might have to drive to the city and find a dealer capable of handling his golden goodie. He should have known these country hicks wouldn't help him; probably just jealous of his good fortune. *Yeah, that was it*. He shook his head knowingly. He should have realized that from the royal eyeball they gave him.

Flicking his cigarette butt out the window, he wiped his nose on his ragged sleeve. He hoped he would get his hands on the cash today and score some fine blow. It had been a mighty long time since he'd been able to afford goodies like that.

Thinking of burning down the gold shop reminded him of his plans. He was on his way home to pack now. First thing tomorrow morning he was going to pay a little visit to the fag lawyer in Newtown.

He spent some time watching the deserted office this morning. They sure weren't doing any business; he must be a lousy lawyer. The only person he saw was the stuck-up bitch, his secretary, what was her name? *Oh, yeah, Tiffany. Baby Tiff.* Well, if he couldn't get his hands on the fag lawyer, then Baby Tiff would do just fine. His face took on a greasy sheen as he thought about the time he might allow for a little fun before he got down to his real business. Unzipping his filthy pants, he drove down the street grinning and giving himself a happy ending as he imagined the look on Ms. Baby Tiff's face when she got a gander at this.

Pulling up to his house, he ran inside to collect some of the necessary tools for his fun time tomorrow. He let himself into Kelly's bedroom to pick through her knife collection. He nostalgically ran his hand over her babies. Selecting one that looked like it would do the job, he thought about Kelly. He had yet to deal with the effect her fucked-up death was bound to have on him. She had been his sister and his best friend. The only one who knew of the pain and torment that had been their companion as far back as he could remember.

Their mother had run off when Kelly was born, never looking back, never heard from again. Kelly had been a toddler when their father, Abe, started locking them together in a wooden box he kept in the cellar. The box, so small they could only lay at the bottom, consisted of rough planed wood that stabbed splinters into their tender skin. They would lie holding each other in the dark until Abe had finished with the latest bar whore or neighborhood housewife on the prowl. He used to call them his juicy little piggies. *Didn't want the piggies seeing his inconvenient brats.*

All they knew was their father and the wooden box. When Armoni turned eight, Abe occasionally sat him in the corner of the room while he and his drunken conquest did their business, amid much slobbering and animal sounds. Sometimes, Abe knocked them around a bit before they got the message. Armoni knew well his father's philosophy about forking out good money to pay a piggy's booze tab without a payback. Didn't matter if they agreed or not. They eventually came round. Armoni thought that the little piggies were the most fun to watch. Just a simple, unknowingly frightening observance from the funny-looking, unnoticed little boy in the corner, huddled and wild eyed, missing nothing. He felt a tug of sympathy for the young boy he had been, remembering being overwhelmed by the spiral of emotions confronting him as a boy and then later, as a teenager.

As Kelly grew older, Abe started to notice her. Armoni also noticed. When she turned thirteen, she displayed a shadow of the attractive young woman she would grow into. Armoni was seventeen. And stone-cold ugly. As of late, when they were locked up, things had changed in the wooden box. Armoni had started to look forward to it. He loved the way Kelly clung to him, softly weeping. He would stroke her budding breasts until she calmed down, kissing her hair, humming to her. His hands loved to explore, Kelly not understanding even when it was too late. She became his obsession. Until finally, he found himself sneaking into her bed at night to fondle her until she woke, then together they would finish the night with physical comfort of the most primal kind.

Until the fateful night Abe came home without a juicy piggy. Armoni and Kelly had not heard him enter. They were fully engrossed, giggles masking Abe's footsteps. The bare bulb hanging over Kelly's bed snapped on. Armoni felt strong fingers digging at his throat, swinging him back over the mussed bed to crash him, naked, against the bedroom wall, leaving a hollow bulge where his shoulders cratered the cheap sheetrock. He lay panting on the floor as his father looked down on Kelly, slowly unbuckling his pants.

"Don't remember giving you permission ta touch something that belongs ta me, boy. Can't say I blame you, though. With your looks, you ain't ever gonna get yourself your own woman." Disdain and contempt distorted Abe's face as he taunted Armoni.

Kelly tried to slip off the bed, her nakedness inflaming Abe. Grabbing her by the hair, he dragged her back to the bed, pinned her down with his weight and slapped her across the face.

"You whore—lying with your own brother. Can't help yourself, can you? Time for this juicy piggy to give her daddy a little payback." He had fumbled with his navy workpants, sliding them to his ankles. Kicking them to the side, he had stood with his erection engorged and craving satisfaction, his dissipated face a tribute to greed and mad fervor. Plunging into his daughter, he had slapped her face again.

"Let's see a little enthusiasm, piggy."

Kelly had lain still, clearly in shock while her father raped her until he was satisfied. Suddenly, Armoni had plowed into him, knocking him off balance and allowing Kelly to twist out from under him and escape the room.

"You mongrel, after all I did for you." Rubbing his arm and rising, he had shot Armoni a vicious look. "Time to teach the pups some lessons." Raising his fist he had struck down violently, landing on Armoni's nose, busting it, blood splattering them both.

Armoni had staggered back, his father pressing forward aggressively, then suddenly freezing. His eyes had flared briefly, valuable air with a spot of blood retching from his lungs over his curled lips as he turned in time to see Kelly, having yanked out the kitchen butcher knife she had gleefully stabbed him in the back with, plunge it into his heart. He had gone down hard.

The cover up had proved easy. Armoni had taken the blame. They had wiped the knife handle clean, replacing it with Armoni's prints. Their father's semen, extracted after Kelly's exam at the hospital, along with signs of sexual activity at a very young age, had helped bolster their claims of incest and rape. Armoni's broken nose and his blood on his father's fist had made the story believable. They had never told the authorities about the wooden box in the basement. The whole town had already known what a lousy father Abe was anyway. The brief investigation had exonerated both of them of all responsibility.

Kelly might have become slice and dice happy as she matured, but it had never caused them any trouble as they strove to duplicate the high they had experienced together the night they had killed their father. He truly enjoyed watching a babe who enjoyed her job. Yeah, he sure missed his sister; no one to share his conquests with now. She was one of a kind. Doubtful he'd ever run across a bitch as good as her again, a tear fell from his eye, landing on Kelly's favorite knife. *Hmm, good omen,* he thought, selecting that same knife as his weapon for tomorrow.

Opening a can of pea soup from the plywood shelves in the pantry, he grabbed a spoon, not bothering to heat it up. He needed thinking time. He suspected he wouldn't be returning to the house after his satisfying moment–*and I do mean satisfying, get it?*—with Baby Tiff. He chuckled to himself over his unique cleverness.

He was reluctant to leave the house with the ripe DNA in the basement. He thought about torching the place along with the gold joint. Considering other methods of covering his tracks, he decided fire covered the best. He couldn't care less if they discovered it was arson. They couldn't prove enough to pin it on him. He would be long gone anyway.

Once he caught up with those motherfuckers that had killed his two best friends, he would have all the gold he needed to go anywhere in the world. After he had his fun with that stuck-up bitch and her weird fucking pet, that is. *Yeah,* he thought, *he would torch that bugger too.* Or stomp him, just like he'd done with the slobbering mutt.

He sucked the last of his pea soup off his finger, enjoying the sensation and letting the can drop to the filthy floor. Kicking it to the other side of the room, he paused. Hadn't he heard the chicks in France were a bunch of whores? Yeah, he would put France on the top of his list. Reaching down to his crotch, he felt for his penis. Stroking it lovingly, he shouted out loud, "Yeah, wait'll they get a load a this!"

The next day dawned early, swirling mists awaiting banishment by a stalwart winter sun. After filling his car with the items he felt worth taking with him, he went through the house, trailing a full container of kerosene, purely to make his job easier when he doubled back to light it up. He planned to be in a big hurry.

Getting behind the wheel, he fought rush hour traffic to find a strategic spot to park his car. Observing Tiffany unlock the office, he decided to wait awhile to ascertain if her boss would show up this morning. Once convinced she alone staffed the office, he crept to the unlocked front door, silently slithering in.

Looking around the empty reception room, he observed cardboard boxes and packing materials piled with files and knickknacks. From the front door he could hear the shuffling of boxes from another room. Unsheathing Kelly's gleaming prize baby, he extracted a pair of handcuffs from his pocket, then locked the front door. The aroma of his staleness and sweat announced him as he opened another door to see Tiffany bending over a box unaware, her back to him, with her miniskirt hiked so far up her panties were winking at him. Licking his slobbering lips, he said, "Hello there, Tiff, my name's Lover."

Two hours later, he had what he needed. Before he left, he dumped out the contents of the boxes, hoping to pass off Tiffany's body as a victim of a robbery gone wrong; or gone right. *Depends on how ya look at things*, he smirked to himself.

Tiff sure was a fun gal, all that squirming while he was on top of her. He only stuck her once or twice with Kelly's baby before she got the message. Just the sight of her arms cuffed above her head as he ran his tongue down to her goody spot made him hard again. Who knew she would like it so much? He could tell by the way she said his name on his command. Slicing into her right titty convinced him of her excitement.

After that, he got all the info he needed, including a mighty fine blow job, although the leaking blood disgusted him. Tiffany finally choked, heaving all over him. Punching her out kinda put a damper on their fun. She had needed to be taught some manners. He thought a fine educated bitch like her would know better than to barf all over him. *Ah, they're all the same*, he thought, shaking his big head in disappointment. *Just cunts and stuck-up bitches.*

Arriving back at his house, he just needed to flip a match where he'd dumped the kerosene and get out fast. Quickly pulling away, he drove to Route 80, knowing he'd be in New York City in less than two hours. Thinking back to the information Baby Tiff had so easily blabbed to him, he wondered what was so special about Sarasota. He certainly didn't relish a long lonely drive to Florida. He wondered how long he could stay on the road without falling asleep. He had to admit, making the long haul in the rickety old Volkswagen was not going to be pleasant. He wondered if he should buy something more befitting a man of his impending stature. He cackled, smacking his hand down on his knee. After he sold the gold in New York City, he should certainly be able to afford any set of wheels he wanted.

He wondered how long it would take. *Probably a few days.* He questioned if a little stopover in the city would put a dent in his plans by slowing him down.

He had never heard of Sarasota before. *Must be another hick town like theirs in Sussex County. Shouldn't be too hard to spot that motley crew of fuckers in a small hick town. It's not like they were going to blend in with that freaky murderous pet of theirs.*

Feeling like a king, Armoni pulled up to the first hotel he found after passing through the Lincoln Tunnel. He decided to make for 42nd Street since it was the only one he'd ever heard of.

Pulling his car under the flashy mezzanine of the Sheraton Hotel, an attendant shouted at him, telling him to move on, he couldn't park there. *What the fuck is he talking about?* Glaring at him, Armoni motioned to the *For Guests Only* sign and walked past him into the lobby of the hotel. Barging up to the reservation desk, he slapped down a wad of money which represented all his net worth and demanded a room.

"May I have a credit card, please?" He didn't like how the pretty front desk clerk with the fussy professional demeanor gave him the ole eyeball.

"What, my cash ain't good enough?" Armoni asked in surprise. Behaving like she smelled something rotten, she explained how he would have to leave payment in advance, in addition to a deposit for incidental room expenditures. Peeling off some large bills, he counted out the amount she requested. It would cover him for a week. Counting what was left, he was surprised to see the dent he had just made in his stash. Oh well, he would be back in the chips soon enough.

Noticing the way the desk clerk stared at him, he kept his mouth shut and wondered if he should do some shopping for new duds while he stayed there. Dropping his car keys on the desk, he ordered her to have his car looked after. Didn't want it stolen his first night in New York City.

Taking the room key the desk clerk had given him, he strolled over to the elevators, gawking at the well-dressed and attractive crowd who all appeared to have very important destinations. *Was he intimidated?* he asked himself. *Nah, just a bunch of stuck-up pussy and sons a bitches.* Fingering Kelly's baby tucked away in his pants, he knew he was the intimidating one.

Arriving at his room, he struggled with the room key until he figured out how it worked. Letting himself in, he heaved his bag with the gold onto the huge bed, looking around the well-appointed room, impressed.

Spotting an advertising directory, he curled up on the bed. Wrenching his boots off, the room filled with a foul foot stench, Armoni completely impervious. Marking the ads for gold dealers, he finally turned to the auto dealers like a house cat that had just taken down a wildebeest. He feasted. Eventually, he found his eyes drooping. Climbing under the covers fully clothed, he drifted off to fuzzy dreams of Kelly and him, speeding down a country road of gold in a cherry-red convertible, laughing their heads off, Tomas in the back seat. Lost in his dreams, he farted and slept the night away.

Chapter 22

Disembarking from her plane, Abby felt disoriented. She followed the stream of fellow passengers as they made their way to the baggage claim, trying to spot Peter. Touching her sunglasses for reassurance, she felt relieved to note she wasn't alone. Everyone wore sunglasses. As she made her way to meet Peter, she tried to quell her nervousness. She almost didn't believe she had arrived safely in Sarasota; her ease with travel almost nonexistent, never before having traveled out of New Jersey. Hardly out of Sussex County or Short Hills either, for that matter. Her eyes roved everywhere as she took in her surroundings.

The airport sparkled, bright and clean. She got goosebumps from the air conditioning, yet everyone dressed casually, in brightly-colored shorts and sandals. They appeared fit, happy and attractive. No signs of poverty here. No downtrodden welfare faces dressed in hand-me-down thrift store clothing. Self-consciously, she smoothed her worn sweater, wishing she could be with Jose and Scotty. She felt undeniably out of her element.

Spotting Peter, she felt a measure of relief. He gave her a quick hug before taking her small bag from her hands.

"I've arranged some time with a personal shopper for you this evening. I hope that was okay?" Peter's timid smile belied his efficiency. Abby saw past his blank owlish face into the intelligence of his unblinking eyes. She felt herself in good hands. Peter's quick competence had enabled Abby and Jose to start knitting a psychological safety net, woven entirely with his help.

"Do we have money in an account here? I only brought enough to pay my hotel bill until the boys get here. I didn't want to carry a lot on the plane."

"My dear, you can spend as much as you please. I have already transferred funds from the two major gold sales to a local bank. The transaction took one day—the money made it to Florida before I did." Handing Abby three plastic cards, he explained how they worked.

"We can activate them with your thumb print before you go shopping. Don't worry about losing them. All vendors provide readers for your print before a sale is wrung up. No one but you can access your card." Changing the subject, he declared, "I'm embarrassed to admit I enjoyed a delightful day yesterday with our realtor. This town is impossible to be depressed in."

"I'm glad you're enjoying the process, I was worried you'd find it tedious. You're so important to us, Peter. We're all so pleased this is working out. Have you completely closed your office in Sussex?" Peter bowed his head, trying to hide his flush of pleasure from her words.

"Yes, the office is closed. Tiffany is shipping my files to my hotel here. I'll store them until we settle on the new move. I turned anything active over to other attorneys in the area. I wonder, what do you think of hiring Tiffany and moving her down here? I think we may need an assistant to do personal errands, shopping etc.?"

"That would be fine. She seems very sweet. Can she leave her family? This is a big move."

"Who would say no to trading Sussex County for Sarasota?" Laughing together, Abby and Peter stepped out into the sunlight.

Peter had a Savanna Rover waiting at the busy curb. As he hustled her out of the terminal, he gave her the low down on their itinerary. First stop, Bird Key and their realtor. Pulling out into the traffic, he dumped sheets of information on her lap, told her to buckle up, and off they went.

Sylvia Wadsworth's enjoyment of her seventy-third birthday had just increased with the execution of the last contract of her long career. It had been two very long days. She fingered the heavy faux pearls draped around the layers of crepe at her throat while her other manicured hand fluffed her perfect blond highlights.

Chuckling to herself, she couldn't wait to enjoy the expression on her third husband's face when he saw this contract and the commission she stood to receive from the sale. What a way to start her long-deserved retirement.

She would have suspected a hoax after meeting the purchaser, had not her stoic attorney accompanied her; a shy respectful young man for sure. Ms. Preston appeared to behave like a lovely young lady, but clearly not from a family of substance. She idly wondered if Ms. Preston might share the name of her stylist, her golden streaks were absolute perfection.

Sylvia did not possess the nerve to inquire as to where the funds for such a purchase had come from. The attorney supplied the proof of funds letter, so she kept her mouth shut. Between the three mansions on pricey Bird Key, the sixty-four-foot Bertram motor yacht, included by one of the sellers, and her fee for coordinating the furnishing of the homes with one of the top designers from Kane's of Sarasota, her purchase would come to $63 million dollars, to close in thirty days. *Nice.*

But what did an unsophisticated single young woman need with these properties? It sure appeared suspicious to her. During her previous appointments with the attorney, he had failed to reveal who he represented. Now, after spending two days together, she knew. But the purchaser revealed very little. *And what's with the constant sunglasses? The girl never takes them off. Like never.* Maybe she should keep an eye on Miss Abby. Wouldn't want any harm to come to her elite community, now would she? Sylvia sniffed, thinking Miss Abby better watch her step if she thought she could break into Sarasota society just because of her flashy new money.

The size of the purchase would certainly be commented on in the real estate section of Sarasota Today. *Everyone in town would be dying of curiosity.*

Preening, Sylvia realized she would receive reflected glory in being the realtor of record. She could sure use a status bump at the country club. Maybe she should be a tad more generous toward the poor girl.

Picking up her cell, she dialed her husband. She felt like celebrating tonight. Asking him to call *Michaels on First* for reservations, she looked forward to an icy cold martini at her favorite restaurant.

Returning to their hotels, Peter dropped Abby off first. His hotel sat just a half mile away, closer to the marina. Working feverishly on his new client's affairs, he hadn't spent much time thinking about the ramifications of this momentous move or his own future. He loved seeing the world outside the small confines of Sussex County. He knew Tiffany would love it, along with the new clients. His fondness for Abby and Jose continued to grow. It was clear in the way that Abby referred to Jose that they were in love. He wished them well, but it made him feel lonely. Perhaps when they had settled into their new homes, he might try to date.

He started to wilt in the late afternoon sun, his shirt sticking to his back and decided to try to adopt a more informal dress. Although he wore them as armor, business suits apparently weren't necessary in the warm climate. Rolling up the sleeves of his no longer crisp white shirt, he entered his hotel. He passed the glamorous pricey shops, available to only the wealthy; the acquisition of their wares now within his means. Who was he kidding? He wore thrift on his soul like a clown wore makeup on his face. Remove the makeup, is the clown really there? Remove the dressing from his profile, is Peter really there?

He sighed over the burden of his personal insecurities. He would just have to find a more inexpensive place to shop.

Entering his room, he turned on the shower in his sumptuous bathroom, the marble unlike anything he had ever seen until Sylvia Wadsworth had introduced him to the finest side of Sarasota real estate.

Tomorrow would prove the wisdom of his advice to move. Jose and Scotty would arrive late this evening. They planned to meet first thing in the morning to go and look at Abby's choice of homes. By the end of the day, he hoped he could maneuver them to a quiet location for a talk.

He planned to ask some pressing questions that nagged anxiously at him. His job description prevented him from questioning the motives or private business of his clients, yet he couldn't dismiss the troublesome premonition that something mystical permeated his clients. He was concerned that he had allowed this phenomenal opportunity to overwhelm his life.

Because of this momentous change, he felt he had a right to ask some questions. He longed to avoid confrontation, yet the clearly unexpected and curious wealth of his clients begged questions. He hoped his interest would not cast him in a venal light. He wanted their relationships to flourish on a more fiduciary, affectionate level. He enjoyed their confidence, but clearly felt an invisible wall of some sort.

And what's behind the infernal sunglasses? Running his chubby fingers through his thinning sandy hair, he realized he didn't believe the congenital eye infection story. It was very disconcerting to talk to someone and never see their eyes. Except the one time that Abby had slipped them off for him. Reflecting on the sudden surprise of their slightly unusual golden quality, he made the astonishing connection that had been eluding him. They all wore a golden aura about them. Their golden-streaked hair, the skin of both Scotty and Jose, all suggested a subtle goldenness. *That's odd.*

Tomorrow would be the first time he'd lay eyes on all three at the same time. *Oh yes, and their two dogs, Barney and Echo. They shouldn't be a problem, Sarasota seemed to be an inordinately tolerant community of dog lovers.* Not intending to offend, he hoped Abby and Jose could take his questions in stride.

Passing the hotel landline sitting on the Chippendale-style desk, he saw a red message light blinking. *Did I miss a call from Abby?*

Dialing into the message center, he found himself ordered to contact the Newtown Police Department at his earliest convenience.

Frowning, he wondered how they knew how to find him as only Tiffany knew his itinerary. Something must have happened to his elderly parents. His father was eighty years old, after all. They knew of his change in fortune, but not the name of his hotel. An only child, his parents relied on him.

Conception had come late for his mother after doctors convinced his parents she could never conceive. The fact that his mother's pregnancy came as she turned forty eight and his father fifty firmly relegated them to the role of shocked and reticent parents, stumbling along, trying their best. It probably contributed to his lack of confidence and reliance on his professional demeanor to formulate his personality. Shrugging off his introspection, he remembered how he loved his parents and quickly dialed their number in Sussex County.

Chapter 23

Armoni hurried back to his hotel, ready to explode with giddiness. The three days it had taken to accomplish the task had felt endless, but the sale had concluded successfully. The gold dealers behaved much more professionally in New York City. They failed to bat an eye when he pulled his lump of gold out of his paper bag. The cash resided safe and sound—except for the wad in his pocket—in the bank.

They tried to talk him into one of those newfangled plastic cards with his fingerprints. Oh no, he weren't no fool. Not gunna let some stupid clerk trick him into giving his fingerprints. He preferred hard cash in his pocket, anyway. Cash always speaks loudest in a crowded room.

Pulling up to the hotel parking attendant, he flipped him the keys to his brand new, two-hundred-and-fifty-thousand-smackeroo Lamborghini SUV, cherry red with a gold-trimmed black lightning bolt down the side panels. Yeah, the snotty, board-up-his-ass dealer sure wasn't pleased about his insistence on the lightning bolt. Slapping his documents from the bank on the dealer's desk sure had changed his tune.

He reached into the back of his new wheels to grab the shopping bags he had accumulated from his riotous shopping spree for the new duds he needed and were befitting for a man of his obvious new stature.

He loved making snot-nosed gay blades dance to the tunes he called as he forced them to run ragged trying to please him. He wouldn't have even bothered with them, but everyone knew they were the best source of what they called *fashion*. Anxious to get himself some *fashion*, he had privately thought his taste as good as the stuck-up blades. Most of the duds he left the store with looked like the same things he had picked out in the first place.

Once the blades realized what he liked, they had bent over backwards to kiss his ass. He had a few numbers that he couldn't wait to try on. Like the red and yellow Anaconda skin shitkickers. He whistled, recalling how they had politely suggested that the 'gentleman's boots might be a tad inappropriate'. Just to show them who was in charge, he bought an additional pair in turquoise and white. *Sure turned their faces green—with envy, of course.*

He couldn't wait to change. *Oh yeah, maybe it would be a good idea to shower up first.* He hoped he might be able to find a willing babe to help him celebrate. He imagined he could have any girl he wanted, now that he was so obviously a man of substance. Cupping his crotch in his meaty hands, he laughed as he entered the sumptuous lobby spotting two uptown ladies with big fake tits staring at his crotch.

Obviously, they're interested in the goods. What girl wouldn't be? They're probably wondering how they can be the lucky ones to celebrate with me.

Strolling right up to them, his bandy legs now shod in his turquoise and white shitkickers, he smacked the nearest one on the ass as he stuck a dirty fingernail between his teeth, removing a piece of his late hot-dog lunch and giving it a quick flick to the floor.

"How 'bout you two hot babes joining me tonight to celebrate our new relationship?"

No sooner had he closed his mouth then all hell broke loose. The broads started screaming. The cops rushed into the hotel, arrested him for assault and took him downtown to get booked. It had taken him all night to convince them it was just a mistake.

A visit from one of the broad's husbands attempting to get to the bottom of the incident had certainly helped. Apparently, they wanted to fly home quickly, finding the whole experience sordid. *Did I hear that asshole say sordid?* They refused to press charges and he was released.

Slinking back to his hotel, tired, confused and deflated, he climbed into his hotel bed, alone and lonely. He felt crushed and disillusioned, not understanding why his recent good fortune did not entitle him to any available female he wanted. Bummed out, he deciding to celebrate tomorrow, quietly, by himself.

Chapter 24

Ginger Mae Shrute sat on the bar stool, scanning her reflection in the expensive mirror on the back bar of the tony *Martini Madness* on Park Avenue. It was a great location to spot lonely business men casually enjoying a quiet drink before dinner.

From the distance, she realized she still projected a glamorous image, even though she leaned toward the mature side. Only up close could you discern the lines around her eyes that even Botox failed to completely obliterate. And yeah, she knew the five extra pounds needed to come off. But luckily, she still projected the look that had helped her face maintain its healthy, pretty girl next door appeal.

Lucky with my choice of plastic surgeons, she thought cynically, having been nipped and tucked for years. She knew she could pass for thirty five, quite a distance from her actual forty eight. She tried to banish the worry about her longevity in her chosen industry, which remained a game for the youthful.

She still managed to rope them in, but she figured she would last *maybe* three years before she faced reducing her fees or starting to risk rejection. Her new priority forced her to save every dollar she could, squirreling it away for the time when she could say *fuck you* to the johns and grab her runaway money to make a last stab at a normal life. As if anyone actually lived a normal life anymore. But she must think of Daisy now.

She checked her emerging grayish-brown roots in the mirror, noting she could get away with them for another two weeks, tops. She had even given up her hairdresser, saving money by coloring her hair herself. Two separate processes. Two separate colors. It looked fairly good. Had to keep her short blond locks natural looking. She had dropped her nail salon too. Glancing at her rosy pink oval nails, she noticed a few chips. A home manicure just didn't hold up half as well as a pro job.

"Excuse me. Is this seat taken?" Looking up into the bright-blue eyes of a friendly and eager businessman, probably from the Midwest, she dismissed him with a cool eye flick. He was clearly not clued in and would be a waste of her valuable time. Probably thought he had found himself a single NYC career girl who would be overjoyed to burn her evening talking to a married Minnesota businessman in the big city without his wife. He would shoo her out his hotel room door in the morning with a promise to call her next time he was back in town, and then zip back to his upstanding wife and children, all the while congratulating himself on his sophisticated daring in the big city.

"Miss, would you care for a cocktail?" asked Mr. Daring Businessman, trying again. She turned to respond as he stuck out his hand to introduce himself. "Hi, I'm Jackson Bonderclod, friends just call me Jack."

Sighing audibly, Ginger Mae tiredly gathered her drink and purse, shot Mr. Daring Businessman a casual *go fuck yourself* look, and left him standing with his hand still proffered, an embarrassed surprised look on his marginally attractive face. She slid off her bar stool, noticing the bartender observe the exchange. Well, this should get his panties out of the knot she had probably wadded them up into as he tried to figure out if he was going to have a problem running off a working girl. What working girl would rebuff Mr. Daring Businessman? *The smart ones*, she grinned to herself, watching the bartender visibly relax as she took a new seat at a small table in the back of the room, all the better to observe her targets from.

She scanned the room, noting the slim prospects. Implementing her new plan required a target of just the right type, easy to manipulate. A dork, hungry to experience what it would be like to have the enthralled attention of the cheerleader that had rebuffed him in high school, the homecoming beauty queen he had secretly beat off to in the privacy of his stinking adolescent bedroom.

She shook her head as she evaluated every man in the room. She knew men better than she knew herself. The disgusting predictability of men always revolved around their cocks.

If she had an extra dollar for every time even the most educated, confident or successful john had said to her, with a nod to their cocks, "So, how ya like it?" she could retire. *If I could just stop laughing first.*

They never understood that a woman judged a man differently. Bright confident smile? Check. Any brains? Check. Can he make me laugh? Check. Does he have a good heart? Check. Does he have any money? Well, can't have everything. These characteristics made the sex good. Not the size of his cock. A woman only cares about the cock if it doesn't work. The johns all think that the bigger the cock, the more a woman will like the sex, therefore, by extension, them.

The only thing Ginger Mae could say about the occasional large dick she had encountered, and she really meant occasional, was that he wasn't touching her with it. She definitely wasn't into pain. And it sure felt miserable, regardless of how hard she faked it. Want to impress a john? Tell him what a sensational cock he had. He would fall in love. If she had realized that when she was eighteen, she would probably own the world by now.

Well, she knew it now. And she planned on making it pay off in a big way while she could still dazzle them. The last time she had found the perfect john, it had lasted five years. She hadn't found it necessary to see any other johns the whole time. He had given her a luxury apartment, charge accounts, elegant dinners, international vacations. All paid for by him.

She had thought it would go on forever. And she had actually grown fond of him. The fact that she had spent all major holidays and most weekends alone mattered little. Just as she was ready to convince him to sign the apartment over to her, she discovered her pregnancy. Foolishly, she had misjudged him. Where she assumed it would only make him feel more responsible, financially of course, she had forgotten how men react when cornered with their own indiscretions.

He had cut off her charge accounts without warning. She had found herself locked out of her apartment and her frantic calls to his cell had stopped being answered. The apartment house concierge had hand-delivered an envelope containing a tersely worded note with $10,000 enclosed. She burned with the humiliating memory. Two words—*Move on.*

And she had, of course. A cheap apartment and back to work, fast, before she started to show. Not that the johns would even care all that much. She had worked up until her seventh month. And then Daisy came. She had given birth alone, in her apartment, no one the wiser. She had planned to take the baby and leave it at the local firehouse, but, inexplicably, she had changed her mind. She had kept the baby, found an Armenian woman from her apartment house to babysit and gone back to work four months after the birth. That was over five years ago and to this day, sadly, her little Daisy had yet to utter a single word.

A clattering at the door to the bar caught her attention. Glancing out the windows, she discovered snow, the flakes backlit by the streetlights like rare mid-summer fireflies. Her attention wandered back to the squat figure at the door. She tapped a slender finger on the varnished tabletop. *Hmm,* she wondered, *let's size this guy up.*

His head bulged out of proportion to his body, his bandy legs were encased in the most ridiculous screaming-yellow cowboy boots. He removed a black leather trench coat trimmed in a silver fur of some sort. Even from her distant seat she could see the buttery texture of the coat. She assumed the boots, although tasteless, had cost a pretty penny. Then he looked up, spotting her staring. She extended a modest smile, trying valiantly to repress her revulsion as she got a clear look at his face. *Oh well, duty calls.* And, quite possibly, he might be the ticket she longed for.

His unsophisticated demeanor stood out like a swarm of hornets at a nudist camp; a real rube. *They made the easiest targets, especially the unfortunate looking ones.* Time to start her act.

Waving wildly to catch his attention, she stood up, dropping her purse in the process. She bent down to retrieve it, allowing him to glimpse the correct amount of thigh. Straightening, she beckoned him to her table again, as he stood there with his mouth open, the dull look in his eyes testimony to slow brain function. She crooked her finger again, encouraging him with another nonthreatening smile. He turned and looked over his right shoulder, then his left. Seeing no one, he hesitantly moved in her direction. As he neared, she pulled out a chair from her table and patted it enthusiastically. Plastering a big smile on her face as he sat, she said to herself, *Okay, Ginger Mae, let's land this big tuna.*

"Hi, I was beginning to think you were standing me up. It's a good thing I waited the extra hour, I thought I might have gotten the time wrong." She opened her eyes wide, batting them charmingly.

"Lady, I have no idea what you're talkin' bout. You must have me confused with someone else." Looking around, he snapped his fingers to summon the attention of the frowning cocktail waitress. "I'm here to celebrate and I don't want no trouble. Ya want something ta drink, since you're here anyway?"

"You mean you aren't my date? You're wearing pretty yellow cowboy boots like Alice told me you would be. And you sure are handsome like she said you would be. Are you saying you're *not* Jonathan Littlecock?"

"*Littlecock?* Are you kidding me?" He laughed so hard, slapping his knee, that the bartender looked up to give them a glare. She joined in with his laughter and with that, the ice broke.

It didn't take Ginger Mae long to convince her new friend that her date had failed to show up. It didn't take him long to convince her to spend her evening celebrating with him at his hotel. She knew she had picked the right guy when they left Martini Madness and he took her to his car, a showy Lamborghini SUV with a tacky lightning bolt decal down the side. Her eyes started tabulating major dollar signs.

She almost blew it when they got into the SUV. The odorously strange stale smell in the vehicle, combined with the alcohol, made her nauseous. When her new friend abruptly slid his dirty fingers up her dress and started pawing around, her automatic response was to pop her blade out of her purse and hold it to his throat.

"Now, little lady," he gasped. "I thought we were friends here. Why don't you put your shiny baby away, so we can work out this misunderstanding?" And they actually did. He really warmed up to her after she put her blade away. Who knew he would have a thing for knives and blondes? Maybe this would be easier than she thought.

"Okay, lover, time to saddle up."

"What did you say?"

She looked at his face in surprise, his tone of voice sounding strangled. His big head sat half in shadow, the streetlights failing to fully dispel the winter darkness.

"You alright, lover?" She placed a concerned hand on his meaty thigh. His big pudgy maw slipped down onto hers and he softly patted her hand. In the shadows, she could see a surprisingly enigmatic smile under his crooked nose. She had him. She didn't know what had just happened, but she knew. She had him.

Armoni fidgeted, glancing at his Rolex. Time to get his hotel room packed up. He floated, high on an emotional cloud. All thanks to Ginger Mae Shrute. His very own high-class dream girl. And boy could she suck cock. *No wonder the guys always wanted the high-class babes. Who knew?* Now he could join the club. A fine babe like her didn't come along very often. And she liked knives. Best of all, she liked him. He hadn't minded a bit when, after their night of fucking, she had needed the bucks to have a limo take her home. Of course that's how she got around town. And, after all, her date woulda taken her home. *Good thing the bum never showed.*

Luck had sure smiled down on him. Packing up all the new things Ginger Mae had helped him buy for himself took a long time. He hoped she wasn't running late, like him. She asked that most of the goodies he splurged on for her go directly to her home address. She planned to send for them after they got to Florida. Yup, she was going with him.

They had fooled around so much that he had decided to delay his trip for a full week. He bent over a box, wincing as the soreness of his cock reminded him of all the fucking they'd done. She sure was hot for him and his cock; definitely a lot to handle for such a sweetie. And he truly sensed something else in her. Something like he felt in himself and Kelly. He fully intended to bring it to the surface. Yeah, his plans for her made him hard. He just had to be careful how he introduced her to them. *She probably nurses some tender sensibilities, a dame like her.*

He filled her in a little, watching closely to see how she reacted to it. He left some of the details vague. Like how his sister and Tomas's murder had gone down. He wasn't really sure how it had happened himself. She knew he lusted for revenge, and she thought he aimed to recover something valuable they'd stolen from him.

She flipped over the idea to go with him, even though it meant she had to quit her important job with a small investment company on Wall Street. He might need some investment advice himself, for sure. Maybe, if things worked out the way he hoped, he'd marry her ass and make her take care of all that.

The only fly in the ointment? Her infernal insistence on all those showers and baths. *For Christ sakes, what a pain in my ass.* He tolerated it only because she let him take a few special sexual liberties; made him feel like a king.

He glanced at his watch, beginning to worry. *What the heck was taking her so long?* He had given her plenty of money to break her lease and pay off her landlord. He expected it to take a while; after all, she needed to put all her expensive furniture in storage. She had admitted to being a spendthrift. Good thing he would get his hands on more gold. At the rate she used money, he'd be broke in no time. *These classy babes demand expensive upkeep. Makes sense*, he figured, *only the best for the best.*

He heard a knock at the door. Relief made Armoni's legs turn to jelly. His girl had made it. He rushed to the door, happiness plastered all over his grotesque mug. As he opened the door, Ginger Mae breezed in with a quick kiss on the lips and an unusually tense look on her elegant face.

His brows scrunched up, a question on the tip of his tongue, when Ginger Mae moved aside, slipping her arm around a frightened little girl hiding behind her skirt: small with dark brown, almost black, silken hair worn loose and long. Her skin pale, almost translucent.

But her eyes, they grabbed him. Her pupils, devoid of almost all color, reflected a piercingly intelligent all-knowing quality. He could see a small resemblance to Ginger Mae, as the girl clearly reflected the same elegance.

"What the fuck is this, Ginger Mae?"

Ignoring Armoni, Ginger Mae knelt down in front of the girl, whispered in her ear and directed her to a blush silk divan in the corner. She turned to Armoni with a contrite and pious look on her face.

"This is my brother's daughter. Her mother ran off after her birth. My brother served in the Army, stationed in North Korea. We lost him during the slaughter in the mist of the Bau Liberation, when Daisy turned six months old. I'm her only relative. She's my responsibility now. She thinks I'm her mother. It's easier that way." Turning to Daisy, she sent her an air kiss.

Continuing in a whisper, she turned back to Armoni. "She's mute. We have to take her with us. I can't leave her behind. Don't worry, she won't get in the way, lover."

"I didn't sign up for no brat to come with us." Armoni started pacing, seeing all his plans go up in smoke. Ginger Mae looked over to Daisy with a reassuring glance. She grabbed Armoni's hand and pulled him into the huge bathroom. She slowly started to remove her clothes, not taking her eyes off Armoni.

"Well, I guess we're going to have to say goodbye then. So let's do it properly. I need something to remember you by."

Armoni watched her body reveal itself. That bitching body belonged to him. He had practically paid for it. He ran his hands over her breasts, squeezing them painfully. The look on Ginger Mae's face showed only sadness and passion.

"Oh baby, give it to me, please, I need you one more time."

Was that a tear falling down her beautiful cheek? She must feel really broken up about this. He stared at her face, those eyes, those cheekbones, wondering how much he would miss her. He felt her fingers at his zipper and the cool moisture of her expert tongue on his cock. Moaning, he ran his fingers through her hair. He melted under her onslaught, helpless to give her up. Exasperated, he realized the kid would have to come. Somehow, he would need to adjust. At least things remained under his control and Ginger Mae still belonged to him. His plan remained intact, with a minor adjustment for the kid. Relieved, he turned his full attention to her breasts, biting down hard enough to hear her muffle a scream. He still needed to remind her who wore the pants. Looking into her bewitching face, he saw it tighten, her eyes flashing an obvious, ill-concealed gleam of contempt. The perpetually obtuse Armoni, mistaking it for passion, excitedly bit down hard again, feeling like he had died and gone to heaven.

Chapter 25

Abby and Jose sat in green and white striped lounge chairs on the flagstone terrace above their natural rock waterfall where they could observe Scotty, happily tossing Echo into the shallow end of the pool. Barney chaotically lunged at the water, jumping back, not sure of the rules of the new game. Changes had come fast for the family in the five months since they had left Sussex County and moved to Mango Lane, their opulent new home and an unimaginable paradise.

They had installed Peter in the 4,400 square foot, custom, red-tile roofed, Spanish-style waterfront home next door to the right. The lemon-yellow art deco gem to their left remained empty, although fully furnished. They hoped Mama Diaz, Bonnie and Emma would join them soon. The house would knock their socks off.

Abby, Scotty and Jose occupied the 6,800 square foot Tuscan olive Mediterranean dream in the middle with lush landscaping, reminiscent of the famous Selby Gardens in downtown Sarasota; over a hundred and fifty palm trees of eight varieties, lush plumeria and giant jungle geranium. Fortunately, because they were on a tiny island less than half a mile wide, they had saved themselves the unpleasant experience of dealing with the tropical snakes that habitually nested in palm trees. The trees and vibrant flowering bushes encompassed the whole property, including across the bay front of the lot. The people who had built the home had sure valued their privacy. The home became a true sanctuary for the beleaguered family.

One of the lovely surprises of the island delighted them all as they enjoyed the presence of a flock of Sand Hill cranes, the most comically amazing birds. Some of the cranes grew as much as five-feet tall with vibrant red caps of feathers on their heads. They imperiously strolled the sidewalks, the streets and the front yards as they pleased. Promenading in pairs or threesomes, they never hurried, they never acknowledged, they never acquiesced. They clearly owned the small island.

Jose stretched in the sun, admiring Abby's tawny tail as it switched languidly behind her lounge chair. Her hair long and lush, full of the golden silk hairs which had first been discovered the wondrous night that had united them. Their exposure in public now seemed a dangerous adventure as they just plain glowed too much. The three of them were now covered with an exceedingly fine layer of golden fuzz from the neck down. From the distance, it looked like skin, but they found themselves unable to avoid the stares that accompanied close inspection from strangers. All three had developed protrusions on each side of their shoulder blades. Comparing their changes with Echo's physiology, they suspected the emergence of wings. The idea thrilled them, but would they work? Would it mean flight? Echo's wings may have functioned at one time, but now they lay lifeless against her furry little back. When asked about the wings, Echo would only reply that she was not an Elder.

Surprisingly, Echo began to pester them with the surprising desire to increase the size of their family—their doggy family. She claimed Barney was lonesome and needed a mate. That's how it started. Poor Peter. He became the official furry buddy locator. To his credit, he never complained, even when Penny, their new springer spaniel, vomited on the front seat of his gleaming BMW.

Penny behaved like a doll. Liver and white with flowing feather-like fur, she loved people, tolerated other dogs, and exhibited an above-it-all attitude when it came to doggy/Echo horseplay. The next addition was Mimi, a black and white Shih Tzu puppy mill mommy. All used up and ready to throw away, she had luckily been rescued by a devoted group of women committed to the effort. Peter had spotted her at the local pet food store, mistaking her for a skunk until she turned her sweet face around. He couldn't resist. Poor Mimi, unfortunately afflicted with cataracts, mammary tumors and food aggression, but, it turned out, also desperate for love. Lucky for her, the inhabitants of Mango Lane had plenty to spare.

Scotty's hands stayed full with the doggy troupe and he appeared to settle into their new environment nicely. He did get a car. A modest maroon Jeep Wolfhound, used mostly on their little island. Jose put his foot down about Scotty driving off the key without being accompanied by one of the adults, including Peter.

Scotty didn't object much as he spent most of his extra time with his outboard motorboat, large enough for Echo and usually one or two of the dogs. Jose's number one rule—no exceptions—demanded life jackets for all; especially Echo and the dogs. Scotty knew how to swim, thanks to a summer recreation program at the local town pool in Newtown when he was in seventh and eighth grades. But everyone knew that the currents in the deceptive bay could be tricky. The dogs could become a handful whenever Scotty lucked on a pod of dolphins to chase, the excitement overwhelming them. Scotty struggled to hold them back, their determination to join the dolphins' play a risk to them all.

The bay teemed with dolphins, all individually known through the studies of the famous Mote Marine Laboratory, located on City Island in the bay in Sarasota. Sarasota Bay, declared by the U.S. Congress an estuary of national significance, boasted an aquarium which opened to the public. The Mote Marine Lab was well known for their studies of sharks, sea turtles, dolphins, red tide, environmental toxins, coral reefs and costal ecology, which beckoned tantalizingly to Scotty. Enlisting Peter, he paid it a visit. A risky business, considering the fact that Peter operated in the dark, still unaware of their true nature.

Jose thought back to his miraculous arrival in Sarasota. Knocking on Abby's door, they had entered her luxury suite at her hotel to find her drawn and frightened. Signs of dried tears had trailed down her pale face. Throwing herself into Jose's arms, she had babbled that Peter's secretary was dead. The police had demanded Peter fly back home for questioning. The words murder and rape had hung in the air. Calming her down, Jose had learned that the police wanted him to return too; ostensibly to discuss the *issues*. Full panic mode had set in, scaring everyone.

Luckily, in all the drama and shock of Tiffany's rape and murder, Peter's requested meeting had failed to materialize. Jose had decided to accompany Peter back to Sussex County. He wanted to stay close to the investigation, hoping Armoni would not surface as part of it. But sooner or later, Jose knew Peter would find the time to sit them all down and start asking questions.

While Peter handled questions from the police, Jose had tried to find Mama Diaz and the girls. Not knowing where or how to start, he had wisely hired a private investigator. He had spent half a day filling the investigator in on all he knew of the Diaz family before his adoption. He had felt certain, with the Internet, that it wouldn't take long before the investigator produced results. Four months later, still no news.

The investigation into Tiffany's killer had landed at a dead end. Jose had reported the small encounter between Armoni and Tiffany, but the police had dismissed Armoni as a suspect. No motive and negligible connection. Oddly, the police had mentioned that Armoni's house had been torched on the same day as Tiffany's murder. There had been no sightings of Armoni since. *And the cops didn't see a connection?* Feeling the heavy weight of dread, Jose thought the coincidence ominous.

Bringing his thoughts back to the terrace, he stood up, surveying the lush tropical property and looking down toward the gazebo-bedecked dock where Scotty's skiff and the colossal green and white yacht swayed gently, water lapping at the hulls.

Captain Cobby glanced his way and gave a friendly wave. Jose waved back, noting Captain Cobby's twenty-year-old son Kane in the water, scrubbing away at the marks left by the waterline. Jose knew nothing of what it took to be a yacht owner. It was said that the happiest days of a yacht owner's life were when he purchased his yacht and then again when he resold it. He had yet to discover the veracity of the saying. He really thought it silly for them to own such a vessel, but for some reason Abby had taken a shine to it.

Truth be told, he didn't believe Abby actually felt happy. He knew something was missing. Not so much about her feelings for him, but something deeper, something profound that she needed to resolve on her own, undoubtedly tied to the death of her mother. It made him sad, knowing he couldn't help her discover the comfort she needed. But he loved her dearly and hesitated to deny her anything.

As he watched Kane scrub the yacht, he hoped Kane and Scotty could get along better. Territorial resentment had blossomed instantly between the two when they moved in. Jose supposed it was natural. They were so close in age, their relationship was bound to go one way or the other. Apparently Kane saw Scotty as an interloper, and Scotty saw Kane as a macho Italian know-it-all. If Kane's sullen attitude didn't improve in time, he would have to talk to his father. They lived in the carriage house behind the art deco home that remained empty. Jose felt having them nearby a great benefit, especially since Captain Cobby also served as security to the property.

Picking up his cellphone, he called Peter for an update on Mama Diaz. Happily, Peter reported the investigator had finally made some progress. They had located the family near a suburb of Short Hills, not far from the area where Abby used to live in as a child, probably a mere coincidence. They both agreed that Jose should be the one to fly to New Jersey to break the news of Tomas's death and convince them to move to Florida. Jose decided to talk to Abby about it later that night. He wanted to keep close, hoping to keep her upbeat. Her moods vacillated so widely these days, he wanted to get a good day under their belt before she learned he would be leaving.

Scotty knew he must always wear a long-sleeved shirt over his swim trunks when he was on the water and around the backyard, but Echo presented a larger problem. She insisted on going with Scotty when he took the skiff out. Abby helpfully took some fabric and stitched together a jumpsuit that disguised most of Echo's uniqueness. Gloves worked fairly well for her hands. A pair of diver's goggles strapped around Echo's face helped greatly, but could not hide her crown of crystal antlers.

Maneuvering quickly away from other boats helped to evade troubling inquiries. So far, the only mishap had occurred when Scotty had forgotten to fill the gas tank before he departed. Forced to use the yacht to rescue Scotty and his posse, Kane had enjoyed his opportunity to gloat as they towed a red-faced Scotty back to the dock.

Trying to explain Echo's unusual appearance took some imagination. Claiming that Abby and Scotty's father, a world-renowned geneticist, had gifted them with Echo, who they no longer needed as a test subject, appeared to work. They claimed Echo resulted from a genetic engineering project regarding gene splicing. Rather than terminate her at the end of the failed project, they made her a family pet. It sounded plausible enough and worked for now. But they still tried to keep Echo's exposure to an extreme minimum, even from the Cobbys. It was one thing to fool a couple of yacht jocks, but anyone with an Internet connection and an inquiring mind could poke holes in their story. Anyone like Peter.

Chapter 26

Abby lay back on her green wicker lounge chair, enjoying the kiss of the sun seeping into her thirsty skin underneath the tiny gold fibers that encapsulated her arms and chest. She found it easier to accept her changes as she watched Scotty and Jose taking them in stride. If she felt uneasy, she hid it well. It had taken her several months to dismiss the meaning of the pronouncement Echo had made to Jose in the limo on the journey to Florida. Her practical side thought Jose may have misunderstood.

Her initial reaction had been to laugh, but Jose tried to convince her that Echo may not have the best interest of humans in her heart. They had lived with Echo for six months now, and Abby had seen no behavior to suggest such a thing. The only disturbing facts were the little matter of Echo and the skeletons. The events that day back in Sussex were so traumatic and fuzzy in her memory that she no longer cared where the skeletons were. Since Echo's reaction had saved her from serious harm, she considered herself lucky. As a matter of fact, Echo seemed unusually attached to them. Not a problem. Since the three of them were all a bit love-starved for family, Echo fit right in.

The changes to their bodies were another matter, and they were not sure how any of them would react if the swellings on their backs developed into wings as they suspected. Lying in the sun in the lap of luxury, healthy as the proverbial horse, Abby reveled in her new lease on life; not at all what had been foretold by her doctors as an abnormally short and difficult life span. She therefore refused to fret as Jose did. See no evil . . . If she must put up with her amazing tail and some cryptic remarks from Echo in exchange, she was willing; outrageously, gratefully willing. She realized she wanted to live a healthy life so badly she would do anything, contend with anything. She wondered what her mom would think if she had lived. Abby ached with the thought of what she could have done for her mother's hard and meager existence, the delight she would have taken in their good fortune. She longed to share her newfound love with her mother. She needed her. When would the pain of her loss go away? And poor Scotty; he still needed their mother's guidance and unconditional love, a critical foundation from which all healthy children developed the courage needed to find their own pathway through an often turbulent and malevolent world.

From out of nowhere, Mimi stood up at the side of Abby's lounge chair, her cloudy cataract eyes unblinking, begging to be picked up. Most of the time, she scurried around like an orphan, afraid she was going to be shown the door. Funny, that was exactly how Abby sometimes felt. Picking Mimi up, she cradled her in her arms, trying to reassure the little dog, knowing no one could. Just like no one could reassure her. Sometimes she felt that if she could just keep her pain sealed up, it would go away. Looking into Mimi's tortured eyes, she knew they could both only hope.

Later that evening, as they clustered around their new eighty-two-inch high-frequency macro digital television, she watched Jose tickling Echo, Barney and Penny on the sofa while Scotty lay on the plush carpet with Mimi. Abby, sitting in her favorite Chippendale-style wing back armchair—the one with the cabbage rose needlepoint—leafed through a vintage Stephen King novel as she tried to ignore the noise of the television. Glancing up, she saw a special announcement regarding the health of the Socialist New World presidential candidate, Omar Nasir's, wife Jane. She reportedly remained in a coma, and it was doubtful she would survive.

The news anchor moved on to another story. A young manatee had been found floating alongside the shore at Philippe Creek. Badly injured by a boat propeller, his tail had been severed. Having little hope of survival, he was rushed to the Mote Marine Laboratory for assessment and care. Moving on to the next story, Abby lost interest. Her thoughts drifted back to the unfortunate Jane Nasir.

When their realtor, the aging but elegant Sylvia, with the ever-coiffed honey-blond hair—expertly highlighted, of course—toured Sarasota with them, she pointed out the mansions of many of the most famous residents of their community, including a mention of the Nasir mansion. Apparently, he did not spend much time there, as he was trying to beat his competition for his party's nomination to run against the Muslim Brotherhood's candidate for the office of the presidency.

At the time, Abby showed no interest in Silvia's story. She was not a political junky like so many others. Today, the media sources in Sarasota were having a field day with the story of Mrs. Nasir's sudden strange illness. Most residents, regardless of their political affiliations, prayed she would recover. The Nasir family were not the only local celebrities this town boasted, but they were the most important.

Abby wondered if Omar Nasir were to win the national election, would it have any effect on the residents of Sarasota? She also thought Jose should check on Peter's progress in locating a diamond cutter. They didn't need more money, but they could use the sale of the diamonds to acquire more property on the island to further insulate them. Just in case.

Seeing Jose try to stand and shake off his furry demons, Abby realized it was time for bed. Admonishing Scotty not to stay up too late, they said goodnight and retired to their bedroom, sometimes the best part of their day. Jose lay down on the purple patchwork comforter, flicking the gold rope trim with his fingers as Abby slipped into her modest cotton nightgown.

Hearing a soft scratch at the door, he rose to let Mimi in. She ran over to the bed, her desperation to get up comical; the bed was a full four feet over her head. Taking pity on her, Jose scooped her up, barely touching her as Mimi used his hands to push herself off and jump to the top. Glancing at Abby, he saw she had noticed.

"Every time I think I have no more room in my heart, along comes something like Mimi."

"Yeah, I know what you mean. I have a weakness for her too. She's my girl," Jose said tenderly. He rolled onto his back, where Mimi promptly walked up the length of his body to rest on his chest where she made herself comfortable, her eyes fastened on him like a laser. Jose, in turn, watched Abby as she prepared for bed.

"I've been thinking a lot lately." Abby scrubbed her face, shouting from their Verde marble bathroom.

"Anything interesting?"

"I don't know. I guess I'm just feeling restless. Any news on Peter's efforts to locate Mama Diaz?" She moved back to the bedroom.

"As a matter of fact, we do have news. The investigators have located them in Short Hills. I want to fly to New Jersey and bring them back with me. I won't feel good again until I know they're safe and sound with us. I can't go on in the dark anymore. Not again."

At the tone of his voice, Abby let the subject drop, surprised at the oblique reference. She knew Jose didn't like to talk about his first family. He had been very young and didn't remember much anyway. Glancing over at him as she brushed her silken hair, she could tell his past rested heavily on his mind, his dark face was tight and tense—he hid tension poorly. The only sign that he physically lay in the opulent room with her was when he buried his face in Mimi's fur, seeking solace. Sadly, she acknowledged that she didn't know how to help him heal his old, deep wounds.

Trying to get his mind off his sad past, Abby slipped into their huge walk-in closet. There she shed her modest nightgown and donned the ivory silk nightie, purchased for just the right moment. Lighting a long wax taper, she carried it into the bedroom to see Jose depositing Mimi on a raspberry upholstered vanity bench. Letting Jose take a long look, she grinned and turned off the bedroom light. Carrying the candle to the bed, Jose took it from her hand, setting it on the carved mahogany side table. Sweeping her into his arms, he kissed her.

"You're all I need right now, babe." Holding her in his arms, he froze, then turned her around. Startled, she let him lift her nightie off her back. He ran his hand over what used to be smooth skin.

"Does this hurt? Your changes are becoming more obvious." Looking closer, he commented on the bony growth that had thickened, flanges sprouting all over the widening surface. "Can you check my back, babe? What do you see—anything new?" Turning, Jose presented his back to her.

"This is way too freaky. Maybe we need to go to the authorities with this?" Looking closely, Abby could see he was further along than her, feathers sprouting all over the flanges that were actually made of keratin. Like fingernails, rhino horn or the framework of a bird's wing. Soon, he would not be safe without a jacket over his shirt. How do you do that in a hot climate?

"*Are you nuts, Abby?* That would ruin us." Lowering his voice, he sounded more reasonable. "They would take all the dogs and Echo away from us. They would probably separate us too. You know you can't trust the authorities, or the government. We're on our own. It'll be okay, babe. No matter what happens, we have to keep a low profile. Things are fine. Let's not rock the boat."

"But how long do you think we can stay cooped up in this house?"

"As long as we need to." She could hear the impatience start to build in his voice. Dropping what she realized was starting to sound like whining, she changed the subject.

"Would you like to think about having a baby?"

"Now? Do you think that's a good idea?"

"I don't know. I guess I just want to hear that you'll consider it— if we can find out from Echo that it's safe."

"As soon as we resolve some of our loose ends, I promise I'll highjack Barney and refuse to give him back until we get some answers from her." Pulling her down on the bed, he blew out the candle, but not before, through the wafting gray wisp of candle smoke, he caught a glimpse of her relieved smile.

Downstairs, Scotty and Echo were making big plans. The evening newscast had not gone unnoticed. Without realizing Echo's manipulation, Scotty decided that tonight held the opportunity they had long awaited. When they were sure Abby and Jose had turned off their bedroom lights, they raced outside the house, down to the quiet dock. The moon hung high and bright in the sky as if a child had cut out a silver circle and pasted it onto a blanket of rich black velvet. The luminescence gave them a lucky break. Scotty lifted Echo and Barney into the shallow skiff, helping them into their orange life jackets before belting them snugly. For the last time, he consulted the map he had pulled off the Internet. He pushed off, gliding noiselessly into the foreboding cold water of the bay, not even a flirty wave to distract them.

Instructing an excited Barney not to whine or bark, Scotty navigated the small skiff through the silent water, eyes peeled for other larger boats, hoping to stay out of the way. The skiff lacked running lights, a huge handicap in the dark. Luckily, Scotty had grabbed a flashlight to use on the other end of their operation. It would come in handy if they needed to announce their presence to another boat, preventing them from getting swamped.

As the skiff settled in the water, making slow progress, they felt the late spring evening rawness in the air. The light scent of brine enveloped them. From time to time, they would hear a solitary splash in the ghostly distance. They listened, all ears to the creepy calm quietude as they glided across the bay.

Nearing their destination, Scotty steered to the shore, hugging the broken rocky coastline so as not to overshoot their destination. Before long, they spotted the aquarium. They quickly docked, pulling the skiff up over the rocks to dry white sand, the moon magically changing it to an unbroken field of snow. Tying Barney to the skiff with instructions to stay put, Scotty and Echo scouted the vacant buildings, looking for the medical unit. Studying the layout confidently shown for the tourists on their website made the search easy for them. But the only entry point they could find was over a wall which supported the seawater tanks filled with sea turtles. The wall loomed too high for Scotty to grab on to, no matter how hard he tried. Looking at Echo, they both realized what they must do.

"If you can't find the manatee, try to find another way to let me in. I'll help. You sure you can handle this alone?"

"Yes, Brother Scotty; I survived alone for over a century until you found me. I will be successful. Thank you for your help." As the mind aura faded, Echo held out her arms and Scotty boosted her up the wall, her leathery feet catching close to the top. Saved by the suction effect of her fingers, she righted herself. She finished the climb and disappeared. Scotty looked up, seeing nothing. Five seconds passed and suddenly Echo's face reappeared. A rainbow aura suffused his mind.

"We are a good team, Brother Scotty—My Barney too." And she vanished again. Shaking his head in amusement, Scotty slumped down on the cold sand to wait for Echo, dampness seeping through the seat of his shorts, goosebumps making the hair on his legs prickle.

Taking any kind of action in their quest to save earth creatures was fulfilling. He paused, reflecting on how much he sounded like Echo when she had first suggested their secret alliance. This was not their first mission, of course. Not far down the coast existed a small shallow beach aptly named Turtle Beach. The green sea turtles' nesting areas were staked out by volunteers, marked to protect them from marauding human profiteers who would eagerly dig them up and sell the eggs to be eaten as delicacies. The efforts of the volunteers were usually fruitless, the poachers cleaning out the nests relentlessly, year after year. As a result, the green sea turtle numbered amongst the most endangered of sea creatures.

One night he had taken the skiff down the coast with his two cohorts. The overcast sky had looked bleak, waves kicking up bitter spray, whipping needle-like in their faces. Echo had located the beach, instructing Scotty to stay on the skiff with Barney, who had tightly hunkered down, shivering. Echo would not be long. Watching from the skiff, Scotty had swallowed his breath, his eyes bugging out in the cold wind as Echo had stood calmly in the coral sand, her crystal antlers peeling apart, releasing a stream of black-red liquid that had surrounded the beach and burrowed under the sand. Echo had announced she was finished, hopped back into the boat and they had sped home, anxious to sneak back to the safety and comfort of Scotty's bedroom.

It had only taken a week before a news story had appeared, commenting on the oddity of a man and woman found on the beach, victims of heart attacks; illegal digging and containment equipment found with them. The reporter had added that they were well known to the police as local poachers. Within a week, three more heart attack victims had been found. Mission accomplished; all poachers exterminated. The baby turtles were then able to climb from their nests, making their run for the ocean unimpeded by avaricious humans.

Did Scotty feel any sense of remorse for his contribution to the deaths of the poachers? Was Echo's influence on a young mind profound enough to make Scotty disregard all he had been taught about law and order? Or was Scotty just reacting with the naive exuberance of an idealistic youth, torn between the never-ending struggle between man, the predator, and wildlife, the prey? Scotty stroked his tail as it unfurled from under his shirt. Was he himself no longer human? Was he now wildlife himself?

Scotty heard a shuffling sound. Looking up, he spied Echo's adorable golden face, her hair standing on edge as she flew off the top of the wall, confidently relying on Scotty to catch her in his arms.

"Gee, how about a little warning, girl? Some day you're going to wind up on my head." He hoisted Echo up under his arm like a football on its way to the homecoming touchdown. They ran for the skiff, where their major domo, Barney, continued to hold his own with the tide. Slipping Barney off his rope, Scotty pushed off and gave the outboard a tug, welcoming the quiet purr of the engine. Echo climbed up Barney's back, their faces to the wind like pirates on the lookout after a particularly difficult raid. The adrenalin in Scotty's bloodstream subsided as they reached home. He wondered where their next rescue would take them.

Chapter 27

Jose sipped coffee from a handmade artisan mug, acquired by their interior designer, like everything else in their dream house. Vapid daylight struggled its way through the celestial kitchen windows, announcing the radiant Sarasota sunshine, still hours away. He scanned the headlines in the newspaper, noting that Jane Nasir had died. Hadn't he heard something about the Nasirs on the television a few nights ago? Glancing at a sidebar, he located a poll result showing her husband was sure to be the nominee for his party during the upcoming presidential election. He wondered how a man could continue with an objective like that when his wife had just died. He thought he'd heard they had a young child. He fought off a brief moment of deja vu.

Scratching his unshaven whiskers, he absently reached for a sweet roll, food no longer the enticement it once was. Was it a side effect of love or perhaps his body's changes? He thought back to their days in Sussex County and realized he couldn't pinpoint when his appetite had disappeared. He made a note to speak to Echo about that later, if he could find her. She and Scotty had sure seemed thick as thieves over the last few weeks. They were developing a bad habit of sleeping late, some days past noon.

Refilling his cup, he turned the page, his eyes coming to rest on the unusual story of the young manatee rescued several days ago, near Philippi Creek. The young manatee's prognosis had been hopeless, having lost its tail to a boat propeller. Propellers created just one of the tragic dangers for the precious ocean wildlife that had to compete with the heavy influx of recreational boating. The article went on to claim that the poor manatee had become a victim of a hoax perpetrated by a malicious prankster. The grievously injured manatee had been taken to the Mote Marine Laboratory for examination. In the morning, mysteriously, the manatee had disappeared and been replaced with a healthy young male, the injured male nowhere to be found. Lab officials were outraged to see a grievously injured creature callously used for a prank. Authorities were not amused.

Sick, Jose thought. Glancing at his new Rolex, a present from Abby for his twenty-fourth birthday, he noticed it was time to get his rear in gear, not wanting to show up late for his meeting with Peter. Finishing his coffee, he ran out the front door, fighting his way through the thick brush of red Peace rosebushes, stately date and royal palms which served as easy access to Peter's house next door.

Ringing the doorbell, Jose surveyed the property. Not bad for a lawyer from Sussex County. Although Jose and Abby retained ownership, Peter lived there as if it were his own. They had allowed him to work with the decorator to select his own furnishings and, as a result, Peter had gone with a very stylized contemporary décor; quite sparse, but elegant.

"Hey, Jose, come on in." Peter stepped back from the doorway, admitting him into a two-story foyer with twin walls flanked by giant fiberglass Siamese cats, backs arched and faux-painted so artistically they looked ready to pounce. Peter looked like he had just rolled out of bed, his sandy-brown hair plastered in three different directions. Removing his frameless eyeglasses he stood, cleaning them on his shirt, his owl-like eyes unblinking, as Jose made himself comfortable on the baby-blue Natuzzi leather sofa in Peter's minimalist living room.

"I would like to get to Short Hills as soon as possible. Can you drop me at the Sarasota airport? I'll be ready to leave late tomorrow afternoon."

"Sure, buddy, just let me know what time, unless you want me to make your flight reservation for you?"

"No, I just need to talk to Scotty first. I'll catch up with you later, thanks." Leaving Peter's house, he headed to the docks to inform Captain Cobby.

Chapter 28

Scotty spread out the newspapers that Jose had left on the kitchen table, noting with a laugh the story of the manatee. He looked up on hearing the French door to the terrace open with Echo hanging on to the doorknob for dear life as it swung into the kitchen. She hung off the floor, her tiny leather hands wrapped around the knob while her scrawny feet dangled in the air. Barney looked up from the terrace where he was playing tag with the rest of the posse. In a jiffy, Barney scooted under Echo, enabling her to drop down on his back, then she slipped down to the floor and ran over to Scotty.

"I would have opened the door for you, girl."

"Yes, thank you, Brother Scotty, but I wanted to do it myself."

Scotty shook his head, turning back to the newspaper. Leafing through, he slowly searched the pages for a lead for their next rescue. Their missions made his life more meaningful. Creatures never turned on him, or called him names, or tormented him. They enchanted him, becoming his friends. Very often, they needed protection. Now, with Echo's prompting, he had found a way to give his life a purpose: hermit by day, hero by night.

Stopping to read a story about recently discovered brutalized dog carcasses which had led authorities to suspect the whereabouts of a sophisticated dog fighting ring, he noticed Echo on high alert, her golden eyes locked on him like a drunk walking out of unsuccessful rehab and spotting an unattended liquor store. How did she know that he had found a story that interested him? Her aura filled his mind.

"I think we will be busy tonight, Brother Scotty."

"Oh, you do? It says here the cops don't know where the gang is warehousing the dogs. So how do you think we can help?"

"Brother Scotty, can I tell you a secret?"

Scotty nodded, intensely interested.

"I know where they are."

"No."

"Yes."

"You can't."

"I can."

"Son of a gun."

"Son of a gum?"

"No. Gun."

"You have no gun?"

"No, Echo, I said son—never mind."

"Are you okay, Brother Scotty?"

Shaking his head with amusement, Scotty realized Echo could frustrate the heck out of him. But—time to get their fly on. "I'm fine, little dude. Midnight then, and you're sure where to go?"

Rainbows flashed their aura as Echo ran out to the terrace with Barney, trailing tentacles of light. "Trust me, my Brother."

At half past midnight, they were on University Boulevard, heading inland. They had passed over the Sarasota border to Bradenton five minutes ago, and Scotty had no idea where they were now. This move was making him nervous. Abby and Jose would kill him if they knew he had gone off the island. Clouds covered the sky: no stars, no moon. The further east they drove, the more the traffic thinned.

"You sure about this, Echo?"

"Yes, Brother, the Womb is never wrong."

Oh yeah, the great mysterious Womb. Scotty decided to let it pass and contemplated the plan. Echo claimed she knew where the dogs were being housed. Once they located the spot, they planned to reconnoiter, then heal any dogs that needed medical care. They aimed to tip off the cops about the location, letting the experts take it from there.

The newspaper said tourists had stumbled over the dumpsite. Over two hundred dogs, in various stages of decay, had been discarded. All of the fighters' skulls had been bashed in by baseball bats and something heavier. It had only taken one blow with the heavy weapon, multiples with the bat. The small dogs ranged from six pounds to fifteen. They were training bait; ripped to shreds. The authorities reluctantly admitted many of the bait dogs had been reported stolen over the last two years.

Scotty figured the live dogs couldn't be far away from the dumpsite. An hour later, they turned off the main road onto a gravel road which led to an empty field. Scotty hadn't seen a house in about twenty minutes.

"Stop here, Brother." The aura swirled in his mind as they got out of the Jeep with a flashlight. Covering the lens, he turned it on and kneeled down, examining the trampled grass and abundance of tire tracks. He surveyed the field, locating an opening at the far end. As they crossed the field, the dark silence penetrated, setting off his chattering nerves and fluttering heart as he tried to remember what he knew about Florida snakes and their hunting habits. He picked up Echo, depositing her on his shoulder as he stepped into the woods on the far side of the field. He could clearly make out a well-traveled path that led deeper into the woods.

"You sure we're in the right spot, girl?"

"Yes, my Brother." They walked another twenty minutes before they heard the sounds. *Barking dogs.* They crept through the woods, trying to be silent while sweat rolled down Scotty's face, attracting bugs that deviled him unmercifully.

Suddenly, they found themselves on the edge of an open clearing. Creeping closer, they could see the shed that housed the dogs; a spotlight fastened to a tree lit up the tableau focused around a bench underneath. To their consternation, a cluster of men milled around the bench. As they watched, one of the men dragged a bloody pit bull from the shed, the dog clearly on his last legs. In one practiced motion, the dog was lifted onto the bench while another man swung a giant sledgehammer over his head and down on the dying pit bull's head with a sickening crunch. Rivulets of blood spattered the jeans of the jostling men. The dog was slung into a waiting wheelbarrow filled with other dead dogs. They heard a guttural cry from the wheel barrel, the victim not yet dead.

Echo's golden aura darkened, grinding with tumult, as Scotty's stomach turned with revulsion. Tears flowed from his eyes as he berated himself for not arriving sooner. They froze at the sound of a round being chambered into a shotgun from behind them.

"Anything I can do to help ya, boy?" Scotty found himself looking down the barrel of a rifle held by one of the fattest black men he'd ever seen.

"Brother Scotty, this is not a good human."

"You're probably right, Echo."

"What'd you say, boy? Get your ass up and start walkin'. Yo, Red, got some company." The man with the rifle lifted his foot, giving Scotty a rough shove. As he fell to his knees, Echo scrambled around to face the man, her stance ready to fight. Unexpectedly, the obese man's hand shot out, grabbing Echo by her antlers, upending her. He threw her over his back and booted Scotty over to the gathered men where he heard the sound of other weapons being cocked.

"Well, looky—"

"Hey—"

"—just a kid—"

"*Quiet.*" A black man, about thirty years old—*kind of hard to tell with the glare of the spotlight*—with dyed red hair stepped forward. He set the sledgehammer down on the ground. Silence settled on the group as Red stepped forward, flexing his rippling muscles. An atmosphere of barely controlled violence clung to him like stink on a skunk. In the background, the soft whining and whimpers from the shed signaled the dogs' sensitivity to the charged atmosphere around the killing bench.

"What the hell you got there, Ton?"

"Don't rightly know." Ton slapped Echo down on the bench, her golden fur soaking up the blood from the dog they had just butchered. Red looked over to Scotty, eyeing him up and down.

"Well, if you don't look like a pretty boy. I think we might have some plans for you. Keys?" He stuck his hand out to Scotty. Scotty looked at Red's hand, struggling to control his adrenaline and interpret the question.

"Car keys, hand them over."

Scotty quickly pulled his keys from his pocket. Red snatched them up, signaling to his men. Scotty felt a punch to his kidneys, the man swearing and holding his hand.

"What the fuc—" Scotty felt his shirt being ripped from his back; his tail unfurled and his wings shook out.

"Holy Mother, bring him to the bench." The men hung back, whispers floating all around him. Red looked from Scotty to Echo.

"What do we have here, boy? Kid, you gonna answer me?" Scotty's knees shook. He needed to sit before he collapsed. He peeked at Echo from the corner of his eye. She just lay there in the dog blood, one of the men holding on to her antlers, the baseball bat in his hand.

"Boss, how 'bout we use the animal for bait? Why waste 'em?"

"Hold on, Trolley. I need some info first. Anybody know you're out here, kid?"

"No." Too late, Scotty realized he should probably have lied.

"What's with the wings and tail? You some kind a freak?"

Scotty said nothing.

"Trolley, why don't you give his pet there a taste a that bat?"

Before Scotty could say a word, the bat came down across Echo's round abdomen, splitting it open, spattering the bench with her golden blood.

"*Nooo.*" Scotty broke away, running to Echo. His tail rose high in the air, extruding its healing membrane. "You stupid fools; you don't know what you've done!" Pressure and the smell of sulfur accompanied Scotty's tail as it healed Echo, knitting her torn flesh and splintered bones together.

The ground began to tremble. The men stood frozen, unable to process what was happening before their eyes. Scotty scooped up a dazed Echo, the ground now rumbling and heaving. He ran to the shed, hunkering down on the ground as the earth near the bench split open, leaving a perfectly round hole from which a thick snake-like monstrosity emerged, shooting up into the night to hang threateningly over the men who cringed like cowards against the wheelbarrow containing the tragic evidence of their greed and brutality.

The monstrosity from the hole undulated and hung poised in the air as if playing with the men, gently swaying as it considered its first victim. Everything happened in a split second. The head of the snake-like thing split open, extruding a thick pulsating membrane, similar to the one that resided in Scotty and Echo's tail. It sprayed the men with a stream of black goop, then dashed into the shed as the goop ate away at the men. Scotty got a big whiff of sulfur from the shed as the membranous snake emerged. It hung in the air, as if debating what to do with them. Slowly, it lowered until it fluttered massively in front of Scotty's face. It moved imperceptibly as if it could smell him. Scotty felt chilled in the humid stinking air, afraid to breathe. It suddenly dipped down, wrapping itself tightly around Echo, drawing her up in the air away from Scotty.

"No. You can't have her. Please." Scotty stood, reaching high into the air. "Please, please, don't take her." Tears dropped from his eyes, desperation clear in his cracking voice. The undulating membrane paused, let Echo drop to Scotty's begging arms and vanished, withdrawing inside the hole, the ground collapsing behind it, shattered dogs and all.

"Echo, Echo, come on, girl, wake up." Scotty held her close, tears dropping down on her face. He felt the aura before her eyes opened. His tears increased. "I love you, girl, don't you dare leave me."

"I would never leave you, Brother." Echo's face looked up at his, her expression solemn and earnest. "We are married. You accepted the diamonds. I will make sure we are always together."

Scotty hugged her, feeling her tiny body shudder in his arms. "We'd better get out of here, pronto." They cautiously peered into the shed, seeing rows and rows of healthy gleaming dogs, mostly pit bulls with a few toy size dogs, set to be used as bait. The cages were covered in dried and fresh blood.

"They're all healed already. From the Womb—it came to save us. It must have known about the evil humans and knew we would need help."

"That was the Womb?"

"Not exactly, merely a manifestation of an arm of the Womb. It came to help us from the Hive."

"The hive in Sussex? You must be kidding."

"No, Brother Scotty. I do not know of kidding. I will be happy to have you instruct me on kidding so we can do it together. Now we must go and alert the authorities before more evil men come."

"My keys, we have to get the keys for the truck." They rushed out to the disaster site, leaving the barking dogs behind them.

Six skeletons lay on the ground in disarray, the bones dry and dissected. The wheelbarrow containing the murdered dogs was turned over on its side, the carcasses gone. Scotty moved frantically through the bones, kicking them with his feet as he searched for his keys. Sweating, he looked at Echo, seeing her bend over in the dirt, then rose with his keys in her hand.

"Good girl. Let's go." Grabbing his ruined shirt, Scotty picked her up, balanced her on his hip and ran for the woods. The sounds of barking dogs faded as they arrived at the clearing, then sprinted across the field to the Jeep. Clambering in, they backed out to race home, stopping briefly at a convenience store so Scotty could give the location to the attendant, instructing him to call the cops. Running out the door, Scotty ran back down the road to where he had left Echo with the Jeep and hurried home.

Sneaking carefully into the house, they raced up to Scotty's bedroom, hoping to avoid waking anyone. It was a comfort to find Barney silently waiting behind the bedroom door, just as they left him, anxiety plain to see in his eyes.

As they all settled down in bed, Scotty sent his mind out to reach Echo. "We did good, girl. How did the Womb find us there?"

"The Womb knows all. As long as we are on earth it can find us. It can reach out as far as it needs."

"The thing, was that the Womb, that monster? Explain it to me."

"No, Brother. It was just an extension of the Womb; a Krayven. The Womb is what you call the Father. You know of it, but not all."

Scotty buried himself in the bedcovers, trying to find a comfortable spot for his wings as exhaustion begged for sleep.

"Someday, will you please tell me what is going on, Echo . . .?" He yawned, his voice trailing off, deeply asleep as Echo answered Scotty's already slumbering brain.

"Why, we are here to exterminate Homo sapiens, of course." Echo rolled over, slipped her arm around Barney and easily fell asleep.

THE END

Introduction to
Species Intervention #6609
Book 3

ARMAGEDDON COMETH

Synopsis for Armageddon Cometh:

Under the guidance of Netty, Abby concocts her plans to abduct the wildlife at the Big Cat Sanctuary in Sarasota. She enlists the help of the handsome Italian yacht captain, Cobby, and his son Kane, forcing her to expose the changes to her body, including her hidden wings. Hiding her plans from Jose, he departs on his own mission to find his adopted mother and sisters, leaving Abby to draw closer to the charming and capable Captain Cobby.

Young Scotty embarks on a romance with a young rich local girl named Chloe who suffers from the mysterious death of her mother and the constant absences of her father.

Life moves expeditiously toward the climax at Chloe's father's mansion on Bird Key as strange connections and revealed identities collide with political intrigue and murder, leaving Chloe and Jose traumatized. Joining them in the frantic dash to a yacht moored on the key, enabling them to make their escape, wildlife and all, to Tampa Bay, is Kenya, a sassy and striking young pregnant black girl; and Peter, their trusted attorney who falls victim to Armoni and Ginger Mae's plot, leaving him dangerously scarred and emotionally ruined. During their escape to Tampa Bay ahead of the cops and devastation from the sky, it becomes clear that Scotty might be the mysterious One, as foretold by Caesar, the iconic Siberian tiger who attaches himself to Echo and Scotty.

Chapter 1
2056 AD

The pounding on Scotty's door came late in the morning.

"Scotty, get out here right now. *Scotty!*"

"Alright, alright." Going to the door, he found Abby and Jose glaring at him.

"What the *hell* did you do?" Jose stood with his hands on his hips, rocking back on his heels, his face purple. Abby's hands held him back, but she didn't look much happier.

"What's the fuss? Hey, can you let the dogs out? I'll be down in a few minutes." He rubbed his eyes, half asleep.

"I'm not kidding, Scotty. You've got five minutes." They turned on their heels, chasing the dogs down the staircase.

Scotty hurried down the stairs, rubbing his sleepy eyes and yawning. Stealing a quick peek out the terrace doors, he could feel the day was a roaster in the making. He glanced around for Echo, seeing Abby and Jose at the kitchen table, scouring the newspaper. Jose picked up the front page, smacking it down in Scotty's direction with such force it fell to the floor. Picking it up, he scanned the headline.

Oh, boy. How in the world did it hit the paper so fast? They must have bumped another story. Scanning the facts, the paper reported the dogs they saved had been taken to the local shelter. Dognapping victims were being advised to stop by to examine the dogs. Human bones taken to coroner; weapons in abandoned vehicles; fighting apparatus; unexplained crime scene; copious amounts of animal blood; authorities stumped etc., etc. . .

Yeah, Scotty thought as he put the paper down. *They know all the facts except who did it and why.* Not surprised, he felt no guilt. No way could either he or Echo have allowed the dogfighting to continue. It was a way of life with those ignorant hillbilly assholes. They didn't change. No second chances for them. They hadn't given the dogs any second chances. No, all they'd received was skulls bashed in with a baseball bat or sledge hammer, or being chewed to death as prey for the fighting dogs.

Tears came to his eyes as he thought about the innocence of the tragic pets stolen from their suburban lawns and loving homes, with no understanding of why they had been torn away. The kind of man who could do this to an animal was on par with a pedophile. They both preyed on the innocent for their own gratification and disposed of the evidence through merciless torture and murder. They were both predators, their predilection hardwired into their brains. The only difference was that pedophiles *knew* what they did was wrong. The other bastards thought they had a God-given right. Well, where the hell was God when the agony and suffering went down? The scum in the woods sure wouldn't be touching another helpless dog again and he *was not sorry*.

"Where were you last night?" Jose looked steamed. Glancing at Abby for help, he knew he was on his own, her face reflected only worry.

"There's no sense denying it, Scotty, the skeletons tell the story. You can't just go around killing people. Was Echo with you?" Turning to Abby, Scotty hung his head. He felt an aura caress his mind as Echo spoke up. "Brother Scotty did not kill anyone."

Jose stood up, disappointment on his face. "Echo, please don't tell me it was you."

"It was not me, Brother Jose. But they *needed* to die. They were very evil."

"Then who was it? How did they die?" Jose sat down, his posture seething with disbelief.

"It was the Womb."

"You saw the Womb? Come on, cut the crap."

"I did, Jose. I saw it."

Jose took a deep breath, a grenade ready to explode. His fingers drummed impatiently on the table, the tempo escalating. "I can't deal with this right now. Can you please keep an eye on him? I'm not in the mood for fairy tales." Jose abruptly rose up from the table and stalked out of the room. Scotty scratched his head, ready to condemn Jose's overreaction.

"What's with him?"

"I don't know, just stress. Promise me you'll stay around the house? Stay out of trouble?"

"Yeah, I'm going back to bed if you don't mind. I have plans later with Echo and the dogs, if that's okay?" Scotty sounded contrite, looking to placate Abby. Why blow up on her anyway? He knew he could always count on his sister to be in his corner first and ask questions later.

"Don't leave the island." She put her hand on his. "You know we have to talk about this sometime."

"Yeah, just later. Please, Ab."

She patted his hand again. "Okay, go back to bed, kiddo." Abby smiled, getting up to give him a quick hug. "I understand. I know how much creatures mean to you. Don't take what Jose says to heart. He's just trying to keep us on the down low and out of the public eye. I'll calm him down. He just isn't as nutty crazy as you are about creatures, so he doesn't get it."

"Don't worry, Ab, I'll convert him, sooner or later." As Scotty left the room to head up the stairs, the entire posse, including Echo, trundled up the stairs behind him, back to bed.

Chapter 2

Scotty slept late into the afternoon, Echo and Barney already outside. Throwing on a pair of denim cutoffs and a terry cloth shirt, he ran down the grand staircase out to the terrace, hunting for his posse.

Putting the memory of last night behind him for now, he allowed himself to get jazzed about the surprise he had planned for Echo. This was just for her. Whistling for the gang, they came running in a pack; Echo holding on tight to Barney as Penny and Mimi brought up the rear. Appearing at the front of the house, Scotty cautiously slipped Echo inside the garage, mindful of unwelcome eyes.

As everyone piled into his Jeep, he lifted a baby carriage into the back of the truck, smoothing down the opaque netting which hung down over the opening. Looking up as he closed the Jeep door, Kane shouted to him from the mouth of the garage, his muscled arms standing out in relief, the sun glazing the sweat beaded on his skin.

"What's you up to, Scotty?" His big sleepy brown eyes squinted into the cool shade of the garage.

"What are you doing here, Kane? Shouldn't you be down at the dock with your father?" Scotty was annoyed, Kane was always trying to suck up or butt in. Penny slipped out of the vehicle and pranced over to Kane where he squatted, rubbing the soft clean fur on her well-formed head.

"Na, he's having a meeting with Jose, so I have a few hours off. Thought I'd offer my services if you wanted to take your little put-put out." Kane smiled innocently.

"I think I'll pass . . . thanks anyway. Penny, let's go, girl." Hearing Penny whine, he saw Kane had taken a hard, fast grip on her. Sizing up the situation, he remembered Kane weighed about fifty pounds more than him, all solid muscle. Uneasy, he tried for a light tone.

"You mind letting go of my dog?"

"Why don't you come get her? Or are you afraid to get your pretty-boy golden curls mussed up?" Kane tensed his muscles, a hard light in his eyes. Knowing a fight was inevitable, Scotty came out from behind the vehicle, noting Echo climbing down from her seat. *Oh, no.*

Before anyone could make another move, Barney bounded out of the vehicle, ran to Penny and lunged at Kane. Caught off guard, he fell flat onto his butt, sprawling on the driveway. Penny and Barney danced back to the vehicle, jumping in as Echo climbed back up to her seat where they all settled down.

With a laugh, Scotty got behind the wheel and started the Jeep. Feeling relieved, he edged out of the garage, giving a jaunty salute to Kane's enraged face, then headed down the road. *He'll calm down soon enough,* Scotty thought, trying to reassure himself. *Too bad he's such an ass.* His life left no time or room for a boat bum like Kane. They shared nothing in common.

Putting Kane out of his mind, he looked forward to the rest of the day. Several weeks ago, Scotty, Echo and Barney had by chance discovered a path from the main road around the island to the water. They had seen a tiny strip of sand that wound unimpeded down a stretch of beach. It begged them to explore. But how to do it without outing Echo in public? Simple solution: *a baby carriage.* Not an ordinary carriage, of course. Forced to take Peter into his confidence in order to obtain the carriage, he had altered the wheels for the beach. They needed to be wider to ride above the sand instead of sinking in. So Peter, the professional that he was, obtained just what he required without asking intrusive questions. What harm could he come to with a baby carriage, anyway?

The unyielding midday sun enshrouded them with its relentless swelter. Scotty slipped on his sunglasses, removed the doctored carriage from the Jeep, and placed a jug of water for the dogs in the storage compartment. Lifting the opaque netting, he boosted Echo into the carriage, pinning the netting to the top so Echo could see out.

"What do you think, girl? Do you like it? It's all yours."

"Is this an automobile, Brother Scotty? An automobile for *me*?" The aura in Scotty's mind swirled with golden fractals, almost blinding him.

"Yes, it's a very old style car, with no engine. It must be pushed and I'm happy to do it. Now we can play on the beach, as long as we're alone." Echo ran her fragile leather hands over the inside lining of the carriage.

"And what is the name of this automobile? Is it Jeep like yours?"

"Nope, a different manufacturer. It's called a Carriage. Modified. Just for you."

"Just for me . . ." The mind aura did not ask a question, it sounded more like a statement of wonder. "I need you in my heart, Brother Scotty." Echo reached out to Scotty. He picked her up, swinging her around in his arms as the dogs danced at his heels.

"Don't worry, Echo, I need you in my heart too." Laughing, he deposited her back in the carriage. Mimi stood on her hind legs, straining to see inside.

"You don't want to miss a thing, do you girl?" Lifting Mimi, Scotty deposited her in the carriage with Echo.

"Brother Scotty, I want My Barney to ride too."

"No, Echo, that boy's just too big. Mimi is perfect. She's too little for the sand and she's your camouflage in case someone comes poking around. You just remember to dive under the covers and pull down the netting. No one will be the wiser."

The whole gang headed for the sand, Scotty pushing the carriage over the scrub weeds until they reached the tiny beach. They were alone except for the closest mansion about five hundred feet away. They were within distant eyeshot of the mansion's deep-water dock, containing two yachts, one a monster for sure. Scotty doubted anyone glancing their way would be able to tell what kind of dogs played on the beach, let alone how many. If approached, he would scoop up Echo and deposit her in the carriage. Little Mimi would languish there, ostensibly recovering from an injury. The ruse gave all of them a small, precious sense of freedom.

Penny loved jumping in the air after the gulls, never getting close, but convinced she was keeping them all safe from the noisy wheeling birds. Mimi watched, glassy eyed and complacent, from the carriage as Echo and Scotty chased Barney around the edge of the water, jumping and playing games of doggy tag. Echo loved being *it*, riding on Barney's back as they chased down Penny and Scotty. Scotty kept his eye on them all, laughing at their antics or tossing a blue rubber ball for them to scramble after.

From out of nowhere, a high-pitched scream came from the direction of the mansion with the yachts, followed by the sight of a miniature chocolate furry bullet streaming toward them on the beach. The bullet was being chased by a young girl yelling frantically for it to stop. How a tiny ball of curly brown fur could keep up that pace in the hot sun was unbelievable. It danced like a ping pong ball, bouncing from one dog to another to Scotty to Echo, where it stopped, panting and staring, its dinky brown paws flush on the sand, its body prone like a sphinx. Scotty scooped up Echo, deposited her in the carriage with Mimi, then grabbed the water canister as the furry bullet's pretty mistress flopped down on the sand next to it.

Scotty poured some water for their furry guest. He sat on the sand, joined by Barney and Penny.

"Thanks for the water, Ted gets carried away sometimes. He loves to show off for people. I'm Chloe. You a dog sitter? They can't possibly all be yours."

"Yeah, they're all mine. What kind of shrimpy mutt is Ted?"

"He's a Shih Tzu/teacup poodle. He's six pounds with a one-hundred-pound personality. Pure alpha. Teddy, come here." Chloe hung her head, shaking it sorrowfully as she watched Teddy climb up Penny's back as she lay in the sand. He was so tiny, fifty-five pound Penny seemed unaware that he was there as he made his way up to her ear, which he straddled and proceeded to mate with.

"I'm Scotty Preston," he said, watching the spectacle in front of him. "We live over on Mango Lane. You live there?" Pointing to the mansion with the deep-water dock, Scotty saw her nod.

"What's in the carriage? You got a kid here?" Getting up, Chloe turned to the carriage. Scotty beat her to it, adjusting the netting.

"No, that's just Mimi, she's a Shih Tzu too, a puppy mill rescue. She can't walk right now. She's recovering from a spinal operation. This helps me get her outside so she can be with us."

Chloe looked in. "Let me see. Oh, she looks like a little skunk. That's so sweet of you."

Scotty grabbed the handle of the carriage and prepared to run. Chloe sat back down on the sand. He relaxed and joined her, appraising her athletic build.

"You must be hot. Isn't that terry cloth? It's okay if you want to take off your shirt."

"No, I'm good."

Chloe and Scotty talked for another hour or so. Scotty felt comfortable with her, common ground easy to find. He sensed a loneliness in her which felt familiar. She was the first teenager other than Kane who he had spoken to in almost a year.

Even though at fifteen she was two years younger than him— although she had mentioned she had a birthday coming up soon—he felt comfortable enough to swap cell numbers, noticing she sure wasn't hard to look at. He wished he could be smoother with the ladies, but he needed a lot of practice before he could set his childhood complexes aside.

"Maybe you can come visit me at my house. We have monkeys, what do you think of that? They don't belong to me, they belong to my uncle. He looks after me when my dad's away. My mom's dead," she said, wiping an unexpected stray tear. I'm sorry, I didn't mean—"

"No, Chloe, I get it. It's okay. My mom died too, about a year ago. My sister and I still aren't normal yet either. That'd be cool if I could see your uncle's monkeys," he said, changing the subject.

Chloe turned away, shading her eyes as she stared past Scotty down the beach. Barney struggled to his feet, running off in the same direction.

"We've got company. Your dog seems happy to see him." Barney was doing his best to lick the hair off Jose's legs.

"That's my sister's boyfriend. He's my best friend too."

Jose reached the group, his eyes searching cautiously in acknowledgment of Scotty's company.

"Where's Echo?" Jose sounded worried. Chloe looked at the dogs.

"Did I miss one?"

"No, Echo's in the carriage with Mimi. She's just a cat we have," Scotty said quickly, jumping up and introducing them, pointing to Chloe's house down the beach.

"I think that little guy belongs to you, young lady?" Teddy was blissfully ignoring everyone, going to town on Penny's ear again.

Getting up out of the sand, Chloe laughed as she detached Teddy from the springer's ear, said goodbye, then headed down the beach to her house. She turned once, giving them all a wave. Jose knelt in the sand, removed his sunglasses and stroked Penny's coppery fur.

"Chloe seems like a nice girl. This the first time you met her?"

"Yeah, we just needed to get away from the house for a while. Don't worry, we were careful. Chloe invited me to her house. I'd like to go. She says her uncle lives there with a collection of monkeys. That'd be cool."

"Yeah, monkeys are cool. I knew a few when I was little, a long time ago." Jose's face took on a distant haunted look, his eyes unreadable. Scotty thought to ask him about it when, just as fast as they had clouded, his eyes cleared. Maybe he had imagined it. Jose's eyes now glowed so golden they were hard to read, anyway.

"Wouldn't mind seeing them myself. Just let me know when you leave the grounds next time." Going to the carriage, he lifted the netting. Two heads popped up.

"Hello, Brother Jose, Look at my new automobile." Echo's colorful aura swirled languidly.

"Your new automobile?"

"Yes, it is a Carriage, modified just for me. I am sorry I cannot give you a ride, but you have your own car. Mine is a gift from Brother Scotty."

"Yeah, real nice, Echo. That Scotty is just full of surprises. Okay, let's saddle up, guys. I need to have a word with Scotty, and you'd better get home now." As they walked back to their cars, Jose told Scotty about his impending trip to New Jersey.

"That's great," Scotty said, realizing Jose had decided to drop the issue of last night's rescue. He must be pretty occupied with the search for his family. They all missed Mama Diaz, being the only adult maternal presence left in their lives. And he missed Emma and Bonnie. They wouldn't care how funny he looked. If Jose located the rest of the family and they joined them in Sarasota, his life would be much more normal. Things were starting to look up. His thoughts drifted back to Chloe. *Yeah*, he smiled to himself, *things are definitely looking up.*

"Let's head back to the house. I'd like us to spend some time together with Abby before Peter takes me to the airport."

"Okay, I'll meet you back there." Jose walked off after making sure everyone was secure; Scotty followed in the baking afternoon sun.

Scotty sat at the kitchen table with Abby, trying to talk to her about meeting Chloe. Jose stood at the kitchen sink, listening to him chatter on. Abby sat in her ornamental pig-iron antique kitchen chair, oblivious to it all. She was staring at Echo who, for some unfathomable reason, sat plucking white hairs out of Barney's fur and holding them up to the sun. She guarded a small plastic jar sitting on the floor where she deposited the hairs. *Well*, thought Abby, *at least Echo's found something to occupy herself with.* Her attention turned moodily to Jose and Scotty, who were both staring at her.

"What?" They both started in on her at the same time.

"What are you guys yelling at me about? For Pete's sake." She lifted her heavy hair off her neck, radiating impatience and boredom.

She stood up suddenly, her chair scraping noisily on the marble kitchen floor. The dogs startled out of their placid late-afternoon snooze, heads swiveling in unison to face Abby.

"Gee, doesn't anyone have anything to do except whine at me all the time?"

"Babe, we weren't whining at you at all, we were just—"

"Oh, so now I'm wrong about my own feelings?" She marched over to a cabinet, took down a glass and slammed it on the counter, inadvertently breaking it. Penny immediately got up to sniff the glass that had fallen on the floor.

"Watch out, Penny. Abby, the dogs are going to get hurt now." Scotty got up to clean the mess.

"So now I'm hurting the dogs? Really?"

Scotty started to open his mouth. Catching Jose's eye, he stayed silent.

"Come on, Ab." Jose moved to put his arms around her.

"Don't. I'm not in the mood." Shrugging him off, she pulled out another glass and let the cold water run, the sound calming her down. Filling her glass, she mumbled, "I'm sorry," then stalked out to the terrace where she remained for the rest of the evening, not even getting up to say goodbye to Jose as he left for the airport.

She hoped she could snap out of her malaise by the time Mama Diaz returned with the girls. Glancing down toward the dock, she saw Captain Cobby sitting alone, watching the sunset. She had been meaning to find the time to chat with him about the tension between Kane and Scotty. Scotty had filled her in on the incident in the garage, and she hadn't liked the sound of what could have been a disaster if Scotty's secret had been exposed in the middle of a fight.

Slipping on her sunglasses, she adjusted her clothing, making sure everything remained properly concealed, then headed down to the dock.

Walking the short plank, she stuck her head in before going on deck.

"Permission to come aboard?"

Captain Cobby hurried to lend a hand, leaving his drink on the cocktail table near the captain's chair at the wheel.

"Ms. Abby, you know you don't ever need permission. The *Lucky Lady* belongs to you."

"I know, Captain, but I do like to observe the niceties where I can. I hope I'm not interrupting your evening."

"No, no, please join me." He led her over to the cocktail area where plush green and white striped outdoor chairs were strewn about. The area could hardly be called intimate as it appeared spacious enough to hold a reception for a hundred people.

Sitting down, she held up an empty Baccarat crystal glass, plucked off the outdoor sideboard. The captain hastened to fill it for her. She held the crystal, twirling it in the waning late afternoon sun, absently noting the similarity to Echo's antlers.

There had been a time when they had counted themselves lucky to have plastic glasses, and if colored all the better. The colored ones hid the scratches which collected on the cheap plastic. She shook her head imperceptibly as she waited for her wine to breathe, reflecting on the grandeur and glamour of the new life which had just been handed to them. Was she dreaming? Just the mere fact that she even knew red wine must breathe, startled her. Nothing about her new life felt real.

"Hope a Pinot Noir is okay."

Nodding, Abby took a sip, eyeing him over her glass. Captain Cobby struck a rather handsome appearance, in an exciting, older, virile Italian kind of way. *It must be the thick, dark, curly hair*, she thought, forgetting that Jose used to have thick, dark, curly hair. They sat together, neither speaking, letting the lapping of gentle waves against the hull weave a calm and intimate ambience around them. Breaking their companionable silence, she asked, "Is Kane around tonight?"

"I'm disappointed. I hoped you were here to visit *me*." Laughing, he gave her a quick wink.

"I *am* here to see you, Captain, I just didn't want our conversation overheard."

Leaning back in his chair, he nodded his head slowly, rubbing his strong weather-beaten hand across his closely cropped beard. He gently set down his wine glass, crossed his tanned arms and looked at her without a trace of humor.

"Is this about my son?"

Taken aback by his quick change of tone, Abby decided to tread softly. "Yes, Captain. I just hoped you and I can do something to bring the boys together, before any blood flies."

Relaxing a bit, the captain adopted a low confidential tone. "Kane has not had an easy go of it in life, Abby. His mother kept me from seeing him, then took off for God knows where. He lived with the notion I was dead. I did my best to find them, but my job on the water was not conducive to raising a child. I gave up pretty easily. When he turned ten, she suddenly showed up to dump the boy with me. You can imagine how it went from there. It's taken me a long time to get Kane to this point. He has a chip on his shoulder because he feels he wasn't wanted. He knows differently, now. But he'll always be that ten-year-old boy who was dumped with a stranger because his mother didn't want him anymore; a mother who betrayed him with a lie for ten years. We've not heard from her since."

Smiling gently, the captain looked deeply into her eyes. "Can I dare to ask you to cut him some slack and let the boys work it out themselves? I promise I'll guide him as much as I can without interfering."

Nodding, Abby stood up, extending her hands to clasp both of his. "I understand, Captain Cobby. I truly do. Scotty's upbringing was not that different from Kane's. Maybe if they each knew that, things would be easier for them. I'll leave the matter with you, after I have a talk with Scotty. Thank you for your time." With that, she released his hands, smiling as he tipped his glass to her in agreement.

Before leaving, Abby filled in a few details of Scotty's loveless relationship with his father and their parents' subsequent divorce. Comfortable with their understanding, Abby allowed the captain to give her a hand across the plank to the dock. With a grateful smile and wave, she walked back to the house, the moon guiding her path.

She marveled at how everyone seemed to have a story of strife and pain. She wasn't the only one. Feeling refreshed, she began to look forward to Jose's return with Mama Diaz and the girls.

That night, Abby's restlessness fought against her desire to sleep. She opened her eyes, noticing it was past midnight. The moon made her uneasy, a quiet crescent gazing into her bedroom window like a peeping Tom hoping to catch her unaware. The shadows of the palm trees, backlit and morphing the yard into an eerie vista of lurking creatures, unnerved her.

Why couldn't she settle down? Her glance lingered on Jose's empty spot in the bed. She leaned over, breathing in the familiar musky smell of his fur, finding it reassuring. Rolling back to her side of the bed, she wrapped her hands around the cool cotton sheet, drawing it under her chin as she scrunched herself into a fetal position, her mind flashing a kaleidoscope of memories, hoping to latch onto a soothing one to lull her to sleep. Feeling her budding wings cramp underneath her, she gave up.

Rising, she shambled over to the windows, her sleeplessness leaving her feeling drugged and lethargic. Rubbing her temples and shaking out her wings, she flexed her tail. *Perhaps my sleeplessness has something to do with my mind's unconscious attempt to avoid reliving the recurring nightmare I've been having for weeks?* The memory of the nightmare sent shivers down her evolving backside, causing her tail to stir reflexively.

Without warning, she found herself reviewing the nightmare as she stood at the window fully awake. She observed herself standing in a deserted parking lot in front of an iron grill, bent and misshapen; the stanchions under which millions of children and adults passed in their quest to discover where the famous Bronx Zoo had once housed their favorite wild creatures. The stanchions no longer supported its proud sign. She scanned the soundless trees, denuded of life. They appeared as if they'd been flattened by a giant fist, pummeling them from the gray and wintry sky. She looked off to the blank horizon: the most famous skyline in the world—gone. Devastation. She felt the bitter cold seep through her golden fur, flakes of dirty brown snow slowly, soundlessly, covering her thick golden hair, even as she somehow knew it was the middle of summer.

She turned back to the ruined zoo, an irresistible compulsion. Without warning, she discovered herself floating over the crumbling exhibits on the zoo's decimated grounds. Formerly home to the many innocent creatures which had found themselves captive to man's misguided attempt to shape, control and destroy the lives of creatures he, in his hubris, thought belonged to him. The vacant exhibits all contained ominous piles of bleached bone ash. All that remained of some of the most exquisite, bio-diverse and marvelous creations ever granted the rights to this planet by their maker. And again . . . brutally and ignobly destroyed by man.

She could feel glacial tears freezing on her cheeks as her emotions remained oddly anesthetized. Finding herself descending to an exhibit, she read the signage proclaiming it to be the home of the magnificent Western Lowland Gorilla. The bitter irony was not lost on her, realizing their home *never* existed here. Sadly, home called from the vanished jungles and watery bais of Western Africa. These sentient gentle great apes were mothers and fathers, babies and youngsters: families. Just like Homo sapiens, for man was a great ape too. But better, of course. Man . . . the chosen one . . . he who shall inherit the Earth. And once again, she noted frightfully to herself, man destroyed.

Her eyes glazed as she noted the complete absence of color, life or warmth around her. The horizon was a palette of black and gray barrenness, benumbing ashen hopelessness and bone-crushing godforsaken loneliness. What had happened here? Such wanton destruction.

Abby struggled, a sudden crush of emotions coalescing, too much to bear. Trying to break the grip of the tableau, she panicked; instinctively calling for her mother, *begging* for her mother. Out of her mind with grief and loss, she confused the emotions in her nightmare with the unresolved heartbreak of her mother's abrupt absence from her life. Here the nightmare always ended, leaving Abby a helpless wreck.

Without warning, Abby felt pulled away from the zoo. She beheld herself in a new and foreign environment, appearing to be a large cavern. Light shone, but the source eluded her. She felt neither warm nor cold. An enveloping layer of something soft and undulating, exuding a smell of organic dampness which clung to the walls of the cavern. How could she smell if she were dreaming?

Further down the cavern, a golden glow approached: a figure. Abby caught her breath, an unexplained premonition sending goosebumps down her arms. The emerging figure formed into that of a woman.

The alluring vision glowed with the fine golden fur draping her body. Like Abby, she sported a long mature tail with a bulbous end floating languidly around her. Her golden-white hair reached, full and glossy, down her back. A pair of exquisite wings framed her statuesque figure. From her hairline, two graceful crystal horns emerged, swirling with silver and gold liquid. Her eyes sparkled with the colors of the rainbow. She smiled benevolently at Abby. With a start, Abby realized she looked familiar. She racked her memory, but could not place the lovely face.

"My dear, we have not met. You are here because you have much to do. We are relying on you. You must save those you can. Time is short. We had hoped to do things differently. Man has conspired, fatally, to abort our plans. We must react quickly. Gather the materials you need and do the best you can."

"Madam, how am I to know what to do?"

Approaching Abby, the woman placed her hand on Abby's shoulder as her right horn split and peeled back, releasing a drop of liquid, its color flashing and filling the cavern. The woman held out her other hand to receive the drop. Reaching up to Abby's ear she placed it inside.

Disappearing, the flashing colors slowly faded as the drop moved deep into her ear. Abby's eyes closed slowly. She blinked, her eyes closing again. They finally opened with a stoic acceptance of realized purpose and clarity.

"I understand completely. I hope to see you again soon," Abby said. Taking Abby into her arms, the woman embraced her warmly.

"You will, my dear. Remember, you have Echo to aid you. I must send you back now."

"Wait. Please, who are you? What shall I call you?" The vision began to recede. She found herself in her own bed, on the verge of waking. From a great distance, she heard the woman's voice. "I was once known as Netty Doyle, my dear. You may call me Netty."

Abby gently drifted into a deep sound slumber, the details of her dream dissipating. She slept soundly.

Chapter 3

Peter pulled his BMW away from the parking lot at Sarasota Airport. He waved to Jose, who stood in line for the security bus to the check-in counter. He was anxious to board a flight to Newark which would hopefully reunite him with what was left of his family.

Peter's happiness for Scotty and Abby knew no bounds. He appreciated how long it had taken them to get this far. As he drove back into town, he observed the night life in Sarasota preparing to heat up as the party hour approached, crowds thickening on the streets. Peter had sampled very little of it, even though the venues of bars and eateries were made to order for a single man.

Some of the most predatory and beautiful women in the country flocked to Sarasota, hoping to land themselves a wealthy husband. Those were the odds any self-respecting singleton would celebrate. Even though he could now call himself well off by most standards, he normally found himself reticent to join the nightly festivities of the crazy rich in this town, and which served as a bizarre escape from the reality of the rest of the country.

But tonight he wanted to flex his muscles. Perhaps his buoyant mood, inherited from Jose's infectious happiness, portended a good omen. Taking a very deep breath, he decided: Tonight would be the night. He felt jazzed up and ready to go fishing for the ladies.

Driving down Main Street proved difficult. Traffic congestion continually hindered his efforts to find a parking place. By the time he found one, discouragement settled in, robbing him of his ebullient mood, which leaked out like a punctured tire. His reluctance to enter any of the most boisterous bars overwhelmed him. Forcing himself to suck it up, he timidly selected one which appeared more discreet and subdued.

As he entered the bar, he relaxed. The atmosphere appeared quiet and non-threatening, although clearly not the place most partiers wanted to be seen in. Definitely down scale. Oh well, it would do fine as a start for him. Scanning the bar, he noticed an empty stool between two other patrons. He started forward, but the stool was quickly taken by another man. As he stood in indecision, he noticed a couple of patrons giving him a quick once over, especially the woman. As his courage began to evaporate, one of the patrons stood up. A short dumpy man, he motioned toward him, offering his seat. Well, that was sure kind. Peter turned to thank him, but the man ducked his face down, hurrying out the door before Peter could even open his mouth.

Getting comfortable on the bar stool, he ordered a glass of wine, then glanced at his reflection in the back bar mirror. His face looked even wider and more owlish than usual. But the mirror failed to hide the quiet, clean-cut, timid man who was finally tired of being alone.

He sat, sulking about his lonely life, and ordered another glass of wine. *A little liquid courage can't hurt.* As people were coming and going, he sat stiffly on his bar stool, unsure what to do next. Feeling discouraged, he felt a bump on the right side of his stool. A patron, the woman who had been staring at him, rose from her own stool, getting ready to leave. She suddenly dropped her purse. Attempting to assist as she bent to retrieve it, they banged heads.

"Ow."

"Ouch." Peter rubbed his head, looking up into the eyes of a pretty blond woman, seemingly a few years older than him. Her nose scrunched up as she laughed heartily at her own clumsiness.

"I'm sorry, that's so typical of me. I'm rather clumsy. Are you okay?" She extended her hand to grip his arm, rubbing softly to reassure him, an intimate gesture. Touched, Peter hastened to assure her of his recovery.

"May I insist you allow me to buy you a cocktail? Just so I can assure myself you're fine?"

Her smile was so lovely, her manner so charming, that he found himself instantly enticed. *A pretty woman wants to buy me a drink. How do you like that?*

When you least expect it, something special comes your way. Looking into her relaxed and friendly face, he felt no qualms about spending time with her. All traces of nervousness disappeared. He began to relax and enjoy himself.

As the evening wore on, they discovered they had much in common. they were both from small towns, both professionals. When she found out he was an attorney, she could not resist inquiring into his intent to sue her for the knot on his noggin. She made him laugh, something unfamiliar to him.

Peter shyly suggested they have dinner together. He wanted to do anything he could to prolong their time together. He just loved how her blond curls shook as she laughed at his lame jokes. *What a doll*, he thought, enjoying how the glow of the bar lights made her eyes sparkle.

They strolled down the street just like all the other happy couples, selecting a nice restaurant, then sharing savory lobster and excellent champagne, frugality forgotten. Her hand lingered on his as she made an occasional point. Peter found himself grinning and laughing so hard the muscles in his face ached.

Finally, they realized the night must end. Suggesting she walk him to his car, she pointed out the high-rise she lived in, within easy walking distance of the restaurant. After arriving at his BMW, he inquired as to whether he could call her for dinner again. Reaching into her purse, she scribbled her cell number, clearly pleased to be asked. Placing the note in his hand, she leaned over slowly, looked into his eyes and placed her lips over his for the softest kiss he swore he would ever feel.

"Goodnight, Peter. This was wonderful. I look forward to hearing from you very soon." Turning, she disappeared into the crowd on the sidewalk.

In a daze, he drove back to Bird Key. Pulling into his driveway, he remained in the car, reliving and savoring the evening. He glowed. *Could she be any more perfect?* Looking down, he stroked the note she had given him, admiring her handwriting. Ginger Mae Shrute 914-555-0436. *How cool is that?* And off he went to bed, sleeping better than he had in years.

*

Ginger Mae walked quickly to the high-rise, not wanting Armoni to wait any longer than necessary. She knew he would be chewing his nails and spitting in anger because he had almost been caught when he had seen Peter walk into the bar, forcing him to make a hasty exit. They could not afford to have Peter recognize Armoni, even though they had only met briefly, months ago. Armoni knew he made an indelible impression on people.

She shook her head, amazed at the irony of the situation. Dining in elegant expensive bars and restaurants every night for months, trying to get a lead on Armoni's enemies could easily have become a drag. But how else could they hope to run into them? Sooner or later, they would show up to eat. Their excellent plan to track them back to their house where Armoni could then reclaim his property had failed to produce results. Not so excellent after all. They hadn't counted on the one night that they had decided to go to a normal, relaxed watering hole, this sudden opportunity would drop right into their laps. Armoni would be very pleased with her results.

She sighed, watching laughing couples pass her on the sidewalk, arm in arm, enjoying each other's company, just as she had enjoyed Peter's. She felt a longing for the unfamiliar life of an upstanding citizen. *Wow, where did that come from? Have I gotten in over my head this time?*

Her big plans for Armoni were slowly turning to ash. Sure, he had taken them to Florida, paying for everything, but he never let her out of his sight. That was not what she'd had in mind. And she could only handle his disgusting habits in small doses. She expected him to set her up in her own place, seeing her when he had the urge (she could handle that) and then get back to his life. But, it appeared, he had no life. As a matter of fact, he seemed to want to turn *her* into his life. *Ugh. Not going to happen.* She hoped that if she helped him recover his property, she could say goodbye and strike out on her own. The wealth and opportunity in Sarasota made her head spin. From the kind of men she met in the bars and clubs, she could clearly see that she and Daisy would be well able to fend on their own, without the odorous Armoni.

But she must be clever. She had come to the conclusion that Armoni kept mysterious secrets to himself. She began to suspect the veracity of his stolen property story.

And then there were his hygiene issues. A godly problem. He must have grown up with wolves. How a man could ignore simple baths, deodorant and oral care blew her mind. She had finally reached the point where she could no longer eat around him for fear of vomiting. So she just drank instead.

Fortunately, his appetite for sex had slowly mellowed. *That was bound to happen as his attention is so focused on getting his property back, thank the Lord.* And she had to consider Daisy's welfare. This was not a good environment for her. Ginger Mae regretted exposing her to Armoni, something she had always refused to do with her johns. This must end, and as soon as possible.

That's why she had said yes to dinner with Peter. She had hoped he would ask for her phone number and then a date. She could find out where he lived and where his clients lived. That should satisfy Armoni. Given enough time, she confidently planned to obtain the information Armoni constantly gnashed his teeth over. Then she would be done with this. She and Daisy would dump this smelly piece of garbage and strike out on their own.

Ginger Mae remembered the trailer trash, horse-faced, fat, little blonde in the gym at the high-rise who had happily bragged about how she had left her loser husband after she had met a wealthy guy on a website for dating millionaires. Within three weeks, she had moved into the millionaire's house. They'd been married within six months. He wasn't exactly a looker, but then, neither was she. But they were happy. What else did they need? At this point, Ginger desperately needed to grab at any straw if it aided her plan to get away from Armoni.

She had started to wonder where his money came from. It wasn't like he possessed any education or skills. Her curiosity about the people who had stolen his property increased. Now, knowing Armoni as she did, she began to have sneaking doubts about his story. After meeting Peter, she didn't think he would, in good conscience, represent thieves. But she was *damn sure* Armoni would steal bones from a puppy. Getting sucked into a crime as an accessory was nowhere on her list.

Her tired eyes flashed lightning bolts as she approached the high-rise. Looking up, she searched in vain for the seventeenth floor where they were residing. She swallowed her dread and went in to face the music.

You can read more by going to Amazon and clicking on Armageddon Cometh, Species Intervention #6609 Book 3.

To You, My Dear Reader,

I want you all to know how heartfelt my appreciation is that you have taken the time to read my books. Being an author is one of the most torturous professions out there. Many of us live on the thanks of our readers alone. If anyone cares to leave me an honest review on Amazon.com, Goodreads.com, Smashwords.com, Kobo.com or Barnes and Noble, I would be ever so grateful. You can leave a review on Barnes and Noble and Goodreads without having made the purchase there. Some of you are unaware that Amazon, in particular, promotes books based on the amount of reviews a book gets. No reviews . . . the book will stay a secret.

Don't be afraid to make suggestions or criticize the writing. How else is one to improve? Stay tuned for the next book in the Species Intervention Series, Armageddon Cometh.

J. K. Accinni

Author's Page

J. K. Accinni was born and raised in Sussex County before moving to Randolph, New Jersey, where she lived with her husband, five dogs and eight rabbits, all rescued, and currently resides in Sarasota, Florida. Mrs. Accinni's passion for wildlife conservation has led her all over the world, including three trips to Africa, where ten years ago she and her husband fell in love with a baby elephant named Wendi who had been rescued by a wildlife group. That baby is the inspiration for the character Tobi, the elephant featured in her fourth book titled Hive.

The character of Caesar is inspired by a real life iconic tiger from The Big Cat Habitat and Gulf Coast Sanctuary in Sarasota. A portion of the proceeds from her third book, Armageddon Cometh, will be donated to the sanctuary in support of the enormous expense required to house and feed the displaced wildlife in their care. Mrs. Accinni invites her readers to visit bigcathabitat.org to view the astounding facility and plan a visit with your family.

Mrs. Accinni also invites you to visit her webpage at www.SpeciesIntervention.com, where information on The Big Cat Habitat and Gulf Coast Sanctuary can also be viewed. Readers are encouraged to comment about the book or your own creature experiences.